CHRISTMAS IN LONDON

Also by Anita Hughes

Emerald Coast
White Sand, Blue Sea
Christmas in Paris
Santorini Sunsets
Island in the Sea
Rome in Love
French Coast
Lake Como
Market Street
Monarch Beach

CHRISTMAS IN LONDON

ANITA HUGHES

St. Martin's Griffin ♏ New York

CHRISTMAS IN LONDON. Copyright © 2017 by Anita Hughes. All rights reserved. Printed in the United States of America. For information, address St. Martin's Press, 175 Fifth Avenue, New York, N.Y. 10010.

www.stmartins.com

The Library of Congress Cataloging-in-Publication Data is available upon request.

ISBN 978-1-250-14579-6 (trade paperback)
ISBN 978-1-250-14580-2 (ebook)

Our books may be purchased in bulk for promotional, educational, or business use. Please contact your local bookseller or the Macmillan Corporate and Premium Sales Department at 1-800-221-7945, extension 5442, or by email at MacmillanSpecialMarkets@macmillan.com.

First Edition: October 2017

10 9 8 7 6 5 4 3 2 1

To my mother

CHRISTMAS IN LONDON

Chapter One

LOUISA NUDGED OPEN THE INDUSTRIAL-SIZED oven and thought nothing smelled as wonderful as cinnamon and nutmeg nine days before Christmas. Everything about the bakery's smooth wooden counters thrilled her: the buttery pie crusts waiting for crisp Granny Smith apple slices and scoops of whipped cream, the eggnog custard nestled in white cups, the cupcakes topped with cream cheese frosting and shaped liked Christmas trees. And she especially loved the croquembouche she had convinced Ellie, the bakery's owner, to let her make on her own time.

She learned the recipe for croquembouche at a cooking course in Normandy and never forgot the cream-filled pastry puffs dipped in caramel and laced with spun sugar. She examined it now and thought the puffs were a little crooked and the cream may not be as rich as she used in Normandy, but when she popped one in her mouth she tasted vanilla and a crust so airy it was like a single fat snowflake drifting down from the sky.

That was one of the things people didn't realize about being a pastry chef. It wasn't just about baking a delicious cheesecake or whisking eggs and flour so a soufflé was firm and delicate at the same time. It was about exploring other cultures. She loved to make lamingtons from Australia with their gooey centers and coconut flakes and panettones from Italy topped with powdered sugar and citrus rinds and toffee pudding from England so thick it stuck to the roof of her mouth.

Her phone lit up with texts and she brushed aside a stray hair and picked it up. Her friends urged her to join them doing all the things twenty-something New Yorkers enjoyed a week before Christmas: ice-skating in Central Park or sipping champagne cobblers at the Monkey Bar or braving Christmas shoppers at Bloomingdale's to pick out the perfect party dress.

But there was always the possibility of falling and spraining her wrist when she ice-skated and champagne gave her a headache and even though she loved Bloomingdale's with its decorated Christmas tree and scents of expensive perfumes, she couldn't afford a pair of silk stockings let alone a whole dress.

And besides, every extra hour she worked brought her closer to her goal. She had been saving for four years and by next Christmas she was determined to open her own restaurant specializing in homemade desserts. She'd already started scouting locations—roaming the trendy streets of Chelsea and venturing to the Upper West Side with its leafy sidewalks and elegant brownstones.

In the summer there would be blueberry tarts and upside-down cake with plums the color of lipstick and almond ice cream torte. And at the Christmas holidays! She would serve Baked Alaska and gingerbread trifle with cognac custard and sliced pears.

She stretched like a cat that had been sitting too long in front of the fire and noticed the rain drizzling on the pavement. If she had brought a proper raincoat she would almost look forward to the six blocks' walk to her apartment.

She thought of all the things she planned to do when she got home: read the chapter on chocolate ganache in Gordon Ramsay's new cookbook, try out a new recipe for key lime pie with limes she bought at the corner market, take a bath before her roommate prepared for a date and spent hours in the bathroom doing her hair and makeup.

Every day for the last week Louisa had staggered up the stairs to her apartment and unlocked the door. She'd flipped through the mail and brewed a cup of orange hibiscus tea. Then she'd lain down on her bed fully clothed just to close her eyes. Hours later she would wake with a crick in her neck and her jacket digging uncomfortably into her side.

A bell tinkled and Louisa realized she'd forgotten to lock the bakery door and change the sign to CLOSED. The kitchen door opened and a man of about thirty appeared. He wore a rain-splattered leather jacket and had short light-brown hair.

"I'm sorry, we're closed." She took the cinnamon rolls out of the oven and placed them on the island in the middle of the room.

"You're not closed, actually." He entered the kitchen. "The door of the bakery was unlocked and the red blinking sign said OPEN."

"The sign is new and I always forget to unplug it," Louisa said. "The cash register is empty and the desserts are put away. I'm afraid you'll have to leave."

"Are these cinnamon rolls any good?" He inspected the tray.

"I really couldn't say," she answered. "I just took them out of the oven."

"They smell delicious." He picked one up. "Do you mind if I try one?"

"You can't just help yourself!" she protested, wiping her hands on her apron. "I spent hours baking them."

The man inhaled deeply and took a small bite. He finished chewing and looked at Louisa.

"Excellent! Not too gooey and with just the right amount of sweetness," he announced. "Possibly the best cinnamon roll I've ever tasted."

"Do you think so?" she asked, suddenly happy despite herself. "I've been working on the recipe for ages. I use a secret ingredient I can't tell anyone about. And the brown sugar has to have just the right amount of molasses."

"Is that all there is?" He waved at the two trays of cinnamon rolls. "Or are there more in the oven?"

"That's two dozen cinnamon rolls! It took me all afternoon." She suddenly remembered that it was 7:00 p.m. and she'd been at the bakery since early morning.

"I'll take the lot." He picked up a tray. "Do you have any boxes? I can't have them getting ruined in the rain."

"Put that down!" she said hotly. "You can't just waltz in here and help yourself to what's on the counter."

"I wasn't going to help myself, I was going to pay you." He reached into his pocket and took out a wallet. "How much are they?"

"They're not for sale." She shook her head.

"Of course they're for sale," he countered. "This is a bakery. You didn't make twenty-four cinnamon rolls to eat before bed."

"They're not for sale now. They're for the morning," she clarified. "They're our most popular item the week before Christmas. People love them with a cup of coffee or hot chocolate."

"I need them now." He riffled through his wallet. "Will one hundred dollars be enough? I can't imagine you charge more than six dollars a cinnamon roll even if this is the East Village."

"One hundred dollars for twenty-four cinnamon rolls!" Louisa gasped.

Ellie had asked Louisa what they should charge and Louisa suggested three dollars apiece. She was terrible at pricing her own desserts. It was a tug-of-war between being grateful people liked them enough to pay for them and wanting Ellie to make a profit. "I'm sorry, you can't have them. I'm not the owner and I'm not allowed to sell the products after hours. I'd be happy to hold them for you when we open tomorrow morning, if you'd like to come back then."

"Two hundred dollars, then." He handed her two hundred-dollar bills. "And an extra fifty if you find me a box."

"That's very generous, but then I wouldn't have any left for the morning rush hour," she explained. "We have to sell cinnamon rolls the week before Christmas. It's our most requested item."

"You have other pastries. They can buy Danish or croissants," he suggested.

"Any other time of the year perhaps, but not now." She shook her head. "People allow an extra fifteen minutes to get to work just so they can pick up a cinnamon roll. It's the high point of their day."

"Have you heard of the cooking show *Baking with Bianca*?" he asked. "We're filming a Christmas special in a brownstone nearby and there was a small fire in the kitchen. The snowball cupcakes look like they were roasted over a campfire and the fig crumble bars are burnt to a crisp. There isn't time to bake anything else and the other bakeries are closed. I need something for Bianca to hold in front of the camera."

"It's the most watched cooking show in New York." She nodded. "At first I was a little put off by Bianca's lipstick. How could you taste your own desserts without getting bright-red lipstick all over the spoon? But I've tried some of the recipes and the steamed gingerbread pudding is delicious."

"Bianca wears waterproof lipstick, it wouldn't come off during a monsoon," he murmured.

Louisa noticed that the man's eyes were blue and there was an ink smudge on his cheek. His cheeks were smooth and when he smiled crinkles formed around his mouth.

"I'm sorry, they're not mine to sell," she insisted. "Ellie, the owner, is at *The Nutcracker* with her daughter, Chloe, and I can't interrupt her. You can try again tomorrow."

"I've got a stylist and a lighting guy and a camera operator who will report this to the union if we go a minute overtime," he pleaded. "And think of the viewers. They're going to tune in to learn how to bake something special for Santa Claus or bring the perfect Christmas gift to Aunt Mary in the hospital and be disappointed."

Christmas was Louisa's favorite time of year because people were so nice to each other. All month the spirit of doing the right thing was intoxicating. People jostled to give up their seat on the subway and when she walked down Fifth Avenue she heard the sound of coins dropping into Salvation Army cans. She wanted to help him, and in exchange Bianca could mention the bakery on the show. It would be wonderful publicity and Ellie would be thrilled.

"I have an idea," she suggested. "What if Bianca says on air that the bakery is one of her favorite spots in Manhattan? Ellie would get free publicity and you would get your cinnamon rolls." She paused. "I will have to come in early and make more, but I don't mind. I'll do anything to help the bakery succeed."

"You're a lifesaver," he said and kissed her on the cheek. "I'm sorry, I didn't mean to do that but you've made me so happy." He stepped back and grinned. "My job is to make everything on the set run smoothly and Bianca was roaming around like a lion with an injured paw. Even our producer, Kate, couldn't placate her. Kate is usually as soothing as a warm brandy before bed."

"That sounds perfect right about now," she said with a sigh. "I arrived so early this morning the homeless man was still asleep. Every evening I give him a stack of blankets and every morning when he wakes up he returns them."

"You give a homeless man blankets?" He stopped. "Doesn't that encourage him to hang around? I'm sure your customers don't want to see him when they're ordering their morning cappuccino."

"No one sees him, he sleeps in the covered alley in the back. Even Ellie doesn't know he comes," she said. "The shelters are so crowded, sometimes it's hard to get a blanket at all. I give him a cup of leftover coffee and blankets I keep in the storeroom." She paused. "No one knows, please don't say anything."

"My lips are sealed. I have to go, or I'll be fired and looking for a handout." He picked up the trays. "I'm Noah, it's a pleasure doing business with you."

"I'm Louisa." She nodded. "I hope it all works out."

He walked to the door and turned around. "You've saved my job, I don't know how to thank you."

Louisa watched Noah cross the street and thought she shouldn't have said yes. Now she'd have to be back at the bakery at 5:00 a.m. Her shoes would barely have time to dry and she wouldn't be able to wash her hair before work. But it was too late now. The cinnamon rolls were gone and she had to get home before the soft rain became a downpour.

She closed the front door and studied the white Christmas tree decorated with gumdrops and peppermints in the bakery window. The red sign still flashed OPEN and she laughed. She unlocked the door and unplugged it. Then she covered her head with her hands and hurried down the street.

Chapter Two

LOUISA POURED A CUP OF coffee from the bakery's silver coffeepot and added cream and sugar. She took a sip and stared at the cup blankly. She had been there so long she couldn't remember how many cups she'd already consumed.

There was the shot of espresso she gulped down when she arrived. The stone floor was freezing under her moccasins and the coffeepot took too long to heat up. She made an espresso in the espresso machine and drank it while she assembled brown sugar and cinnamon.

Then there had been the cup of coffee with a splash of vanilla she sipped after she handed the cinnamon rolls to Danielle, who worked the bakery's counter. That was the best cup of the day. It was fresh and hot, and she could savor it slowly.

But then Danielle needed a tray of pecan crescent cookies and Louisa groaned and returned to work. Now it was early afternoon, and the coffee was so stale it needed a large dose of cream and two packets of sugar just to swallow it.

The kitchen door opened and Louisa looked up. Noah wore a long wool coat and blue jeans.

"Not you again!" she exclaimed. "Because of you I woke up so early, I banged my foot on the radiator in the dark. I had to hobble six blocks and when I arrived the bakery was like the inside of an igloo. I made two trays of cinnamon rolls and three cranberry logs and a persimmon pudding. If you have any designs on my pecan crescent cookies, you better think again. They're for the evening rush, and I'm not going to make more."

"They look excellent but I'm not hungry." Noah glanced at the tray. "And I'm sorry you hurt your foot. I'm in a bit of trouble and need your help."

"I'm a firm believer in helping others, especially at Christmas." She poured the coffee in the sink. "But everyone has their limits. I was about to drink coffee that is so stiff you could put it behind a frame and hang it on the wall. I'm afraid this time you'll have to solve your own problems."

"The cinnamon rolls were a huge hit. The crew fought over who took them home and the producer, Kate, said they were the best she ever tasted," he began. "Kate is very particular, she's worked with Anthony Bourdain."

"Anthony Bourdain!" Louisa's eyes were wide. "Did she really say they were good?"

"Her exact words were 'they are so rich and flaky they should be served at afternoon tea at the Waldorf.'" He paused. "Are you happy?"

"Very happy." Louisa imagined getting a plug on national television for her restaurant when it opened. Then she studied Noah suspiciously. "But I'm exhausted. If you need more cinnamon rolls you'll have to wait until tomorrow. As soon as I finish these crescent cookies I'm going home."

"The only person who didn't react favorably to the cinnamon rolls was Bianca." He lifted the lid of the coffeepot and inhaled. "She took a few bites to show the camera how delicious they were and an hour later her lips blew up like a blowfish. Whatever you used, she was allergic."

"It must have been the nutmeg, that's my secret ingredient!" she gasped. "Some people are allergic. I should have told you. I'm sorry, it's my fault."

"Unfortunately she has an extreme case," he finished. "Her doctor said she'd look like that for a week."

"I feel terrible. Should I send an apology note or a fruit basket?" She stopped. "But why do you need my help? I'm the last person Bianca wants to see."

"Tonight the whole crew is flying to London to prepare to film *Christmas Dinner at Claridge's*. Top chefs from around the world are going to prepare Christmas Eve dinner at one of the most famous hotel restaurants." His eyes darkened. "Bianca was supposed to bake her layered fruitcake with crème fraîche frosting. Except now she's going to be lying in a dark room watching *Scandal* and drinking milkshakes with a straw."

Louisa's cheeks paled and a shiver ran down her spine. "Oh, I see," she breathed. "That does create a problem."

He glanced at the clock above the oven. "In four hours and thirty-six minutes I have to be at the British Airways lounge at JFK. Before I hand over my boarding pass and receive my complimentary glass of champagne, you're going to help me find Bianca's replacement."

"How would I do that?" Louisa demanded. "I'm a twenty-seven-year-old pastry chef at a bakery on the Lower East Side.

I don't know any famous chefs and I've never been invited to a restaurant opening." She turned back to the crescent cookies. "I'm happy to write an apology, but I can't find a replacement."

"You don't understand," he urged. "I'm the one who brought the cinnamon rolls to the set. If I don't show up with Bianca's replacement, I'll be fired."

"Aren't you overreacting?" she offered. "You didn't mean to make Bianca's lips blow up like a blowfish. She must have insurance for these situations."

"Insurance doesn't cover the press releases that have been sent out, and the promotional ads that have been filmed, and the fact that working alongside those chefs will be a huge boost for Bianca's career," he spluttered. "Someone has to take the blame, that's how television works. It will be my head rolling around the network floor like a cabbage at Trader Joe's."

"If I could help you I would." She opened the oven door. "But I have to finish these crescent cookies and then I'm going to go home and take a bath. My hair hasn't seen a shampoo bottle since Tuesday and I've run out of clean shirts."

She placed the cookie tray in the oven and pushed a stray hair from her cheek. Noah was watching her as if she were an animal at the zoo.

"Why are you looking at me like that?" she asked nervously.

"Do you always wear your hair in a ponytail?" he wondered.

"When I'm baking," she answered. "I had it cut at the beauty school and she cut it too short. No matter what I do, it slips out of the elastic band."

"What color are your eyes?" he squinted under the lights. "I can't tell if they are brown or green."

"They're hazel," she replied. "Why do you ask?"

"And would you say you're five foot four, give or take half an inch?"

"I've been five foot five since my senior year in high school." She wiped her hands on her apron. "What does any of this have to do with finding Bianca's replacement?"

"Looks are important. Her replacement's face will be broadcast in twenty countries," he pondered. "But you have bone structure a camera loves, you just need some mascara and lipstick. And a new haircut of course, possibly with some highlights. I can't see your figure underneath that apron, but you have good legs."

"What are you talking about?" She suddenly felt naked.

"Do you really know a lot about baking?" he asked. "That's very important."

"Of course I do," she bristled. "I've always wanted to be a pastry chef. When I was seven years old, I received a Fisher Price kitchen for Christmas. I tried to like the gift. But I longed to bake real fudge brownies instead of ones made of plastic. I attended the Culinary Institute in Hyde Park and since then I've worked as a dishwasher at a seafood restaurant in Chelsea and as assistant to the assistant pastry chef at a French patisserie in Union Square," she continued. "I work ten-hour days and I'm saving all my money. Next Christmas I'm going to open my own restaurant specializing in desserts."

"I know the feeling." He sighed. "I work all day on the show and go to law school at night. It will be worth it when I pass the bar and hang my own shingle. I'll be doing something useful instead of tracking down nail polish to match Bianca's raspberry trifle."

"Any kind of work is useful," Louisa countered. "You said that millions of viewers count on Bianca to teach them how to make chocolate truffle layer cake."

"You're absolutely right, and I can't afford to lose my job!" He nodded vigorously. "That's why you're going to be Bianca's replacement."

"Me!" Louisa exclaimed. "I can't just waltz off to London at Christmas. And I've never been on television in my life."

"Being on television is easy. All you do is stand on a piece of tape." He shrugged. "And you'll be working with the best chefs in the world. Pierre Gagnaire, who owns Osteria Francescana in Paris, will be there and Andreas Caminada whose restaurant in a historic castle is the only three-star Michelin restaurant in Switzerland. It took Kate months of buttering up the organizers to get this invitation. It's going to be televised around the world and the British prime minister and her husband will dine there," he finished. "But I forgot it's Christmas. I assume you have a boyfriend. Tell him that when you return, the show will pay for you to have a belated Christmas dinner at the St. Regis."

"I don't have a boyfriend, I'm too busy."

"Do you have a cat?" he asked.

"I'd like one. We had a gorgeous tabby when I was growing up," she mused. "But I'd never see it. Besides my roommate is allergic."

"You don't have a boyfriend or any pets. And you have a roommate to make sure the radiator doesn't catch fire. I don't see the problem." He stopped. "Unless you don't have a passport. But Kate could fix that, she's good at coaxing people in high places."

"I have a passport," she said. "I can't go because the week before Christmas is the busiest time of the year for the bakery. Leaving Ellie in the lurch would be an awful thing to do."

"Surely she can find someone else," he urged. "We'll pay your airfare and expenses and put you up at Claridge's. You'll have five days to explore London. Have you ever been to Harrods Christmas Grotto? It's like entering Santa's workshop. Or you can ice-skate at Hampton Court. Henry VIII's sixteenth-century castle is lit up at night and it's the most magical place you've ever seen."

An all-expenses-paid trip to London at Christmas! She always wanted to visit the food halls at Selfridges and see the Changing of the Guard. And the fresh scones with marmalade and clotted cream at the Savoy were supposed to be heavenly.

"I've never been to London. Who wouldn't want to see the holiday lights on Oxford Street and the countdown to Christmas at Trafalgar Square?" She sighed. "But Ellie has bills to pay. I can't desert her because I want to visit Buckingham Palace. Though I always dreamed of meeting the Duchess of Cambridge and giving her one of my cupcakes. She is serious about helping others and her children are gorgeous."

"If you're so concerned with helping others you might start with me," he reminded her. "It is because of you this happened."

"We went over this, it was an accident." She suddenly felt guilty. "I'm sorry, but I have to get back to work. Leave me your number and if I think of anyone, I'll call you."

"It's too bad your cakes won't be featured on TV." He glanced at the counter. "Can you imagine if viewers saw your croquembouche. When you open your restaurant, there would be lines around the block."

"How did you know that was a croquembouche?" she asked. "Most Americans have never heard of it."

"We filmed a segment of the show in Paris," he explained. "Yours looks better than the one baked by the chef at the Hôtel de Crillon."

"Do you think so?" She pulled off a puff and handed it to Noah. "Here, you can take a piece with you."

"It's fantastic," he said while biting into the pastry. "The cream is sweet without being cloying."

"That's what I was hoping to achieve." She brightened. "It would be wonderful to serve it at Claridge's. And of course, I'd love the publicity."

"And you'd be working alongside Digby Bunting. I've never met him, but I heard he's the best pastry chef in England. Kate says his crumble pudding is perfection."

"Did you say Digby Bunting?" Louisa gasped.

Digby was in his midthirties and was one of the most revered pastry chefs in the world. Louisa tried to master his cherries jubilee, but it always came out a bit tart. And she was dying to ask him how he stopped the meringue on his chocolate meringue cake from flaking all over the plate.

"Didn't I mention that Digby was invited?" Noah asked. "Apparently he's the IT chef in London. When he gives a cooking demonstration, it's like the second coming of the Beatles."

"I could ask my friend Lenny to fill in for me," she wavered. "We were classmates at the Culinary Institute. He's on vacation, but if I promise to pay him double he might do it."

"Why don't you call him?" Noah suggested. "The network will pay him, you don't have any excuse not to come."

Louisa pulled out her phone and entered the storeroom. She returned to the kitchen and her face broke into a smile.

"I had to promise him my macaron recipe on top of his fee, but he'll do it."

Noah leaned forward and kissed her on the cheek.

"I don't mean to keep doing that but being around you is like riding a roller coaster," he said. "One minute you're flying high and the next you feel like you're plunging to certain death. I have to tell Kate and book your flight. We'll work on your wardrobe in London and I'll call ahead to get a hair appointment at Taylor Taylor."

"My hair is fine if I wash it." She touched her hair and suddenly wondered what she had gotten into. "And I'm sure I have a black cocktail dress in my closet."

"Leave it all to me." He beamed. "Write down your address and a car will pick you up and take you to the airport." He took off his wool coat and handed it to Louisa. "One more thing, this is for you."

"What's this for? It's a little big and I don't need a wool coat." She frowned.

"It's for the homeless man who sleeps in the alley," he explained. "There won't be anyone here to give him blankets."

Louisa noticed a speck of cream on Noah's collar. She wetted a napkin and dabbed it gently.

"What was that for?" He looked down.

"I didn't want you to leave with a stain on your shirt."

"Thank you." He smoothed his collar and smiled. "We're going to have an excellent working relationship."

Louisa smiled back and felt a shiver of excitement. "I agree."

Noah left and Louisa glanced at the clock. Noah said he had four hours and thirty-six minutes to get to JFK and that was half an hour ago! That meant Louisa had exactly four hours to finish the crescent cookies and race to her apartment and pack. She had to tell Ellie the news and call her parents and leave a note for her roommate.

The counter was littered with powdered sugar and chopped

pecans and she wondered whether she had done the right thing. Then she pictured the windows of Liberty filled with Burberry sweaters and Oxford Street strung with fairy lights and the aisles of Fortnum and Mason stocked with shortbread.

The rain fell outside the window and she hugged her arms around her chest. The first thing she would do when she arrived was buy a raincoat and wellies. She was going to spend Christmas in London!

Chapter Three

FOURTEEN HOURS LATER LOUISA SANK onto a red velvet sofa in her suite at Claridge's and let out a small sigh. She felt like a puppy that had played with a ball and now was happy to curl up with a favorite blanket. If she never left her suite and explored London at all, she'd be perfectly happy.

The suite's living room had crown moldings and white pillars and art deco mirrors. The walls were painted yellow and the parquet floor was scattered with geometric rugs. Scarlet armchairs were arranged around a glass coffee table and a crystal vase held the tallest flowers she had ever seen. The valet said the arrangement was replaced daily by McQueens, one of the most famous florists in London with a shop inside Claridge's.

And the bathroom! Louisa pictured her bathroom in New York with the sink jammed against the shower and the fire escape outside the window. The suite's bathroom was like entering Atlantis. The floor was heated white marble and the walls were painted ivory and everywhere you turned there were mirrors. The ceiling was mirrored and the side of the bathtub was mirrored and the walk-in closet had so many mirrors she felt dizzy.

When the front desk manager handed her the gold key for the Mayfair Suite, Louisa said there must be a mistake. Noah couldn't possibly have reserved a one-bedroom suite with a baby grand piano and furnishings designed by David Linley. She didn't need a balcony with a view of Brooks Mews, and a sideboard set with raisin scones and Marco Polo jelly.

The canopied king-sized bed in the master bedroom was so large, sleeping in it would be like being stranded in a rowboat in the middle of the ocean. And the ivory quilted bedspread made her nervous. What if she got face cream on it and it never came out?

But the manager explained the suite was reserved for Bianca and it was the only available room. It was completely paid for: she could eat anything from the minibar and every morning there was a complimentary room service breakfast of pink grapefruit juice and brown eggs scrambled or poached, with grilled tomatoes.

Noah had dropped her off at Claridge's entrance to run an errand and Kate stayed at the airport to locate a missing suitcase, so Louisa had no one to ask. Finally she gave up and followed the valet to the elevator.

She was so tired she could spend the whole morning soaking in the bathtub. Maybe in the afternoon she'd venture down to the lobby. She read all about the Map Room with its red-lacquered walls and burgundy carpet and curated library of books.

And she couldn't wait to poke her head in the Foyer with its creamy beige décor and plates of smoked salmon sandwiches and Cornish lobster salad. Noah said it was the perfect place for celebrity watching and it would be fun to bump into Nigella Lawson or David Beckham.

But she hadn't slept on the plane and she felt as if there was an orchestra playing inside her head. Noah and Kate had boarded the plane and pulled out eye masks. They wrapped themselves in cashmere blankets, downed two glasses of champagne, and fell asleep.

Louisa had never been in the business-class section of an airplane. She hadn't wanted to miss the movies showing on her personal iPad or the assortment of expensive lotions handed out by the flight attendants.

Now she walked to the marble sideboard in the suite and filled a brandy snifter with golden liqueur. There was a knock at the door and she answered it.

"Do you mind if I come in?" Noah asked. "I was afraid I missed you and you were already sightseeing." He glanced at the glass in Louisa's hand. "Isn't it a little early for a drink?"

"I wasn't going to drink it. I'm going to inhale it." She held it to her nose. "It's the perfect cure when you haven't slept. The brandy wakes your senses and makes you feel warm and alive."

"I did say you should sleep on the flight." Noah entered the living room. "It's important to adjust to local time. Eat a good lunch and drink lots of coffee. If you stay awake until 10:00 p.m., you'll be fine."

"I'm not the least bit hungry and the thought of coffee makes my stomach turn," she groaned. "I'm going to run a bath and take a long nap. Then I have to finish my recipe card for Ellie's daughter, Chloe. Chloe and I usually bake a different kids' Christmas dessert every day of the week before Christmas. She comes in after school in the middle of my shift. I'm not there, so I thought I'd send her one recipe card every day. It will be a bit like the Twelve Days of Christmas but instead of partridges in pear trees and drummers drumming there will be mini elf donuts and Christmas tree pops." She picked up the embossed Harrods stationery. "I'm starting with Rudolph's Shortbread. The short-bread is simple to make and you add M&M's for the reindeer's eyes and pipe cleaners for antlers." She beamed. "The cards won't arrive until after Christmas, but I told her she could save them and we'd bake them together. It will be so much fun."

"That's a wonderful idea. I'll tell you what I'll do," Noah suggested. "Give the card to the concierge each day and I'll make sure it is overnighted to Chloe. But I'm afraid you'll have to finish the card later. I have today's entire itinerary." He examined his clipboard. "At twelve thirty we'll meet your personal shopper at Harrods. We shoot B-roll around London all week: you shopping for ingredients at Selfridges and posing with the wax figure of Julia Child at Madame Tussauds.

"You'll need a selection of cashmere dresses and shoes. We should stay away from beiges, and we need to make you a bit taller, so we should find pumps with a heel.

"You have a three o'clock makeup session with Daniel Galvin. It's just preliminary, we don't know what will work until you're in front of the camera. But he can shape your eyebrows and see if we can get your cheekbones to look a little narrower.

"Lastly, we'll select a few pieces of jewelry at Asprey. They're only on loan, of course. It is Christmas at Claridge's; you have to look glamorous. A classic Asprey watch, the camera zooms in on it when you're mixing a bourbon sauce." He put down the clipboard and grinned. "That should bring us to the evening when there will be cocktails with the other chefs in the Fumoir."

"I'm not going to do any of those things! I never wear jewelry when I bake. What if I get molasses on a bracelet or an earring falls into a chocolate mousse? And if I'm going to be traipsing around London, it's going to be in comfortable boots, not pumps with a heel." She stopped and her eyes watered. "And I'm so tired, I couldn't possibly try on dresses. Can't I do all that tomorrow?"

"Tomorrow morning you have an interview with BBC One, followed by hair and highlights at Taylor Taylor." He looked back at the clipboard. "I wanted to get the hair done first, but we're lucky they squeezed you in. This is the most important culinary event of the season and you're one of the star chefs. Do you really think you get to lie around in a Claridge's robe and slippers?"

"I just wanted one day." Louisa dragged herself off the sofa. "I didn't realize how tired I was until I sat down. I feel like there's a bus sitting on my chest. And I don't want to disappoint Chloe and not send the recipes. It's bad enough that I left the week before Christmas."

"As long as you finish the card by this evening, I promise it will be overnighted in tomorrow's mail. Speaking of buses, I want to get some B-roll of you riding a red double-decker bus," he said and smiled. "We'll find one on the way to Harrods."

Noah waited while Louisa showered and slipped on a sweater and pair of slacks. She forced herself to eat a cucumber sandwich and gulped a cup of Earl Grey tea. They took the elevator to the lobby and suddenly Louisa felt silly for wanting to stay in her suite.

She had been so exhausted when she arrived she hadn't appreciated the black-and-cream-diamond marble floors and beveled mirrors. Glass vases were filled with white roses and an original Gainsborough hung over a stone fireplace. And the Christmas tree! It reached the ceiling and was made out of gold and silver metallic umbrellas.

"It's magnificent! Look at the way the light from the chandelier reflects off the umbrellas." She tilted her head. "It seems like it's actually raining."

"It's a promotion with Burberry," Noah explained. "Every year Claridge's partners with a fashion brand to create the most extravagant Christmas tree. They used one hundred umbrellas and it took three days to install."

Women crossed the lobby swathed in cashmere and carrying Harvey Nichols bags and Louisa felt a building excitement. She reached forward and kissed Noah on the cheek.

"What was that for?" he asked.

"I'm sorry I complained, I want to thank you for bringing me to London," she said. "I'll be the best chef Claridge's ever had, and I'll do everything you ask."

"Let's start by getting out of here." He guided her to the revolving glass doors. "If we miss your appointment with the private shopper, you'll be appearing on television in a sweater and moccasins."

· They passed the snowy expanse of Hyde Park and chic galleries on Bond Street. Piccadilly loomed in the distance and taxis were plastered with advertisements for Cadbury chocolates.

The bus stopped on the corner of Brampton Road and Louisa caught her breath. Across from her was a five-story building with stone turrets. It reminded her of a chocolate marzipan cake with HARRODS scrawled in gold frosting. She looked more closely at the store windows and had never seen anything so unusual.

Reindeer were dressed in knitted sweaters and red booties. Instead of pulling a wooden sleigh, they were attached to bright-red sports cars. There was a Lamborghini brimming with presents and an Aston Martin adorned with a gold bow. Fake snow dusted the tires and silver ornaments dangled from the bumpers.

"I thought I was jet-lagged and seeing things," Louisa laughed when they crossed the street. "How did they get the cars into the store, and whoever would have imagined a reindeer pulling a sports car?"

"No department store in the world celebrates Christmas like Harrods." Noah glanced at his watch. "Can we admire the windows later? We have to get to the fourth floor."

"I have to send Ellie a picture." Louisa handed Noah her phone and stood in front of the display. "Her daughter, Chloe, is seven. She'll think I landed in some incredible version of Santa's workshop."

"You're not wearing makeup and you haven't done your hair." He hesitated. "Why don't we take photos later?"

"I don't care what I look like. I'm at Harrods at Christmas!" She waved at the window. "Just take the picture."

Noah snapped the photo and they entered double brass doors. The throng of shoppers was so thick, Louisa could barely see the counters. Men in overcoats carried giant shopping bags and women wearing knee-high boots examined lipsticks and perfumes.

"Look over there." Noah took her arm.

Louisa pulled her eyes from a display of Christmas crackers and followed him to the middle of the store. The Christmas tree was five stories tall and seemed as wide as an ocean liner. Every branch was decorated with ornaments: teddy bears hanging from gold ribbons, and snow globes and toy trains. There were painted reindeer and a red telephone box.

"That looks like Cinderella's slipper." She pointed to a slipper on a lower branch. She peered closer and gasped. "It can't be made of real diamonds!"

"It is made of diamonds. And there are ruby angels and stockings made of emeralds and sapphires. You can see every ornament after we choose your wardrobe." He steered her toward the escalator. "It's going to take us ages to get upstairs. The escalator is more crowded than the subway at rush hour."

They reached the fourth floor and entered a lounge with plush carpet and high-backed velvet chairs. There was a plate of scones and glasses of apple cider.

Louisa sank onto a chair and pushed a stray hair from her forehead. She looked at Noah and her eyes sparkled.

"You promise not to wake me?" she asked.

"What do you mean 'wake you'?" His cheeks paled. "You can't fall asleep now!"

"I mean don't wake me from this whole dream," she laughed. "A suite at Claridge's and the whole afternoon at Harrods. Any minute I'll wake up in my apartment with the radiator spitting water and cracks in the ceiling."

"You're not dreaming," Noah said and Louisa noticed his eyes were bluer than she remembered. He was about to say something when a woman in a navy suit appeared.

"It's a pleasure to have you join us." The woman nodded. "Where would you like to begin? Some gorgeous Herve Leger dresses just came in, and we have a fabulous selection of Balmain blazers."

Louisa followed the woman and her shoulders tightened. Cashmere sweaters were piled to the ceiling and there were racks of wool slacks and silk blouses. Mannequins wore satin evening gowns and glass cases were filled with patterned scarves.

Suddenly she wished she was sitting in the bathtub or curled up on the sofa writing Chloe's recipe card. The last thing she wanted to do was stand in front of a mirror and fiddle with zippers and buttons. But Noah trailed after them like an overprotective parent and she didn't have a choice.

"That dress looks nice." She waved at a kelly-green knit dress. "I guess we can start with that."

The woman led her to a dressing room and handed her Burberry sweaters and Alexander McQueen dresses. There was a sequined sheath that was so sheer, Louisa was embarrassed to look at her reflection. She slipped on a magenta evening gown and a coatdress made of Shetland wool. Finally the saleswoman carried away her selections and Louisa joined Noah.

"Most women would give anything to be handed St. John dresses without worrying about the price tag." He looked up from his clipboard. "You look like you had a tooth filled at the dentist."

"I wore a gorgeous dress to my cousin's wedding and it's important to dress up for birthdays and Christmas." She shrugged. "But I'm happiest when I'm baking. You can't wear a pretty blouse when you're making crust for a peach tart. It will end up covered in peach juice."

"Is baking the only thing you care about?" he asked curiously.

"I love romantic movies. And I adore animals, though I'll never have a pet in Manhattan." She paused. "But there isn't time to be passionate about more than one thing. If you want something in life, you have to sacrifice everything else to get it." She looked at Noah. "Aren't you passionate about something?"

"I'm passionate about the law, I guess," he answered. "It's fascinating to read hundred-year-old cases that affect our laws today. When I'm in the midst of a case study, I don't think of anything else."

"You see, we're the same," she mused. "We're both happiest when we're doing what is important to us."

"What about love?" he asked suddenly.

"What do you mean?" she wondered.

"Most people our age want to get married and have babies."

"I haven't thought about it," she said slowly. "I don't have time to fall in love."

"But if you did?" he prompted.

"I don't know," she replied and suddenly the room felt a little warm. "Right now, I'm too tired to think about anything except going back to Claridge's and taking a bath and finishing my recipe card."

"You can't show up for cocktails at the Fumoir in moccasins." He glanced at her feet. "First we'll tackle Harrods's shoe department. Then you can take a bath."

They rode the escalator to the second floor and entered the shoe department. Noah pulled out silver stilettos and satin pumps and ankle boots made of the softest suede. There were ballet slippers with diamond bows and a pair of red Louboutin pumps with a jeweled sole.

"You want me to try on all these?" she asked dismally. "Can't you choose? I'll close my eyes and you can pick whatever you like."

"You can't stand on the set with pinched toes. And if you don't practice walking in high heels, you'll fall on your face," he insisted. "Shoes are very personal. You have to try them on."

"If they're so personal why can't I wear the ones I have?" she grumbled. "No one will see them on television and the chefs at the cocktail party won't notice. We'll all be busy discussing the Christmas Dinner menu."

He took a pair of Gucci pumps out of the box and handed them to Louisa. "Don't you ever worry about what you wear?"

"I don't have time to go out to dinner, and I'm always too tired to go dancing," she explained. "Besides, a pair of designer pumps costs a week's salary."

"Well, tonight you're having cocktails at Claridge's." He handed her the pumps. "Please hurry. We have to be at Daniel Galvin's in an hour."

Louisa tried on shoes until her ankles burned and she could barely walk. Finally Noah was satisfied and gave the tower of boxes to the salesgirl.

"Kate just sent me an urgent text." He pulled out his phone. "I need better reception. Stay here and I'll be right back."

Louisa leaned against the cushions and closed her eyes.

"One more thing." He turned around.

"Yes?" Her eyes flickered open.

"I just wanted you to know, you look lovely in moccasins." He grinned. "I'm only doing my job."

Louisa peered over the marble balustrade and saw the Food Hall with its gleaming glass cases and festive decorations. The scent of mulled wine and gingerbread drifted up the escalator and people milled around as if they were at a symphony opening.

The delicacies she had read about! Scottish salmon and suckling pig and thick slices of ham. There was a chocolate shop with chocolate teddy bears and a chocolate Santa Claus with a white frosting beard. A patisserie baked éclairs like you found in Paris and an Indian counter sold curries that made your eyes water.

She couldn't leave Harrods without visiting the place she had been dreaming of since she became a pastry chef. It would be like waiting months for a reservation at Eleven Madison Park and leaving before dessert.

It would only take several minutes to walk around the Food Hall. She wouldn't see everything, of course. But she could sample sticky puddings and bittersweet-chocolate tarts.

The shoeboxes were stacked on the counter and she told the saleswoman she'd be right back. The escalator deposited her at the entrance and she was so excited, she wanted to hug every vendor in his striped apron and colorful cap.

The ceilings were painted with gorgeous frescoes and the floors were black-and-white marble and iron grillwork covered the walls. But it was the food displays that took her breath away. All the Google images didn't prepare her for pyramids of cheeses and buckets crammed with lobsters and fruit stalls stocked with kumquats.

She sampled a ricotta cheese that was as creamy as the finest ice cream. The chamomile flower tea made her feel like she was in an English garden, and the Turkish coffee was the strongest coffee she'd ever tasted. And the pastries! There were trays of custards and vanilla slices and raspberry cheesecakes.

She noticed a familiar packaging and stopped. It was the French butter she had discovered in Normandy. Ever since she returned to New York she had tried to replicate it. But American butters were plain and thick, like processed cheese on white bread.

"Can I help you?" a man asked.

"Is that really Echire butter?" she wondered. "I ate it one summer in Normandy. I never had French butter before, it was the best thing I ever tasted."

"It's because of the amount of butter fat," he explained. "And French butter is made from partly soured cream to give it a tangy flavor."

What if she bought a package and kept it in the suite's minibar? The croquembouche she was baking for *Christmas Dinner at Claridge's* would be superb. But the line at the cash register snaked halfway down the Food Hall. If she weren't in the shoe department when Noah returned, he'd be furious.

"Would you like to buy some?" the man asked.

"Perhaps another time." She hesitated. "I'm in a hurry."

"We run out quickly during the holidays." He shrugged. "It's a popular ingredient for Bûche de Noëls."

Noah had every minute scheduled; she might not return to Harrods for days. And she still had time—her makeup appointment wasn't for an hour.

"I'd like two pounds of butter please," she announced, ignoring the nervous flutter in her stomach.

Louisa clutched her package as if she'd won some incredible prize. But the wait at the cash register was even longer than she thought and it took ages to pay. When she returned to the shoe department it was an hour later and the stack of shoeboxes was gone.

"Have you seen my boxes?" she asked the salesgirl anxiously. "I left them right here."

"The gentleman came back to collect them," the woman said.

"The man wearing a navy sweater?" Louisa gulped. "Do you know where he is?"

"He was here, but then he left," the woman answered.

"Did he say anything?" Louisa urged and a prickle ran down her spine.

"He didn't look very happy," the woman remembered. "Is something wrong?"

"Just a silly misunderstanding." Louisa flushed and hurried down the escalator. She raced across the marble floor and through the revolving doors. But Noah wasn't in front of the window or underneath the Harrods sign. She didn't see him at the taxi stand or the bus stop across the street.

Her phone hadn't been switched to international calling and she couldn't remember the name of the makeup artist. Jet lag engulfed her and tears pricked her eyes. She had made a mess of her first afternoon in London.

But Noah would understand when he tasted her croquembouche. After all, she was replacing Bianca at the most important culinary event of the year. He would want her dessert to be delicious.

The sun filtered through the clouds and she suddenly felt brighter. She was in London at Christmas; of course she wanted to do some sightseeing. And *Christmas Dinner at Claridge's* wasn't for six days.

She strolled down Brampton Road and noticed tour buses stopping in front of iron gates. She looked more closely and realized she was in front of Buckingham Palace.

What if she entered the grounds and had a quick look around? She already missed the makeup appointment and there was plenty of time to take a bath before cocktails. She couldn't pass Buckingham Palace and keep walking!

She called the front desk of Claridge's and left a message for Noah telling him she would be back soon. Then she bought a ticket at the kiosk. The woman handed her a guidebook and she followed the signs to a marble corridor. The State Rooms had ornate mirrors and dazzling chandeliers and silver candelabras. Paintings in gilt frames lined the walls and the ceilings were so high she had to crane her neck to see the gold-flecked frescoes.

She saw the Throne Room where the Duke and Duchess of

Cambridge took their wedding photos, and the White Drawing Room where the royal family gathered before official engagements. There was a whole exhibit of Queen Elizabeth's fashions including her wedding dress designed by Sir Norman Hartnell and the lace gown she wore to her coronation.

And the Royal Mews! She could have spent hours in the stables with their sleek horses and black-and-red carriages. She fully expected Cinderella to descend from a horse-drawn carriage and meet her Prince Charming.

A clock chimed five o'clock and she gasped. How did it get so late? She only planned on taking a quick tour. She raced down the palace drive and strode the few blocks to Claridge's.

"Good evening, Miss Graham," the valet greeted her. "I hope you had a pleasant afternoon."

"London is wonderful, but there's so much to see." Louisa sighed. "The whole day flew by."

A fire flickered in the lobby's fireplace and bellboys carried packages wrapped in silver paper. Guests in chic evening wear mingled around the Christmas tree and there was the heady scent of pine needles and expensive perfume.

She took the elevator to the fifth floor and fiddled with her key. The door of the suite opened and Noah stood in the living room.

"What are you doing in my suite?" she demanded.

"What am I doing here?" he seethed. "I waited in the shoe department for thirty minutes and then searched every floor of Harrods. I spent an hour humoring one of the most important makeup artists in London. I've been sitting here so long, I memorized the books on the bookshelf."

"I'm sorry I'm late. But you could have waited in the lobby," she said, wondering if she'd left out any bras or underwear.

"And have you sneak by like some international spy?" he spluttered. "You're not late. Late is missing your subway stop and arriving ten minutes after a meeting started. Late is hitting the Snooze button on your alarm and calling your boss to apologize. Late is not disappearing from the shoe department of Harrods and arriving at your suite three hours later."

"I couldn't call, my phone didn't work." She sank onto the sofa. "I was only going to take a quick look around the Food Hall, but then I discovered they had Echire butter. I couldn't leave without buying a package."

"You stopped to buy butter?" He wrinkled his brow.

"It's from France and it's the best butter in the world," she insisted. "It's because of the rich soil they feed the cows. I'm going to use it in my croquembouche."

"In half an hour you're supposed to be at the Fumoir and you're wearing slacks and moccasins," he fumed. "I don't care if it was the butter Marie Antoinette ate with her last omelet, you could have bought it another time."

"I've stood in the pouring rain at the Chelsea market to buy peaches and took the train to Brooklyn to get the perfect baking chocolate." Her eyes flashed. "I'm a chef. There is nothing more important than my ingredients."

"If you remember, I borrowed two trays of cinnamon rolls and ended up giving Bianca an allergic reaction. Then I promised Kate you would be the perfect replacement and she paid your airfare and accommodation. Now there is a camera crew waiting to film you at a cocktail reception." He jumped up. "I don't care if your croquembouche is made of Styrofoam. If you're not downstairs in half an hour, I'm out of a job."

Noah paced around the room and suddenly Louisa felt guilty.

What had she been thinking? Just because clothes and makeup weren't important to her didn't mean she could ignore them.

"Where are the boxes from Harrods with all the dresses and shoes?" She glanced around the suite.

"The valet delivered them to your bedroom." He waved his hand.

"I made a mistake, but I promise I won't let you down," she said. "Give me twenty minutes and I'll make you and Kate proud."

"What are you going to do?" he asked.

A smile crossed her face and she was so happy to be in London. "Don't come in until I'm ready. I don't want to spoil the surprise."

Louisa spritzed her wrists with perfume and rubbed her lips with lipstick. She touched her hair and wondered why she felt anxious. Then she pictured the disappointment in Noah's eyes. She hated to let him down; it wasn't like her at all.

Was that why she felt the same nervous excitement as when she got ready for her senior prom? She couldn't think about it now. If she took any longer to get ready, Noah would never forgive her. She sifted through the boxes for a chiffon wrap and opened the door.

"What do you think?" she asked, entering the living room.

Noah stood next to the fireplace clutching a shot glass. He placed it on the sideboard and rubbed his forehead.

"You don't like it," she said anxiously. "I shouldn't have chosen the red dress. It's too bright for a cocktail party and the fabric is practically see through. I'll go change, it won't take long."

"The dress is perfect." Noah stopped her. "You said you don't have any makeup and the hairdresser ruined your hair. You look like . . ."

"Like what?" she prompted, and for some reason felt unsteady.

"You look like a movie star," he finished.

"You're exaggerating," she laughed, relief flooding her chest. "I never said I didn't have any makeup. Most women carry mascara and lipstick in their purse. And a curling iron does wonders with hair." She paused. "Do you think Kate will be happy?"

Noah started as if he forgot the time. "Only if we are downstairs in three minutes," he began. "I'm sorry I snapped at you. I convinced you to drop everything and fly to London. Then I didn't care that you were tired and scheduled every minute of your day."

Louisa smiled and suddenly felt better.

"Apology accepted," she conceded. "With your itinerary, we're going to be stuck together like sprinkles on a birthday cake. It would be nice if we got along."

"We can work out a truce later." He grinned. "There's a two-man camera crew and some of the most important chefs in the world downstairs. We don't want to keep them waiting."

Noah opened lacquered double doors and Louisa gasped. Entering the Fumoir was like walking into a 1920s speakeasy. Purple velvet love seats were arranged around beveled glass coffee tables and photographs of Marlene Dietrich and Clark Gable lined the walls. An art deco mirror stood behind the bar and patterned rugs covered oak floors.

Everything about the room was stunning: the pearl cigar cases and horseshoe-shaped bar lined with bottles of Armagnac. Crystal vases shimmered under the low light and flickering candles gave the tables a warm glow.

A small group gathered near the fireplace and Louisa recognized Pierre Gagnaire and Andreas Caminada. Her stomach turned and she wanted to race upstairs.

Could she really chat with chefs who were on the cutting edge of the culinary scene? She knew nothing about reduction sauces or plate equilibrium. She didn't work in a kitchen filled with gleaming cookware like a restaurant kitchen on a movie set.

But when would she get a chance to learn from chefs who earned Michelin stars and wrote glossy cookbooks? And besides, she and Noah agreed to get along. He wouldn't be happy if she suddenly had a headache and went to her suite.

"There you are." A woman turned around. "Noah was frantic. He thought you had been kidnapped or fallen asleep in the back of a cab."

When Louisa had arrived at JFK there had only been a few minutes until the plane boarded and she barely met Kate. And the moment they touched down at Heathrow, Kate rushed off to solve a crisis. Now Louisa noticed how beautiful she was.

Kate was in her early thirties and had blond hair knotted in a chignon and green eyes coated with sparkly eye shadow. She wore a silver sheath that complemented her long legs and a hint of pale lipstick. But it was her smile that made her lovely. It was bright and sincere.

"Please don't blame Noah," Louisa urged. "It's entirely my fault. This morning I was so jet-lagged, I could barely stand up. Then I got sidetracked in the Food Hall at Harrods and missed my makeup appointment. There's so much to see, Christmas in London is thrilling." She paused. "I promise it won't happen again. From now on I'm sticking to the itinerary."

"As long as you are here now." Kate nodded. "I can understand. When I don't sleep on the plane, I'm like a bear forced out of hibernation."

"It is overwhelming." Louisa glanced at waiters wearing black bow ties and white gloves. They carried trays of quail eggs and potted shrimp. "The Mayfair Suite and giant Christmas tree in the lobby and having cocktails with world-class chefs," she said with a sigh. "What if I say the wrong thing and everybody laughs?"

"Use my trick," Kate offered. "When I produced my first show, I had to speak at a board meeting in front of a roomful of executives. I stood next to my PowerPoint presentation with the Empire State Building behind me and forgot my notes."

"What did you do?" Louisa asked.

"I imagined everyone sitting in their underwear."

"That doesn't work," Louisa laughed. "It's what they do in movies."

"It cured me immediately," Kate insisted. "It helps if you imagine something ridiculous: boxer shorts with Santa Clauses or penguins."

"What could I possibly have to say to some of the most famous chefs in the world?" Louisa asked and noticed a man standing next to the fireplace. While the other chefs wore blazers and ties, he was dressed in a cashmere V-neck sweater and navy slacks. His blond hair fell over his forehead and he held a champagne flute.

"Is that really—" she began.

"Digby Bunting?" Kate followed her gaze. "I haven't met him, but he's quite notorious. They call him the British Cooking Casanova. At his last book signing they had to hire security to keep the women away."

"I don't care about that. His recipes are delicious." Louisa shrugged. "I'm dying to ask him how he gets the right consistency in his Opera Cake. When I make it, the whipped mascarpone cream falls flat."

"I'll introduce you," Kate suggested.

"Now?" Louisa panicked. What if she said something embarrassing? Like she adored his chocolate truffle layer cake and he said that wasn't in the cookbook, she must be thinking of Alain Ducasse.

"You're going to be cooking beside him," Kate reminded her. "Don't worry, he's just like the rest of us. He probably had acne as a teenager."

"Let me get a drink first." Louisa accepted a martini from a passing waiter and glanced around the room.

She looked for Noah but he'd disappeared. There was no reason for him to stay; his job was to make sure she made it to the Fumoir. He was probably at Claridge's bar sipping a Dubonnet or in his suite taking a nap. She was surprised that his absence left her suddenly deflated, like when she baked a perfect cheesecake only to discover the blueberries were sour and she didn't have a topping.

Digby glanced in her direction and she flushed. She should be excited. She was standing in Claridge's about to meet one of the most famous pastry chefs in the world.

"I'm ready." She turned to Kate. "Let's meet Digby Bunting."

Chapter Four

KATE SAT IN A BOOTH in Claridge's Reading Room and picked at a tomato and Parmesan salad. She hadn't eaten anything except an egg sandwich since the plane landed this morning and now it was past 10:00 p.m. But she moved bacon around her plate and realized she wasn't hungry. She should have spared her expense account and ordered a cup of tea.

She was rarely hungry when she worked because there was so much to think about: whether the camera crew was getting the right angles or the wireless microphones were picking up sound. The reception in the Fumoir ended at ten and everyone went to bed. Noah left early and she couldn't blame him. Being responsible for Louisa must be exhausting.

Kate could tell Louisa was out of her depth. It was bold of Noah to pluck her out of a bakery kitchen on the Lower East Side and put her on a plane. But they didn't have a choice, and now they were all in it together.

Kate fiddled with her glass and knew worrying about Louisa wasn't the only thing that made her lose her appetite. And it wasn't the excitement of being in a foreign city that let her exist on the occasional sandwich and endless cups of coffee.

The magazine was propped up on the silver bread basket and she picked it up. It was the picture on the cover that made her heart beat a little faster.

A British country manor with stone statues and English rose gardens stared back at her. A woman wore riding boots and her chestnut hair was tied in a ponytail. Beside her stood a man in a navy blazer and tasseled loafers. The caption read: "Sir Trevor Skyler and his wife, Susannah, great niece of Queen Elizabeth, at home at Yardley Manor in Sussex."

But it hadn't been Sir Trevor when she knew him at St Andrews ten years ago. It had been Trevor with hair that was too long and fell in his eyes, and pants that were too short because they were castoffs from a wealthier friend.

Trevor helped her get through applied mathematics because the math was completely different from what she'd learned in high school in Santa Barbara. She and Trevor spent hours studying on the lawn in front of the Student Union while other students played Frisbee. The Scottish autumn was so short; you had to take advantage of good weather.

Trevor didn't mind. He was as allergic to exercise as he was to peanut butter. But Kate watched young men with floppy dark hair and girls with fair complexions laugh and toss the Frisbee and wondered why she came all the way to Scotland for university if she was going to bury her head in a textbook.

And she had helped Trevor in return. He wouldn't have passed freshman English if she hadn't shown him how to decipher *Beowulf*. He refused to read anything in Old English, and he wrote a paper trying to convince the professor to start with Shakespeare. He got an F on the paper and Kate couldn't help laughing.

She remembered all the afternoons they spent exploring the alleyways of St Andrews. The university was spread out through the town, like daisies popping up in a field. Stone buildings with stained-glass windows and peaked roofs were wedged between the butcher with pork hanging in the window and a newsagent selling girlie magazines and Violet Crumbles.

They took long walks on the sand dunes of West Sands beach that adjoined St Andrews golf course. When she arrived, she thought that color green couldn't be real. It was like the emerald in a priceless pendant.

How did the boy who would rather eat cold meat pies in his room than attend festive communal dinners in McIntosh Hall marry a minor member of the royal family who was famous for her house parties?

The article said every year Sir Trevor and his wife held a house party that lasted the whole week before Christmas. The Duke and Duchess of Cambridge were known to attend and there was hunting and fishing.

Dinners were served in Yardley Manor's dining room and a well-known chef created each meal. Jamie Oliver prepared sweet potato and cardamom soup and Marco Pierre White served venison with beets and heritage carrots. The whole estate was decorated for Christmas: a Fraser fir tree with ornaments from Harvey Nichols and stockings hung from massive stone fireplaces and a toy train set that took up the entire library.

She hadn't seen Trevor in ten years. And she'd taught herself not to think about him. Her memories of St Andrews were packed away with her yearbooks and the tartan scarf Trevor gave her for her birthday.

She put down her fork and thought she should be upstairs planning tomorrow's schedule. They were going to film Louisa strolling past the boutiques on Carnaby Street and examining the Christmas hampers at Fortnum and Mason.

She glanced around for a waiter and saw a man standing in the lobby. A trench coat was folded over his arm and he scribbled on a note card.

Even before he looked up, she knew it was Trevor. Somehow she wasn't surprised; the article mentioned that Claridge's was Trevor's favorite hotel in London. Perhaps he was giving a lecture or attending some holiday function. Where else would he stay when he was in town?

Once early in their friendship, Trevor marveled at how they had the same tastes. They both had porridge with sliced peaches for breakfast and didn't eat big lunches. In the evenings, while other students played drinking games and danced on tables at the pub, they found each other sitting on the fire escape, looking up at the stars.

Should she get up and say hello? Afterward she'd need a large scotch. But she was a grown woman and her job was to tackle difficult situations. She couldn't slink away like a wallflower at a dance.

She searched her purse for her charge card and heard a male voice. She looked up and Trevor stood next to the table. His suit was tailored and he had an expensive haircut, but he had the same brown eyes and narrow cheekbones.

"Kate?" he asked incredulously. "What are you doing in London?"

"Trevor! I was just reading about you." She pointed to the magazine. "'Sir Trevor was knighted by Queen Elizabeth for his contribution to the field of mathematics. The ceremony at Buckingham Palace was followed by a private party at Annabel's given by his wife, Lady Skyler, and attended by London's fashionable set.'"

"One can never trust the media to get it right." He sighed. "Do you remember when you subscribed to *Hello* and complained they made the stories up?"

"Which part did they get wrong?" she asked.

"That Lady Skyler is my wife," he said slowly. "We're separated."

"Separated!" she exclaimed.

"To be fair, it hasn't been announced." He shrugged. "It's a recent development."

"I'm sorry, I had no idea," she answered.

"Do you mind if I sit down?" he asked. "I've driven from Sussex in the rain. My suite isn't ready and I don't feel like sitting in the bar and listening to Christmas music."

"I was about to go upstairs," she stammered. "Perhaps we could meet for breakfast or—"

"Kate." He stopped her. "We haven't seen each other in ten years. We have time for a brandy."

Trevor was right. They had been close for four years; she could manage one drink.

"Why not? I can never sleep after a transatlantic flight and a Brandy Alexander sounds delicious."

The waiter set down two Brandy Alexanders and she fiddled with her hair. This was a bad idea; she didn't know where to start. Did they talk about St Andrews or the last day they saw each other?

"Is it still Kate Crawford?" He glanced at her hand. "Or are you one of those modern career women who has a husband and four children but doesn't wear a wedding ring?"

"I'm not married." She felt the brandy warm her throat. "I'm the producer of a television cooking show. It's like being a surgeon and attorney and parent at once. There's always some disaster to stitch up and crisis to solve and feelings that need soothing."

"I'm not surprised, you were the most capable person I knew. Member of the History Society and Save the Elephants Society and Mermaids Theatre Committee." He fiddled with his drink and his eyes darkened. "You were even capable of breaking my heart."

Kate put down her glass. "It's late, I should go."

"I'm sorry, I'm overtired," he urged. "I've been sleeping in the den because the bedrooms are full for Susannah's house party. She doesn't want her friends to know about the separation so I had to sneak down after everyone went to bed. The central heating doesn't work in the left wing and the blankets were spoken for," he said. "I finally gave up and booked a suite at Claridge's."

"A last-minute suite at Claridge's the week before Christmas?" Kate raised her eyebrow. "You must be important."

"Terribly important," he laughed. "Prize-winning mathematician and related by marriage to Queen Elizabeth. If you come back next summer, I can get you a box at Wimbledon."

"I'm sorry about your marriage." She waved at the magazine. "I read the whole article. Thirty-room Sussex manor and stable of hunters and summer home in Spain."

"Did they mention the dogs?" he asked. "In the end, they were the only ones who talked to me."

"What happened?" she asked.

"When Susannah and I met, I won the Hirst Prize for Mathematics. I was different from her set who worked in The City and drove flashy cars. Susannah can be lovely when she's alone, but when she's with her friends she becomes another person." He sighed. "A mathematician who would rather spend his evenings looking through a telescope than drinking Taittingers at London clubs wasn't a suitable husband."

"Do you have children?" she wondered.

"We were planning on it. But Susannah hadn't scheduled it around her gymkhanas." He ran his hands through his hair. "I'm not going to cry into my brandy the week before Christmas. We were from separate worlds, it was like parking a Volkswagen in the garage of Buckingham Palace."

"You must have been in love to get married," she said and stopped.

Trevor's eyes flickered and he stabbed his drink with his straw.

"I'm sorry, it's none of my business." She stood up. "I'll have the waiter add my drink to my check. It was nice to see you."

Trevor stood up and she remembered how tall he was. Except at St Andrews his clothes hung on him like a skeleton at Halloween, and now he filled out his suit.

"I'm tired too." He leaned forward and kissed her on the cheek. "You look beautiful, Kate. Being a successful producer agrees with you."

Kate entered the living room of her suite and slipped off her pumps. She was grateful that Claridge's upgraded her to a suite. The eggshell satin walls and white wool rugs and bouquets of roses were so soothing. Even looking at the art deco bar with its bottles of aged cognac and chocolate truffles made her feel better.

She filled a brandy snifter and stood at the window. It was past eleven and silver Bentleys idled outside the entrance. Men and women wore elegant evening wear and there were flashes of diamond earrings and gold watches.

She felt as rattled as when they filmed a show in Paris and her cameraman came down with the flu. She had to find a doctor who made house calls, and then run to a pharmacy in the pouring rain.

But she didn't mind; that was her job. This was so personal. Her heart hammered and she could barely breathe.

The hotel phone rang and she started. She unclipped her earring and picked it up.

"Kate," a male voice said. "It's Trevor."

"Trevor!" She flushed. "Why are you calling? We just said goodnight."

"I was wondering if you'd like to have dinner tomorrow night," he began. "We can go to Quaglino's, it's one of the most famous restaurants in London. Princess Diana used to sneak in through the kitchen and diners have been known to pocket ashtrays as souvenirs."

"I don't have time for dinner," she said quickly.

"You have to eat, you taught me that," he laughed. "You used to hide my textbooks until I went to the Student Union and ate a sausage roll. Then you'd make sure I didn't throw half of it away so I could get back to solving algorithms."

"You were so thin, you couldn't afford to miss meals," she remembered.

"We're both alone in London the week before Christmas," he

urged. "It would be a shame if we spent every night sitting alone, pushing steak tartare around our plates."

"You must have other friends in London." She fiddled with her glass.

"Susannah and I had friends, but they're all at Yardley Manor taking long walks and playing charades."

"It's not a good idea," she insisted. "And I really am busy, we have a tight schedule."

"We've always enjoyed each other's company and I'll tell you what to see in London." He paused. "Let's make a deal. We won't talk about the past. We'll eat chicken liver parfait and I'll give you tidbits for your show—who serves the best Bloody Mary and where to spot young royals: Loulou's and Bunga Bunga and The Brown Cow."

"We really won't talk about the past?" she gasped.

"It's a promise." His voice softened. "It's only dinner, Kate."

"All right, dinner." She nodded. "I'll see you tomorrow night."

Kate hung up the phone and replaced her earring. What had she done? She really didn't have time and they had so much history. But Trevor was right: she was alone in London at Christmas. It might be nice to explore Oxford Street without a clipboard.

She sipped her brandy and the past washed over her, like the sea at White Sands beach. God, they had fun! Walking down South Street and eating so much tangy cheese at the Old Cheese Shop she was sure she'd get a stomachache.

She met Trevor during her third week at St Andrews. From the moment the taxi dropped her off at McIntosh Hall, the town enchanted her. Cobblestone streets were crammed with narrow houses with bright orange roofs. Wooden planters were filled with pansies and shop windows displayed Shetland sweaters.

And the bicycles! Students left them propped against fire hydrants while they browsed inside Waterstones bookstore and ate eggs Benedict at Taste café. Kate bought a yellow bicycle and rode to Blackfriars Chapel and down to the sand dunes to watch the sunset.

The sunsets took her breath away. She'd look back at the town with the ruins of St Andrews Cathedral rising in the distance and St Andrews golf course laid out like a magic carpet and think the whole world consisted of stone turrets and picturesque shops and fishing boats bobbing in cozy inlets.

Kate hopped on her bicycle and rode down North Street. It was one of three medieval streets at the center of town and it was so narrow, she was afraid of getting sideswiped by a taxi.

Her college advisor had shown her the brochures for St Andrews. Her parents were hesitant: Kate was in the top ten of her class; she could have gone to UCLA or even Stanford. But when she read about the six-hundred-year-old university nestled in a fishing village on the North Sea, she didn't want to go anywhere else.

Everything about St Andrews was new and exciting: the Botanic Gardens with its lush ferns and university museum filled with fifteenth-century artifacts. She spent whole afternoons admiring pottery in quaint galleries and exploring fishing villages on the Fife Coastal Path.

She waited at the stop sign and realized she forgot her math homework. She was in enough trouble with math; she couldn't afford another bad grade. She turned back and parked her bicycle in front of Mitchells Deli.

A young man sat at the wooden table. His sandy hair fell over his forehead and he tapped on a calculator.

"Excuse me." She approached him. "I left my binder here, did you see it?"

"It's right here." He took it out of his backpack.

"You took my homework?" Kate was startled.

"I was going to return it, your name is on the back." He handed it to her. "I corrected it for you. You got most of the answers wrong."

"Did I?" she said and sighed. "No one told me applied mathematics is completely different from what we learned in America. No matter how much I study, I can't get it right."

"Would you like help?" he asked.

"I can't afford a tutor." She shook her head. "I've used up my allowance."

"I won't charge you," he answered, erasing a number on his paper.

Kate often had men offer to carry her bags at the airport, or allow her to cut in line at the supermarket when she was in a hurry and only had one item. But the offers usually came with a request for her phone number and phone calls asking her to dinner.

But he couldn't be interested in her. He barely looked up, and she was wearing jeans and no makeup.

"You have your own homework," she said. "Why would you want to help me for free?"

"It's math," he said simply. "I enjoy it."

"All right, I'm Kate." She smiled, relief flooding through her. She noticed his angular cheekbones and thin wrists beneath his shirt cuffs. "But let me buy you a plate of chips and Parmesan. It's the best thing I've eaten since I arrived in Scotland."

"Trevor." He held out his hand. "And a plate of chips and Parmesan sounds great."

Kate glanced at her watch and gasped. She had been listening to Trevor so closely, she hadn't kept track of time.

"This has been wonderful, but I have to go." She gathered her books. "I'm late for the Gilbert and Sullivan Society and then I have a meeting of the Music Is Love committee and tonight I'm assisting at the student film festival."

"You have three events in one afternoon?" he asked. "Doesn't that make your day a little crowded?"

"The societies are the best thing about St Andrews," she countered. "You meet students from all over the world and become interested in subjects you never imagined. I also joined the Sherlock Society and Children's Teddy Bear Society. We deliver teddy bears to local hospitals."

"Charity work is worthwhile but most of it seems like a waste of time." He shrugged. "If I want to study Sherlock Holmes, all I need is a book."

"You must belong to some societies," she urged. "How do you make friends?"

"I tried the Mathematics Society, but the members were more interested in drinking Hendrick's gin at Sandy's Bar," he replied. "Most societies have members who spend Christmas holidays at a Scottish castle and summer vacations on large yachts. They have jobs waiting for them in family banks or trust funds large enough so they never work at all. Attending St Andrews is just moving the party from London and Surrey to their own private club on the North Sea."

"I've never been to a castle and didn't know a single person when I arrived," Kate argued. "Everyone is friendly and I'm having so much fun."

"You're a pretty American; it's different," he said. "My father teaches science at a grammar school in York and my mother is a nurse. That hardly qualifies me to rub shoulders with guys who grew up on polo ponies and girls whose diamond earrings cost more than my parents' house."

"Why did you come to St Andrews if you don't like anything about it?" She was suddenly angry.

"A few reasons," he said thoughtfully. "The math program is internationally regarded, but it's more than that. When I stand on the Old Course and gaze at the grass tinged with purple and yellow and the sun reflecting on the Castle Course Clubhouse, it's the most beautiful place in the world."

Trevor pushed his hair off his forehead and Kate noticed his eyes were brown and flecked with gold. Her voice softened and she smiled.

"The golf course is my favorite spot. Sometimes the light is perfect." She stood up. "Thank you for your help. I'm sure I'll see you again."

"Kate," Trevor called.

She turned around and he waved a paper in the air.

"You forgot your math." He grinned. "It would be a shame not to turn it in. You got all the answers right."

Kate sat at the desk in her dorm room and thumbed through a copy of *Beowulf*. It was past midnight and the moon glimmered on the playing fields. Footsteps clattered across the cobblestones and there was the sound of laughter.

She never needed much sleep; it was one of the reasons she excelled in high school. It wasn't unusual for her to study for a chemistry exam until 2:00 a.m. or stay up all night reading F. Scott Fitzgerald.

There were so many things she loved to do at St Andrews that it was impossible to fit it all in. Just this evening, she welcomed a well-known Swedish film director and watched a performance of *The Mikado*.

She sipped a cup of lavender tea and heard a knock on her door. She pulled a fisherman's sweater over her T-shirt and opened it.

"Trevor!" she exclaimed. "How did you get up here? The residence hall is locked after 10:00 p.m."

"What a strange coincidence, I live down the hall." He waved at a door. "You have a telephone call on the house phone."

"A phone call?"

Her friends would call her cell phone and she'd already talked to her parents this evening.

"His name is Byron." He handed her a notepad. "He said it was urgent."

"His name isn't actually Byron, it's George." She glanced at the note. "My bicycle got a flat tire and he pumped it up. He told me his whole life story: his father expects him to take over the family stock brokerage but he wants to be a poet," she explained. "He asked where I lived, but I didn't think he would call."

"Would you like me to give him a message?" Trevor asked.

"Do you mind?" she wondered.

Kate sat cross-legged on the bed and waited for Trevor to return.

"It's all fixed." He entered her room. "He wrote a sonnet and wanted to deliver it to you in person. I told him you fell into a bush and got poison ivy." He chuckled. "It is particularly bad and very contagious. If he wants to see for himself, he can come tomorrow. From the speed he hung up, I doubt you'll be hearing from him again."

"First you save my math homework and now you chase away would-be poets," she laughed. "How can I thank you?"

Trevor rubbed his forehead and a smile crossed his face. "Follow me, I want to show you something."

"I'm not dressed and it's past midnight." She pointed to her sweatpants and bare feet.

"No one will see us." He opened the door. "Trust me, it will be worth it."

They strode across the quad and climbed the steps of a stone building with a domed roof. Trevor pushed open double doors and she followed him inside.

The foyer had a tile floor and rounded plaster walls. Trevor started up a spiral staircase and Kate suddenly panicked. What was she doing alone with a stranger in the middle of the night?

"Don't look so alarmed." He waved his flashlight. "It's perfectly safe."

Kate wanted to say she wasn't worried about falling and breaking her neck, she was afraid he was going to kiss her. But he had behaved like a gentleman. And if she were wrong, they'd both be embarrassed.

They reached a landing with floor-to-ceiling windows and a domed ceiling. Trevor pointed and she gasped. The space was taken up by the biggest telescope she had ever seen.

"You asked me why I came to St Andrews and this is one of the reasons." His eyes sparkled. "The James Gregory Telescope is the largest telescope in the United Kingdom and is being used to study extrasolar planets."

"It's amazing!" She admired its gleaming surfaces. "I've always wanted a telescope. In Santa Barbara, my favorite thing to do is lie on the beach and look up at the stars."

"Somehow, I knew you'd appreciate it." His smile was as wide as a boy's. "Look through the camera."

Kate squinted into the lens and the stars were so close, it was like looking through the wrong end of a kaleidoscope. The sky was milky velvet and the moon was a golden ball.

"You should join the Astronomy Society." Kate turned to Trevor. "They meet at the observatory every Wednesday. Once a month they have a pudding and hot chocolate social."

"I'd much rather use the telescope when no one is here." He shrugged. "Astronomy is like math, it's best appreciated alone."

"You brought me here," she reminded him.

"Friends are important," he said slowly. "But it has to be someone you have a connection with, not because your names are on the same lists. You're different."

"Different?" she wondered.

"You care about your grades. Your light is on in the middle of the night because you're studying, not because you're passed out and forgot to turn it off." He paused. "You love the sunsets on the Old Course and you're not afraid to leave your dorm at midnight and try something new."

"Those are the qualifications for a friend?" she laughed.

"They are for me," he said seriously.

Kate gazed out the window at stars that looked like a diamond necklace and thought St Andrews was even better than she imagined. She turned back to Trevor and felt light and happy.

"They are for me too."

Kate sipped her brandy and gazed out the window of her suite at Claridge's. Hyde Park was lit with twinkling lights and she could see Big Ben and Westminster Abbey.

What had it been like to be eighteen and not have made any mistakes? She shouldn't have accepted Trevor's invitation. But he agreed not to talk about the past and it would be nice to sit in an elegant restaurant and talk about London and New York.

She entered the bedroom and slipped on a robe. The four-poster bed had monogrammed sheets and royal-blue pillowcases. A beveled mirror rested against the wall and Tiffany lamps stood on walnut bedside tables.

Now wasn't the time to think about Trevor; she had to concentrate on *Christmas Dinner at Claridge's*. She climbed into bed and flicked on her laptop. It would be impossible to sleep. At least she could catch up on her work.

Chapter Five

LOUISA SAT AT A TABLE in the Foyer Restaurant at Claridge's and consulted the breakfast menu. There was so much to choose from: smoked salmon and scrambled eggs, omelets with haddock and Mornay sauce, French toast with berries and clotted cream. The waiter named so many tea flavors it made her head spin, and the scones and *pain au raisin* sounded delicious.

She put down the menu and smiled. Two days ago she had been wearing wet moccasins and drinking cold coffee at a bakery on the Lower East Side. Now she was dressed in cashmere and sitting in one of the most elegant restaurants in London.

The Foyer was like an illustration in an Eloise book: elegant arches and marble columns and art deco lights illuminating starched white tablecloths. A Christmas tree stood in the corner and silver bows adorned the stone fireplace.

Louisa was tempted to flee back to her suite and have a cup of instant coffee and an apple from the minibar. She was so nervous. What if she dropped her fork on the parquet floor by accident?

But she had the morning appearance on BBC One and then her makeup and hair appointments. In the afternoon she was going to visit the Christmas markets in Hyde Park and the Tate. Noah would be furious if she didn't stick to the schedule and she couldn't disappoint him again.

The cocktail reception at the Fumoir had been fabulous. The other chefs were welcoming and she learned so much. Pierre Gagnaire had earned three Michelin stars and owned restaurants in Paris and Tokyo and Dubai. Andreas Caminada was the top chef in Switzerland and his restaurant in an eighteenth-century castle in the Swiss Alps sounded like something out of a storybook.

And Digby Bunting! He was so knowledgeable about British desserts; she could listen to him for hours. He told her how to make the perfect pastry for a trifle tart and that an Eton mess might have a strange name but it was the best thing she'd ever taste: strawberries and meringue with fresh cream.

A young woman wearing a red wool dress appeared at the doorway and Louisa recognized Kate's blond hair. It was eight o'clock in the morning and Kate looked like she was dressed for a fashion show.

"There you are." Kate approached the table. "I was hoping we could chat before your interview."

"Please join me," Louisa offered. "All the other tables are set with feasts that look like they're prepared for Henry VIII. I usually manage half a cinnamon roll and coffee for breakfast," she said sighing. "If I just order a side of stewed fruit, they'll ask me to leave."

"I'm not a breakfast eater but we can cobble something together." Kate sat across from her.

"I was just finishing a card to Ellie's daughter, Chloe." Louisa pointed to the card next to the menu. "I promised I'd send her a Christmas recipe every day. When I get home we're going to bake them together." She picked up the embossed stationery. "Today's recipe is for Gingerbread Sweaters, I found it in a cooking magazine at the hotel gift shop. You spread the gingerbread biscuits with white icing and green and red sprinkles. It resembles a Christmas sweater and it's so festive."

"That's a lovely gesture. Chloe is lucky to have you as a friend." Kate glanced at the card and then looked at Louisa. "You look lovely. Noah's shopping expedition was a success."

"I still feel guilty about abandoning him at Harrods," Louisa admitted. "But I'm a chef. I don't need my hair lightened or my eyebrows shaped or an Asprey watch. People will only be interested in whether my croquembouche is sweet and flaky and melts in your mouth."

"Do you really believe that?" Kate asked.

"No one cared what Virginia Woolf wore to write *Mrs. Dalloway*, and Tchaikovsky could have been sitting at the piano in his pajamas when he composed *The Nutcracker*," Louisa said earnestly. "I'm not comparing myself to them of course; I'm just a pastry chef. But I did attend cooking school and I'm serious about what I do. The only thing that is important is what comes out of the oven."

"*Baking with Bianca* is seen by millions of viewers and everything on the set has to be pleasing. We can go through three cartons of ice cream getting a shot of a banana cream parfait, because the ice cream keeps melting. The lighting has to be perfect on a holiday log or it looks like a plain loaf of bread." Kate paused. "No one wants to see Bianca in sweatpants and sneakers. She has to be like the food she presents: polished and lovely so you can't take your eyes off her."

"I hadn't thought about it like that." Louisa hesitated.

"This wool dress itches but the hotel maid took my other dresses and hasn't returned them. I can't stand wearing panty hose and I'd much rather leave my hair down," Kate continued. "But when I meet the producer at BBC One, I'm representing the show. Right now you are the star of *Baking with Bianca* and you have to do what everyone on television does: make the camera fall in love with you."

"I feel like an ungrateful child," Louisa said guiltily. "I'm so lucky to be here. Any chef would kill to be part of *Christmas Dinner at Claridge's.*"

"I don't expect you to master everything at once." Kate smiled. "But this job is important to Noah and he discovered you. If the network executives aren't happy, he could get fired."

"I would hate Noah to get in trouble, from now on I'll stick to the script," Louisa said. "The hairdresser can make my hair stand up like a soufflé and I'll get those French nails that look so perfect they must be fake." She looked at Kate. "I do have a question. How do you keep your panty hose from falling down?"

Kate glanced around to make sure no one heard her. "Reversible Scotch tape around the waist."

Louisa laughed and signaled to the waiter. "I'll have to try it."

They shared a tomato omelet and talked about Claridge's. The doorman could make a reservation at any restaurant in London and the concierge kept tickets to *The Nutcracker* at Covent Garden in his desk. Louisa stirred cream into her coffee and saw a man standing under the arch.

"This is a very appealing picture." Noah approached the table.

"Baccarat water glasses and Waterford china and a silver bread basket of raisin scones."

"Would you like to join us?" Kate offered.

"I thought you'd never ask. My expense account only stretches to Starbucks coffee and a sticky bun." He grinned and turned to Louisa. "I'm surprised to see you up this early. I was afraid I was going to have to instruct the maids to fill your bath with ice water."

"I took your advice and didn't let myself go to sleep until 10:00 p.m.," Louisa said. "I slept like a baby and feel completely refreshed."

"I'm glad. We have a busy schedule." Noah consulted his clipboard. "After the interview with BBC One, you have a hair appointment at Taylor Taylor. I had to promise Daniel Galvin two tickets to *Hamilton* when he's in New York, but he agreed to reschedule your makeup." He paused. "In the afternoon we'll film you at the Tate and finish at the Winter Wonderland in Hyde Park. You will sample bratwurst in the Bavarian village and sip coffee with schnapps in the après-ski chalet. Oh, and I spoke to the concierge and instructed them to send all postcards to Ellie and Chloe by overnight mail," he said to Louisa. "Chloe should receive the first card tomorrow morning."

"That's wonderful." Louisa beamed. "I appreciate it."

"I changed the Winter Wonderland to this evening," Kate cut in. "Digby Bunting called. He offered to show Louisa the Winter Wonderland. He thought it would make excellent footage: the top British and American pastry chefs seeing London from the Giant Observation Wheel and watching Christmas pantomimes."

"Digby Bunting called?" Louisa was startled. "How odd! We

hardly talked about my baking at all. And I'm not the top pastry chef in America, I'm a complete nobody."

"Apparently Digby was quite taken with you," Kate continued. "He was very excited about the feature. He'll meet you in front of the Magical Ice Kingdom at 6:00 p.m."

"We can't change the schedule because Digby Bunting wants to visit an amusement park," Noah cut in. "Viewers don't want to watch Louisa tossing a ball to win a Christmas bear. They want to see her sampling spotted dick pudding."

"We were going to film at Winter Wonderland this afternoon," Louisa reminded Noah. "And you said we're going to shoot all over London: in front of Big Ben and Westminster Palace and the British Museum."

"It was going to be a brief segment." Noah stabbed his pancake. "And those are London monuments, not a giant amusement park with couples holding hands and eating fairy floss."

"I agree with Louisa, viewers want to see London at Christmas," Kate said. "And we can't turn down Digby Bunting. Our ratings will go through the roof. Every woman who watches the show while baking Christmas cookies will be glued to the television."

"What if Digby wants his own camera crew or isn't happy with our microphones?" Noah demanded. "Two celebrities on the same show is a recipe for disaster."

"I'm not a celebrity, I'm just someone who made good cinnamon rolls," Louisa said. "It's very kind of him. I'd give anything to learn his secret for Lord Mayor's Trifle. His recipe uses chocolate jelly and coconut sponge and vanilla custard, but mine always comes out too sweet."

"You're worrying about nothing, it's a fabulous idea." Kate ate the last bite of omelet. "Why don't you and Louisa pick out some playful accessories to wear: a Burberry scarf or some sparkling earrings?" She stood up. "I have to send a few e-mails. I'll meet you at the television studio." She smiled at Louisa. "I have complete confidence in you. If you can impress Digby Bunting, you are going to be dazzling on television."

Louisa was tempted to say she was coming down with the flu and have Kate take her place. Kate was poised and beautiful and knew everything about the show. But then she remembered Kate saying Noah's job was on the line. She had to stop acting like a child and do everything they asked.

"I hope so." She drained her coffee cup and gulped. "Because I feel like a complete imposter."

Louisa stood in front of the David Hockney exhibit at the Tate Britain and tried to smile. But her toes were pinched in her new pumps and the cashmere dress was too warm and she had been smiling so long, her face froze.

Tears filled her eyes and she realized it was more than that. No matter what she did, Noah wasn't happy. When she asked what was wrong, he just consulted his clipboard and hurried to the next location.

It started this morning at the BBC One morning show. After she got used to the bright lights and director talking into her earpiece, she actually enjoyed herself. The host, Maryanne, was lovely and they talked about the difference between British and American desserts. Louisa promised to send her a carrot cake with cream cheese frosting when she returned to New York.

Noah joined her in the green room after the show and criticized the way she had fiddled with her hair. Her forehead had been shiny and she kept crossing her legs.

He even reprimanded her for telling Maryanne how many pounds of butter to use in a New York cheesecake recipe when the British measured in grams. Louisa retorted she never measured in grams in her life. Noah said it was her job to do research and get it right for the television audience.

She tried to make it up to him by letting the stylist at Taylor Taylor do whatever he liked with her hair. She didn't complain when she had to sit for an hour under a plastic shower cap, or when the girl washing her hair got her neck stuck in the sink.

She had to admit her new haircut was lovely! It fell just under her chin and framed her face. Her eyes seemed larger and the uneven ends were smooth and glossy. She thought Noah would be pleased, but he grumbled it had taken too long and they were behind schedule.

From the hair salon they went to Daniel Galvin's and after lunch they visited Liberty Department Store in the West End. The windows were decorated like a life-sized dollhouse and Louisa had never seen anything so pretty. A child's room had a sleigh bed overflowing with presents and a stuffed giraffe and pink-canopied bed. There was a drawing room with a white Christmas tree and a library filled with Peter Rabbit books.

The interior of the store was so enchanting: glass cases filled with soft gloves and leather purses and elegant hats. Louisa tried on a red Philip Treacy hat and Noah scowled and said she'd spent hours getting her hair done, and now she messed it up.

They stopped in Kitchen Accessories, and Louisa was dying to buy a sterling silver spoon rest or nut splitter for Ellie for Christmas. But Noah tapped at his watch and Louisa bit her lip and agreed to come back on her own time.

It was when they reached the women's department that Louisa knew something was wrong. She was determined to do what Kate asked and buy a festive scarf. Noah said he had to make a phone call and she had to pick one by herself. When she showed him the Liberty London scarf she chose, he said snowflakes danced on television and made her return it and get something else.

Now she looked up at the David Hockney landscape and pretended she had never seen anything more interesting.

"You're standing on the wrong side of the painting," Noah said. "And you could be more enthusiastic. You look like a schoolgirl on a very boring field trip."

"I was excited when we spent twenty minutes at the Turner exhibit and I looked happy when I strolled along the Thames in the freezing cold. And I looked delighted when I stood in the middle of Piccadilly Circus even though I was terrified of being hit by a double-decker bus." She glowered. "But now my feet ache and I haven't eaten a thing since lunch. Please get your shot so I can take a break."

"I would never put you in danger, the light was red and the cars weren't moving," Noah retorted. "This is what television is about. It looks glamorous but it can be as tiresome as watching a baseball game from nosebleed seats."

"I don't mind any of it, but you found fault with everything I did," she fumed. "You criticized my performance on the breakfast show, and you didn't like my haircut and I chose the wrong scarf. I can't even admire a painting to your satisfaction."

"Your haircut is lovely though I do miss your long hair. And Kate was very happy with your appearance on BBC One," Noah said, stumbling. "It's just . . ."

"Just what?" Louisa asked.

"Yesterday I couldn't get you to try on a dress. You blew off your makeup appointment to buy French butter at Harrods Food Hall. Then you were gone from Claridge's for so long, I thought you'd been kidnapped or run over by a bus." His voice rose. "When actually you'd decided to visit Buckingham Palace!"

"I apologized," Louisa said stiffly. "I was jet-lagged and everything was brand new."

"I forgave you. But today you didn't mind sitting still while Daniel Galvin applied powder and lipstick and you swooned over your new haircut like a fashion model." He stopped. "And it's all because Digby Bunting invited you to Winter Wonderland."

"What did you say?" Louisa demanded.

"The minute Kate said his name, your ears pricked up like a puppy with a new ball," he said.

"I am excited to see Digby Bunting. He has been my idol since I baked my first Pavlova," Louisa interjected. "But what does that have to do with my hair and makeup? I'm only interested in his raspberry trifle and tapioca pudding."

"I watched him at the cocktail reception. He's one of those men who spends half his time looking at women and the other half gazing at his reflection in the mirror," Noah snapped. "His assistant probably creates his recipes and he shows up to sign books. You said yourself you're not a famous chef. The only reason he wants to be with you is so he can rub knees on the Christmas Coaster."

"I don't know why you are being cruel," Louisa gasped. "Digby

Bunting is a professional and so am I. If you are quite finished, I'm going to meet him at Winter Wonderland." She waved at the painting and strode to the exit. "I never liked David Hockney anyway, his colors are washed out."

"You can't just leave." Noah ran after her. "What good will it do if you arrive without a camera crew? The point is to film a segment of *Baking with Bianca*."

Louisa hopped into a taxi and slammed the door. She rolled down the window and glared at Noah.

"Then I suggest you get in a taxi and follow me."

Louisa leaned against the vinyl and tried to stop shaking. She had been about to tell Noah she had her hair styled and her makeup done because Kate said Noah was worried about his job. But then Noah implied Digby wasn't interested in her culinary skills, and she was so angry, she didn't say anything at all.

The taxi deposited her at the entrance of Winter Wonderland and she entered the park. It was like a small city with a giant Christmas tree and booths selling toys and sweets. There was a circus and a train that rode through Santa Land.

Louisa searched for Digby but couldn't find him. The traffic had been terrible and now it was after 6:00 p.m. What if he'd gotten tired of waiting and left?

A man in a leather jacket walked toward her and she recognized Noah.

"Put this on." He handed her his jacket. "Your lips are blue and you're shivering."

"No, thank you," she said sharply. "Digby will be here any minute and your crew can start filming. It wouldn't look professional if I'm wearing a leather jacket on television."

"We're not filming," Noah said. "Digby isn't coming."

"If you called him and told him it was a bad idea, Kate will be furious," Louisa warned him.

"I did nothing of the sort." He showed her his phone. "Kate forwarded me Digby's text. Something came up and he had to reschedule."

"I see." She glanced at the text and wondered why she felt deflated. "You must be glad, you have the evening off. You can ask the Theatre Desk at Claridge's whether they have a ticket to *Phantom of the Opera*. I'm going to buy a snow globe for Ellie's daughter." She walked toward the Christmas markets. "I'll see you later."

"Louisa!" Noah ran after her and handed her his jacket. "It's freezing, you should have brought the coat we bought at Harrods. Take this. If you catch pneumonia, we can't film tomorrow. And if you insist on staying, I'll join you," he said. "Kate said I'm not allowed to leave your side until I return you safely to the hotel each evening."

"I left my coat in the taxi by accident. I'll call the cab company when I return to the hotel." She accepted his jacket. "You want to explore Winter Wonderland together?"

"Why not?" He shrugged. "I never have time to see the Christmas tree at Rockefeller Center or go ice-skating in Central Park. It'll be fun."

They examined fragrant candles and colorful trinkets in the Fairies Market. They drank mulled wine in the Ice Bar and marveled at the tables and chairs made of solid ice. They stood in line to see Sooty's Children's Show and shared a bag of caramel toffees.

Noah suggested they ride the Giant Observation Wheel and they squeezed onto the hard seats. It stopped at the top and all of London lay before them. Big Ben sparkled with a thousand silver lights and she could see London Bridge and Westminster Abbey.

"Oh, it's gorgeous," Louisa breathed. "I thought London was like a Dickens novel, but it's the most beautiful place I've seen. Buckingham Palace is a fairy-tale castle and Harrods looks like the top of a wedding cake and there's Kensington Gardens and Park Lane."

"I'm sorry that Digby didn't show up." Noah rubbed his hands. "I know you were looking forward to it."

"Meeting Digby Bunting was one of the reasons I came to London," she agreed. "But he's not why I got my nails done or spent ages choosing the right scarf." She looked at Noah. "This morning Kate said if the network isn't happy with me, you could lose your job. I promised I was going to do whatever anyone asked."

"It's my turn to apologize," Noah said. "You handed two trays of cinnamon rolls to a complete stranger and didn't ask for anything for yourself in return. You agreed to fly to London at Christmas when I'm sure you had plans. Today, you were led around London like a pony at a children's birthday party and didn't complain." He looked at Louisa. "I was just afraid you would be swept up by Digby's charm and forget why you are here."

"Why am I here?" Louisa suddenly felt unsteady.

"Because when viewers see you on *Baking with Bianca,* your restaurant is going to be a huge success," he urged. "And because it's Christmas and what better place to spend it than Claridge's? You deserve heated marble floors and a sideboard set with nuts and cheeses."

"Whose turn is it?" she asked.

"Whose turn is it for what?" he wondered.

"When I gave you the cinnamon rolls you kissed me on the cheek to thank me for saving the show. When I agreed to fill in for Bianca, you kissed me on the cheek again," she replied. "When we arrived at Claridge's, I kissed you on the cheek because I'd never been anywhere so fabulous." She looked at Noah. "Whose turn is it to kiss the other person on the cheek?"

"I guess it's mine." Noah brushed her cheek and then his lips found her mouth. He tasted warm and sweet and they jumped apart.

"I'm sorry, I shouldn't have done that," Noah said hurriedly. "It's so beautiful up here and I got carried away. It didn't mean anything."

"Of course it didn't." Louisa put her hand to her mouth.

The wheel tilted and Winter Wonderland tipped toward them like an airport landing strip. The attractions were strung with glittering lights and the Christmas booths were a row of toy houses.

They stepped off the ride and Louisa felt strangely unsettled, like when she went on Space Mountain at Disneyland as a child. She hadn't thought she was frightened, until the ride ended and her legs were wobbly and her stomach felt queasy.

"What would you like to do next?" Noah asked. "We could see the *Nutcracker on Ice* or search for polar bears in the Magic Ice Kingdom. If we find a bear, we can take our picture with it."

The air smelled of spun sugar and all around her people were sipping hot cider and carrying oversized Christmas bears. The unsettled feeling disappeared and was replaced by a wonderful lightness.

"We have to visit the Ice Kingdom," she laughed. "I've always wanted to have my picture taken with a polar bear."

When they returned to Claridge's it was 10:00 p.m. and Noah went to check on the film footage. Louisa entered her suite and sank onto a red satin love seat. The lights were dim and there was a tray of scones with honey and strawberry butter.

It really had been a lovely evening. The Winter Wonderland was dazzling and entering Claridge's lobby was like returning to an elegant cocoon. Men wore white dinner jackets and women were dressed in chiffon gowns and there was the scent of pine needles and expensive perfume.

Noah had the whole day tomorrow scheduled: They would start at St Paul's Cathedral, at the highest point of the city. Then they would visit the Tower of London and see the crown jewels. Just the thought of being so close to the eight-hundred-year-old Coronation Spoon and one-hundred-carat Koh-i-Noor diamond was thrilling.

In the afternoon, the chefs would gather in Claridge's kitchen to go over the menu. Louisa would see Digby and could ask him all her questions: How did he achieve the consistency in his rice pudding and what flavor jam did he use in a roly-poly?

Noah had said such unkind things about Digby; it wasn't like him at all. And Digby couldn't be interested in Louisa; they barely talked to each other. She remembered Noah's kiss on the Giant Observation Wheel and had a funny feeling, as if she'd entered a cinema halfway through a movie.

A fire crackled in the fireplace and the air smelled of lemon polish. She was sitting in a suite at Claridge's six days before Christmas. A smile crossed her face and she wondered if she was dreaming.

Chapter Six

KATE GAZED OUT THE TAXI window and admired the Georgian mansions with their creamy stone facades and iron gates. Lampposts were wrapped in Christmas lights and store windows were decorated with gold and silver ornaments.

Mayfair really was the prettiest section of London. Bond Street was lined with smart galleries and Savile Row had exquisite tailors and there was the Royal Academy of Arts and Dorchester Hotel.

Trevor suggested meeting at Claridge's but Kate said she would join him at The Arts Club. She felt a little silly; they could have shared a cab. But it would be better if the evening began in a noisy bar rather than the backseat of a taxi.

She didn't know why she agreed to have dinner with Trevor at all. She should be in her suite, checking e-mails and having a room service lobster salad. But Trevor knew her so well; he could tell if she made a flimsy excuse. And it was only dinner. What could go wrong with waiters hovering over them and asking how they liked their steaks?

The taxi stopped in front of a brick building with ivory pillars.

There was a lacquered front door and plaque with THE ARTS CLUB in gold lettering.

"Good evening, Miss Crawford," a doorman greeted her. "Sir Trevor is expecting you. He's waiting in the drawing room."

She walked down a marble hallway and entered the drawing room. Gray satin love seats were arranged around a glass coffee table and orange rugs were scattered over parquet floors. Silk drapes covered tall windows and bookshelves were lined with leather-bound books.

"Kate," Trevor welcomed her. "I was afraid you weren't coming."

"The taxi driver wanted to show me every street in Mayfair," Kate said and laughed. "How did the doorman know my name?"

"It's one of the benefits of belonging to a private club. Gerome makes it his job to know the name of every guest." He grinned. "I did mention a beautiful blonde was joining me for dinner. So perhaps I gave it away."

"I assumed we were going to dine at a restaurant." Kate glanced at the regency desk and paintings in gilt frames. "To be honest, I never thought you belonged to . . ."

"A private club?" Trevor asked. "The gentlemen's clubs are London's best inventions. Susannah kept Yardley Manor so full of guests, I couldn't think. Even the dogs retreated to the garage because there were always people milling around in tennis whites.

"The club is surprisingly relaxed," he continued. "Once you're a member, no one cares what car you drive or where you bought a holiday villa. They just want a quiet place to have a brandy and read the paper."

Trevor gave her a tour of the library bar with its polished walnut tables and cigar lounge decorated with art deco furniture and courtyard with a stone fountain and ivy-covered trellises.

"The Arts Club was founded in 1863 as a gathering place for men in the arts and sciences." He led her into the brasserie. "Charles Dickens and Anthony Trollope were members, and so was Degas."

"Your life has certainly changed." Kate raised her eyebrows. "Member of a private club and married into the royal family."

"Susannah is only a second cousin, but we got invited to the occasional tea at Buckingham Palace and shooting party at Balmoral Castle. And endless weddings." He picked up the menu. "You could spend your whole life fastening the cuff links on your morning coat."

"Have you really been to Balmoral Castle?" she asked.

"The Queen holidays there from August to November." He nodded. "There are picnics, and corgis running around your feet. I'll miss it, now that we're separated. The Queen is lovely and no one in England has experienced so much history." He sipped a glass of ice water. "Tell me about you. What did Kate Crawford do after she tossed her tasseled cap in the air and left St Andrews?"

"I moved to New York," she said. "It's the usual story: I rented an apartment with three roommates and a pullout bed. I worked at television jobs that paid less than my school paper route and had longer hours than a law firm. Then I met Bianca and got my lucky break. The pay is still low by New York standards, but I have a driver and expense account." She paused. "And I love what I do. It's everything I wanted."

"And men?" he asked. "Surely there's a hedge fund manager escorting you to industry events, or an artist waiting at home with a chicken and baked potato?"

"There have been men," she admitted. "A poet at Columbia who took a position at a college in Ohio. A tech genius who moved to Silicon Valley and forgot to tell me our long-distance relationship wasn't working." She winced. "I found out when he posted a photo of his new girlfriend on Instagram."

"That's his loss." He leaned back in his chair. "You're very beautiful, Kate. Any man would be lucky to have you."

"Trevor, I . . . " she began.

"Yes?" he asked.

Kate opened her mouth and stopped. Saying anything would be like releasing a tightly wound spool of thread.

"I'd like to order." She consulted the menu. "The grilled Dover sole with truffled potatoes sounds delicious."

They ate a blue cheese salad and grilled sole in hollandaise sauce. Trevor ordered a bottle of Taittinger and they talked about Sussex and New York. The champagne was wonderfully smooth and Kate felt light and relaxed.

"You'll never guess who I ran into on our holiday in Spain," Trevor said when the waiter set down a platter of fruit and cheeses. "Ian Cunningham."

Her chest tightened and she gripped her champagne flute.

"He looked the same as he did at St Andrews. His blond hair didn't quite look like it came out of a bottle and there were lines around his mouth." He fiddled with the cheese knife. "Apparently he had a failed nightclub in Knightsbridge and ran through his inheritance. He and a partner decided to try again in Spain. He married a Spanish girl and they have a baby."

"Trevor," Kate said warningly. "We agreed not to discuss the past."

"He was very friendly. He offered us free entrance to his nightclub and bought us a round of sangria," he continued as if he hadn't heard her. "Isn't it strange. One would have imagined Ian would be having dinner at The Arts Club with a beautiful blonde instead of me."

Kate put her napkin on her plate and grabbed her purse. "This has been lovely, but I have to go."

Trevor ran his hands through his hair and for a moment he was the boy who could spend hours helping her with a math problem.

"I'm sorry, that was wrong," he apologized. "Please stay. After dinner we can take a tour of the upstairs drawing rooms. There's an autographed copy of *Great Expectations* and an original newspaper clipping of Churchill's victory speech."

"All right. I'll stay this time, but you have to promise not to say anything like that again," she relented and smiled. "When will I ever get another chance to eat at The Arts Club?"

They wandered upstairs and Trevor showed her a study with first-edition books by Kipling and Wilkie Collins. There was a signed sketch by Degas and antique silver used by Rodin when he dined at the club.

"I know we said we shouldn't talk about the past, but do you remember when we spent all our evenings at the museum at St Andrews?" Kate asked. "I wanted to go dancing but you thought that was as crazy as boarding a spaceship to Mars."

"Why would anyone want to stumble around in a drunken blur when there was so much history at our fingertips?" he recalled.

"We were young, it was important to have fun," she insisted. "The point of being at university was to make friends."

"I already had a friend." Trevor turned to Kate. "All I needed was you."

They walked back downstairs and Trevor retrieved their coats from the coat check. He folded his Burberry overcoat over his arm and helped her on with her jacket. He stood close enough for her to smell his cologne and her whole body tingled.

"It's good to see you after all this time, Kate," he said and touched her wrist. "You don't know how lovely you are."

Kate turned around and their eyes locked. Suddenly he pulled her close and kissed her. His mouth was warm and he tasted of champagne and berries.

"I had a wonderful time, but I have to go." Kate pulled away. "I'll ask the doorman to call a cab."

"Don't be silly, we'll go together," Trevor suggested.

"I'm not sure that's a good idea." She smoothed her skirt and smiled. "Thank you again. I'll see you later."

Kate hurried down the steps and turned onto Dover Street. If she waited for the doorman, Trevor might rush out and stop her. Why did she agree to have dinner with him?

The night air touched her cheeks and she wondered if she was overreacting. They were both tipsy and a little nostalgic. The kiss was as harmless as a kiss under the mistletoe at a holiday party.

Kate passed a bar and noticed a crowd of young people at the entrance. The girls wore their hair long and straight and were dressed in boots and miniskirts. They were joined by young men in blazers and khakis. They all had white teeth and keys to expensive sports cars.

A young man at the center of the group looked up and caught her eye. Kate gasped and noticed how much he resembled Ian Cunningham. His blond hair brushed his forehead and he had the kind of smile that was irresistible to women.

A girl tugged at the boy's sleeve and Kate looked away. She

entered a café and ordered a cup of coffee. It was too cold to keep walking and she had to clear her head.

It had been foolish to think they could have dinner without talking about Ian. He was like a photo spread in a men's fashion magazine. Blond hair and chiseled cheekbones that belonged on a Roman statue.

She remembered the first time she saw him, eating a baked potato at the Old Union Coffee Shop. It was Trevor's fault she got involved with Ian. If Trevor had taken her to the Snowdrop Ball, none of it would ever have happened.

Kate jumped on her bicycle and rode quickly down South Street. It was November and really too cold to ride a bicycle. She couldn't wait to tell Trevor her news, and he would probably be solving algorithms at a café until nightfall.

The glorious Scottish fall weather had been replaced by bitter nights and mornings with frost covering the playing fields. Everyone said the climate in St Andrews was milder than other parts of Scotland because of the North Sea. But Kate pictured November in Santa Barbara with the breeze wafting through the palm trees and sun glinting off the Pacific and had never been so cold in her life.

She didn't mind having to use extra blankets at night or warm up her hands before class. She loved the university's majestic buildings and quaint courtyards. The town of St Andrews was so charming with its cobblestone alleys, and Fife Coastal Path had views of the whole coastline.

And she had a best friend! She and Trevor did everything together. They quizzed each other on French pronouns and studied for chemistry tests. They explored the ruins of St Andrews Cathedral and watched classic movies at the cinema on Market Street.

The only thing Trevor wouldn't do was listen to the jukebox at Cellar Bar or play billiards at Criterion. Every Friday night, Kate begged him to join her and he refused. He had a point. The pub was so noisy you couldn't hear anyone talk. And if you managed to find a quiet corner, the other person usually kept looking around for someone more interesting.

Kate often returned to McIntosh Hall at midnight, dejected and smelling of smoke. Trevor made hot chocolate and mumbled I told you so. Kate insisted it didn't matter if it was enjoyable; it was part of the college experience.

She parked her bicycle in front of Zizzi's and entered the café. This time she was determined to convince Trevor to accompany her. The Snowdrop Ball was the most important event of the semester and she couldn't go alone.

"You're the only person who isn't eating anything." She approached his table. "I'm surprised they don't kick you out."

"I come because of the pizza oven, it keeps the room warmer than anywhere on campus." He waved at the brick oven. "I did eat a side of pumpkin mozzarella. It was all I could afford and I finished it ages ago."

"I'll order a pizza with all the toppings to celebrate." Kate handed the invitation to Trevor. "After you read this."

" 'St Andrews Student Union requests your presence at the annual Snowdrop Ball. November twenty-fifth at the Old Course Hotel,' " he read out loud. " 'Formal dress is required.' "

"I'm not sure what we're celebrating." He set the card on the table. "That sounds as appealing as a seventeenth-century Scottish torture chamber."

"It's invitation only and it's an honor to be included as a freshman," Kate gushed.

"I'm glad your membership to committees and societies paid off, but I don't know what it has to do with me." He turned back to his equation.

"You're going to take me," she pleaded. "There will be a twelve-piece orchestra and hot chocolate station. The ballroom will be decorated with gold and silver snowflakes and it will be like a scene from Narnia."

"It sounds horrifying. Everyone will drink flasks of whiskey they sneak in their socks." He shuddered. "By midnight half the crowd will be throwing up and the other half will be pawing each other like animals. I'd rather watch an episode of *Wild Kingdom* on television."

"It will be wonderful and elegant and they're going to perform Scottish dances," she corrected. "I need a date and I don't have anyone else."

"Kate." Trevor looked at her. "You could wave the invitation in the middle of the Student Union and half the guys would jump at the chance."

"I don't want to go with someone I barely know." She fiddled with the card.

"I'd have to rent a dinner jacket. I never took dancing lessons and I don't know anything about wine." He shook his head. "There's a performance that night of Music in the Museums. We'll attend that instead. Now I have to finish these problems. Afterward we can quiz each other on geography."

"Just because you study math night and day doesn't make you superior." She was suddenly angry. "Attending balls is as important as solving logarithms."

"It might be for the students who only care about the leather in their parents' Aston Martins," he said icily. "But it isn't for me. When I graduate, I actually want to have learned something."

"There's time to do both. You're an intellectual snob and you won't admit it." She grabbed the invitation and stood up. "But if you won't come, I'll take your advice."

"Where are you going?" he called after her.

"To find someone who doesn't think escorting me to the Snowdrop Ball is worse than coming down with the chicken pox."

Kate jumped on her bicycle and rode down South Street. Why was Trevor being difficult? Just this week she missed a meeting of the Ivanhoe Society to proofread his paper on Spenser's *Faerie Queene*. All she wanted was for him to accompany her to the ball.

The frigid air touched her neck and it was too cold to ride back to McIntosh Hall. She parked her bicycle in front of the Old Union Coffee Shop and walked inside.

She found a table in the back and ordered a hot chocolate. A familiar-looking man sat at the counter, nursing a pint of beer. He was like a model in a Ralph Lauren ad, all blond good looks and eyes as blue as sapphires.

He looked up and she realized she had been staring. She opened her purse and fiddled with her lipstick.

"Do you mind if I join you?" He approached her table. "I hate eating alone. The food loses its flavor if you don't have someone to talk to."

"I'm not eating, I only ordered a hot chocolate." She flushed.

"That's a shame. They serve the best stuffed baked potato in town." He placed his plate on the table. "Here, you can share mine."

She took a bite of baked potato stuffed with cheddar cheese and it really was delicious.

"You're in my poetry seminar. But we haven't been formally introduced." He appraised Kate carefully. "Which at this moment seems like a terrible tragedy. Because you have truly remarkable legs."

"I'm surprised you noticed," she shot back. "You're usually surrounded by a flock of girls like seagulls on the beach."

"I'm a gentleman. It's not polite to exclude others from a conversation." He held out his hand. "I'll make amends now. Ian Cunningham."

"Kate Crawford." She shook his hand and his palm was smooth as butter.

"And what is Kate Crawford with an American accent and smile that belongs in a toothpaste commercial doing in our little medieval town?"

"I didn't want to spend four years attending football games and fraternity parties," she explained. "Here you meet students from all over the world. And people are so involved. I'm a member of the Wildlife Society and the Harry Potter Society and lots of other societies."

"I see you have an invitation to the Snowdrop Ball." He pointed to the card sticking out of her purse. "That's a coveted document."

"How do you know what it is?" she asked.

"I received one too," he admitted. "I'm president of the Fine Food and Dining Society and a member of the James Bond Society."

"I haven't heard of the James Bond Society. I must join!" She laughed and suddenly thought of Trevor. "I'm not sure if I'm going to the Snowdrop Ball."

"Why not?" he asked. "The music is excellent and the wine selection is from the university's private cellar."

"I don't have a date and it's not the kind of event you attend alone," she said. "Couples eat dinner at the Adamson and exchange corsages and boutonnieres."

Ian sipped his beer and looked at Kate. "I'll take you."

"I don't even know you!" she exclaimed. "And I'm sure there's already some girl picking out her satin dress and pumps. I can't imagine Ian Cunningham going stag to the Snowdrop Ball."

"I might have been about to invite someone, but I can invent a toothache." He shrugged. "I even have a note from my dentist. I can't turn down a beautiful American, it's bad for international relations."

"We just met." She hesitated. "What would we talk about?"

"I don't have my curriculum vitae handy but I can give you a rundown: Born in Surrey and attended Harrow School. Did a gap year in Spain so even though I'm twenty, we're in the same year. Mildly ambitious and determined to do something worthwhile with my trust fund." He paused and looked at Kate. "I forgot the most important thing. I'm a great admirer of female beauty and you have the loveliest green eyes." He set his beer on the table. "Am I a satisfactory escort?"

Ian was everything Trevor disliked. He was much too good-looking and the band on his Patek Philippe watch was so worn, it must have belonged to his father. He cared more about clubs than his studies, and instead of having to find a job, his only concern was what to do with his trust fund. And he was willing to take her to the Snowdrop Ball because of the color of her eyes and shape of her legs.

"Yes." She nodded and ate another bite of baked potato. "You'll do just fine."

Kate stood in front of the mirror and admired her silver gown. Ian was picking her up in an hour and she still had to do her makeup.

The week leading up to the Snowdrop Ball had been so much fun. She took the bus to Edinburgh and bought a dress at Debenhams. In the afternoon she visited the Royal Botanic Garden and Edinburgh Castle and ate mince and tatters at George Hotel.

She wanted to ask Trevor to accompany her but they barely talked to each other. She was still angry with him for refusing to attend the ball, and he wasn't happy with her choice of date.

Edinburgh Castle was magnificent! Trevor would have loved the Half Moon Battery with its fifteenth-century cannons and prisons where they used to keep pirates.

She wished he were with her when the guide described the Scottish charge at Waterloo. And she debated buying him a book on Mary Queen of Scots at the gift shop. He would have enjoyed the chapter on Mary's dog hiding beneath her skirts during her execution.

Tomorrow the Snowdrop Ball would be over and they could go back to their routine of brisk walks and long hours in the library and gazing at the stars.

There was a knock at the door and she opened it. Trevor stood in the hallway. His backpack was slung over his shoulder and he clutched a paper sack.

"What are you doing here?" she asked.

"I have something for you," he answered. "Could I come in?"

"I'm very busy," she said tersely. "Perhaps another time."

"It will only take a minute." He followed her inside. The dorm room only had two places to sit and he chose the wood chair. His long legs stuck out in front of him and she noticed his pants were too short.

"The other day you said I was an intellectual snob, but you were wrong," he began. "I can't compete with others on the polo field or by picking up the bill at an expensive restaurant. All I have is my brain. If I interrupt my homework to drink at the pub or watch some silly pantomime, someone else will get ahead."

"Being at university isn't a contest," she snapped. "It's about having experiences and discovering who you are."

"That's fine in America where all you need is a big idea and decent work ethic to get rich," he responded. "It's different in England. The other students attend their fathers' boarding schools and belong to the same private clubs and eventually have adjoining boxes at Wimbledon. I don't want those things, but I do want to afford a nice home and family," he finished. "The only way I'm going to get them is by being the best at what I do."

"You still have to have fun," she insisted. "We're young and without responsibilities. We're supposed to enjoy ourselves."

"I love solving equations. And algorithms aren't some impossible puzzle; they are as simple as a child's building blocks. What I didn't realize is that keeping our friendship is as important as achieving my goals." He paused. "When I'm with you I'm happy. I've never experienced that before." He reached into the paper sack and took out a plastic box. "This is for you."

Kate glanced at the rose corsage and frowned. "It's beautiful, but I have a date to the Snowdrop Ball."

"I know. Even if you didn't, I still wouldn't go," he said. "But that doesn't mean I won't be thinking of you." He admired her blond chignon and diamond earrings. "You look beautiful, Kate. I hope you have a wonderful time."

"The rose is lovely." She put the box on the desk. "But what if Ian gives me a corsage?"

"You'll figure it out." He stood up. "I do have a question."

"Yes?" she asked.

"Tomorrow I'm going to hike in Tentsmuir Forest. Would you like to come?"

"Yes, I'd love to." Kate nodded.

"Good." He turned the door handle and grinned. "You can explain the plot of *As You Like It* to me. I'm a great admirer of Shakespeare's business acumen, but I can't understand a word he writes."

Kate put down her coffee cup and reached into her purse. It was late and if she drank any more coffee she'd have a terrible headache. They had a busy schedule tomorrow and the last thing she needed was to be popping aspirin.

It was hard to believe that Ian was married with a baby. To her he was still the overly handsome, frustratingly outgoing boy who never let a group dissolve without planning an impromptu picnic or late-night pilgrimage to some pub in town.

Of course that was silly; they were all ten years older. She was a television producer and Trevor had been knighted by the Queen and Ian owned a nightclub in Spain. Then why after all this time did Trevor's kiss feel exactly the same?

Her phone buzzed and she picked it up.

"It's Trevor," a male voice said. "Gerome said you left without letting him call a cab. I wanted to make sure you got back to Claridge's."

"I'm fine." Kate smiled. "I just needed some air."

"Kate, I'm sorry for kissing you," he said. "I got caught up in the moment."

"You don't have to explain." She squeezed the phone.

"I have two tickets to *The Nutcracker* at Covent Garden tomorrow night," he continued. "It's a private box and Susannah and I were supposed to go together. Would you like to join me?"

"I have a busy day tomorrow. . . ." She hesitated.

"You're in London at Christmas," he urged. "You can't turn down an invitation to Covent Garden."

"All right, I'll go," she agreed.

"Excellent," Trevor said. "And Kate, wear your hair the way you did tonight. You've never looked so beautiful."

Kate walked out of the café and hurried down Dover Street. She shouldn't have said yes to Trevor. But she adored *The Nutcracker* and she couldn't pass up a box at Covent Garden.

Being with Trevor was like slipping on her favorite dress, comfortable and pleasing against her skin. Then why did his kiss unsettle her and why did he apologize?

The doorman at Claridge's greeted her and she strode through the lobby. She was going to take a hot bath and catch up on her e-mails. She'd think about Trevor tomorrow.

Chapter Seven

LOUISA GLANCED AROUND CLARIDGE'S LOBBY and shivered with excitement. It was four days before Christmas Eve and the buzz in the air was electrifying. Bellboys balanced boxes from Harvey Nichols and families carried soft leather luggage and the odd teddy bear that couldn't be left at home.

The morning sun glinted through the revolving glass doors and outside the sky was bright blue. Tourists in buses craned their necks to get a glimpse of Claridge's and Louisa felt like she had been invited to some incredible party.

She had slept wonderfully and woke up light and refreshed. A silver tray of hot coffee and English muffins stood at the door and there were fresh towels in the marble bathroom. She slipped on a crepe dress and applied lipstick and mascara. The mirror caught her reflection and she felt elegant and sophisticated.

Now she slipped the card she had been writing to Chloe into a gold envelope. It was for one of her favorite recipes: candy cane lollipops made with peppermint candy canes and dipped in white chocolate. They were so easy to make and Chloe could give them out to her friends. She had to thank Noah again for making sure the cards were overnighted to Ellie. It was so thoughtful.

She looked toward the elevator and wondered when Noah would appear. She was determined to make up for not following his directions yesterday, and do something nice for him. She had asked the concierge to prepare a picnic of ham and cheese sandwiches and key lime pie. She even stopped at the gift shop and bought Noah a packet of Mentos. He sucked them so quickly; he was always running out.

A young woman wearing a plaid dress crossed the lobby and she recognized Kate.

"There you are." Kate approached her. "It's a gorgeous day. The view from St Paul's Cathedral will be magnificent."

"I read all about the cathedral," Louisa gushed. "The original St Paul's was destroyed by the Great Fire of London and Sir Christopher Wren was commissioned to build a new one. It sits on Ludgate Hill and the dome can be seen from anywhere in London." She smiled. "Not that Noah will let me sightsee. We were on such a tight schedule yesterday; I couldn't catch my breath." She took a pair of flats from her purse. "I brought these so I can keep up between locations, and asked the concierge to pack a lunch so we don't have to eat horrible salad sandwiches. Yesterday's sandwich was so soggy, Noah grumbled all afternoon."

"British kiosks aren't known for their gourmet foods," Kate laughed. "Didn't Noah tell you? He's not coming."

"Not coming?" Louisa repeated.

"He texted and said he had to get the lens fixed on a camera." She shrugged. "I suggested he send it out, but he insisted on going himself. He might make it to the Tower of London, but he'll miss St Paul's Cathedral."

"Who will be at St Paul's Cathedral?" Louisa asked and wondered why she felt disappointed.

"I will," Kate said and walked toward the entrance. "Let's get a taxi before the doorman is overwhelmed by guests asking where the best shopping is. Claridge's might be one of the most refined hotels in London, but right now it feels like Grand Central Station."

St Paul's Cathedral was built in the baroque style and had huge arches and stone pillars and stained-glass windows. The ceilings were inlaid with mosaic tile and the altar was supported by gold-and-black-marble columns. It was the dome that took Louisa's breath away. It was like some fabulous treasure chest filled with precious gold jewelry. The frescoes were blue and gold and the windows were gold flecked and the plaster walls were decorated with gold leaf.

She missed Noah telling her what to do. She could almost hear him say she resembled a stork when she craned her neck to see the ceiling; she had to be graceful like a ballerina. She didn't have to shout when she was in the whispering gallery; the whole point was to whisper and your voice carried throughout the cathedral.

And she wished he were there to tell her not to look frightened when she entered the crypt. The tombs had been there for hundreds of years and they weren't going to pop open. She couldn't help it; she was never good at being in small spaces.

The view of London from the Golden Gallery at the very top of the dome was stunning and it would have been nice to share it with someone. But Noah would have said they didn't have time to admire Piccadilly Circus and Trafalgar Square, that she could buy a postcard at the gift shop.

Finally the cameramen collected their gear and Louisa noticed Kate in the pew facing the altar.

"I'm sorry I wasn't more help." Kate glanced up from her phone. "I had some e-mails that needed answering."

"We got everything we needed." Louisa sat beside her. "Isn't it magnificent? Winston Churchill's funeral was held in the cathedral and so was Prince Charles and Princess Diana's wedding. Diana's wedding dress was stitched with ten thousand pearls and had a twenty-five-foot train. It almost didn't fit in the glass carriage and it took her three and a half minutes to walk down the aisle."

"The British are wonderful at pomp and circumstance," Kate agreed. "I remember watching the Duke and Duchess of Cambridge's wedding at Westminster Abbey on television. The pageboys were dressed in velvet outfits and flower girls wore satin ballet slippers and it was like a fairy tale. Unfortunately, in real life love seems as difficult as solving the *New York Times* crossword puzzle. Just when you think you've got it right, there's a letter missing and you have to start again."

"Someday, I want to get married." Louisa sighed. "But right now love is an impossible luxury, like the heated towels in Claridge's bathroom. It's lovely to wrap myself in a warm towel after a bath, but I can dry off with the hand towel hanging in the shower of my apartment just as easily. I'm saving up to open my own restaurant and don't have time to date."

"Do you really use a hand towel after a shower?" Kate raised her eyebrow.

"Well, it feels like a hand towel. It started as a proper towel but it's been washed so often, I'm positive it shrunk," Louisa admitted. "I don't even own a cat because I work such long hours, it would starve. I'm not going to stop now. Everybody has to give up something to achieve what they want, that's how the world works."

"My job isn't very conducive to relationships either," Kate mused. "There's always some crisis that needs solving and my hours are impossible. Men aren't very understanding when you cancel dinner because the Baked Alaska collapsed and we have to reshoot the whole segment."

"I don't believe it. You're beautiful and worldly and have a fabulous career, any man would be thrilled to go out with you." Louisa turned to Kate. "Is the man you had dinner with at Claridge's someone important?"

"What do you mean?" Kate asked.

"It's none of my business but after the reception at the Fumoir, I saw you having dinner with someone," she continued. "And last night you were walking through the lobby. You looked so stunning in that red dress, I wondered if you had been on a date."

"I ran into an old university friend." Kate flushed. "It's nice to have company."

"He was gorgeous," Louisa prodded. "Like the male lead in a series on Masterpiece Theatre. He had that sandy blond hair and English complexion that make women swoon."

"Discussing my love life isn't very exciting, because there's nothing to tell." Kate stood up and laughed. "We better get to the Tower of London or Noah will complain we messed up his schedule."

"He's not here, so he'll never know," Louisa said and felt like she made a friend. "But I am dying to see the Cullinan diamond. It's 530 carats and the largest diamond in the world."

Louisa paced around the living room of her suite and blinked away tears. The Tower of London had been a disaster. Kate had to rush back to Claridge's and Louisa continued without her. The guard snapped at Louisa for getting too close to St Edward's Crown. And just when the cameraman was satisfied with her pose in front of the Sovereign's Sceptre, a group of schoolchildren walked into the shot.

She asked the cameraman if she could check the footage and was appalled. How was she to know that if she smiled too wide she resembled the Cheshire cat? And her yellow crepe dress made her look like she was recovering from cholera. If Noah had been there he would have noticed right away and told her to wear something else.

Now she was supposed to be in Claridge's kitchen in half an hour and they hadn't rehearsed. Noah promised to help her practice answering questions: Who were her influences as a chef, and which spices were in her pantry?

What if she got nervous and forgot her croquembouche recipe? Or her throat closed up and she couldn't say anything at all?

There was a knock at the door and she opened it. Noah stood in the hallway. He wore a wool coat and carried a red Liberty bag.

"How nice of you to show up, but you missed the whole morning," she snapped. "At St Paul's Cathedral, I had to enter the crypt and almost had a panic attack. And at the Tower of London, I got too close to the glass case and set off the sensors. The guard was so furious, I expected him to lock me up."

"They don't actually use the Tower of London as a prison anymore." Noah took off his coat.

He noticed the way her hair curved around her chin and her cheeks were brushed with powder. "Your hair is different and someone did your makeup."

"I did it myself." She touched her hair. "I was trying to make your job easier. I even ordered a picnic so we wouldn't have to eat salad sandwiches, and bought Mentos so you're not always rummaging through your pockets. But then you didn't show up and Kate was busy, and there was no one to direct me."

"You're right, it's my fault," Noah said. "I left you in the lurch and I apologize."

"You do?" Louisa turned around and the afternoon light reflected off the glass coffee table.

She was reminded of how stunning the suite was. The walnut sideboard was freshly polished and the scarlet sofa was scattered with silk cushions. A silver tray was set with a porcelain coffeepot and platter of soft cheeses.

"I had to get the camera lens fixed. It's very fragile, one has to handle it like a baby." He handed her the shopping bag. "But then I stopped at Liberty and bought you a present."

"You bought me a present?" she asked.

"For the show, of course," he clarified. "You were so enamored by the nut splitter, I decided you need a signature baking utensil. Martha Stewart wears her striped aprons and Bianca uses mixing bowls given to her by the pastry chef at the Ritz in Paris." He pointed to the bag. "Go ahead and open it."

Louisa unwrapped tissue paper and discovered a silver cake server.

"It's for your croquembouche." He turned it over. "I had your initials engraved on the handle."

"It's gorgeous." She looked up and her eyes were bright. "I never had anything like it."

"I didn't think the bakery on the Lower East Side came equipped with sterling silver utensils." He grinned. "But you're at Claridge's now. You need something special."

Louisa was about to kiss him on the cheek and stopped. She remembered the kiss on the Giant Observation Wheel and suddenly felt like a girl who was too old to have sleepovers with her male best friend.

Big Ben chimed in the distance and she gasped. "We're supposed to be downstairs, and I haven't brushed my hair. Is my lipstick okay?"

"You look perfect the way you are," Noah said. "I was wondering if—" Noah's phone buzzed and he glanced at the screen. "It's a text from Kate. The missing camera arrived at Heathrow and she wants me to get it. I'll have to join you later."

Louisa wanted to say it wasn't just his direction that she'd missed this morning. Exploring London wasn't as much fun without him. Perhaps they could do something tonight: see a pantomime or listen to Christmas carols at Westminster Abbey. But Noah was already walking to the door.

"Thank you for the cake server," she called. "I can't wait to use it."

"The other chefs may have fancy cookbooks but you have something unique." He turned around.

"What's that?" she wondered.

"Your cinnamon rolls are the best in New York, but it's more than that." He paused. "I saw the footage and your smile lights up the screen. You made the camera fall in love with you."

"You picked out my clothes and arranged my haircut and scheduled my makeup." She fiddled with the tissue paper. "I just did what you told me."

"Whatever it is, it's working." He grinned. "Let's not change a thing."

Louisa entered Claridge's kitchen and felt as excited as when she visited FAO Schwarz as a child. The space had creamy stone floors and yellow plaster walls and a range with a mosaic backsplash. Gleaming surfaces were scattered with carving knives and ceramic mixing bowls and rows of sparkling stemware.

The pastry area had silver whisks and a selection of rolling pins. And the measuring cups! They were stacked together like miniature houses and there were so many, she'd never have to rinse one mid-recipe. Usually no matter what she did, a little flour stuck to the bottom of the cup.

There was a fridge bigger than the bathroom in her apartment and a stove that turned on so easily, it must be magic. She remembered coaxing the stove at the bakery to turn on like a lover rekindling a lost love. Eventually she would grab a match and hope she didn't burn down the whole kitchen.

The other chefs appeared and they sat at a wooden table and discussed the menu. There would be the usual Claridge's Christmas starters: roasted goose salad and salt-baked parsnip. Pierre would make his single oyster in a consommé with fennel and wild mushrooms, followed by blue lobster in a foaming bisque with turmeric and cauliflower.

Andreas was going to prepare saddle of venison with spice bread and carrot puree. There would be pigeon with onions and rhubarb, and side dishes of sweet-and-sour plums and fruit chutney.

Then it was her turn and she remembered when she was in first grade and forgot to bring something for show and tell. The other children displayed a guinea pig in its cage or favorite doll. Louisa pulled the ribbon out of her hair and mumbled something about the pretty colors.

She took a deep breath and explained how she learned to make croquembouche during a summer in Normandy. The eggs came straight from the chicken, and the butter was the best she ever tasted. The pastry cream was mixed with semisweet chocolate and espresso powder.

She described how she let the caramel simmer until it hardened and arranged the puffs in a pyramid. The whole thing was wrapped in spun sugar like a Christmas tree decorated with priceless yellow diamonds.

It was only when someone's cell phone buzzed that she realized the whole kitchen had gone silent. Everyone was listening to her as if she was a famous opera singer.

"I would fast all day so I could enjoy that croquembouche," a male voice said. "And I'm usually a terrible snob about French desserts. They're all butter and flour, without any flavor."

She looked up and Digby Bunting leaned against the door frame. He looked like a movie star in a black leather jacket and tan slacks. His shoulders were broad and he had a cleft in his chin.

"I'm sorry I'm late." He entered the kitchen. "I seem to have missed the most delightful dessert. Perhaps Louisa can let us sample her croquembouche."

"I couldn't bake one now." She flushed. "I don't have all the ingredients and it takes ages to make the puffs. They have to be so hard they crunch in your mouth." She paused and realized she was rambling. "*Croquembouche* means 'crunchy' in French."

"I'm fascinated." Digby sat beside her. "Tell us how you get the pyramid not to collapse."

Louisa wished Noah were there. He would tell her not to reveal her secrets. But she couldn't say no to Digby. Sitting so close to him was like being asked on stage at a rock concert.

"Surely there are other things to talk about: whether we should make traditional sides like cauliflower cheese and whether we'll serve a Christmas pudding." She glanced around the table. "I know we're all from different places, but *Christmas Dinner at Claridge's* has to include a Christmas pudding. That's what a British Christmas is all about."

Louisa gulped and put her hand over her mouth. What if Digby planned on making one of his impossibly complicated desserts: a velvety chocolate mousse with almond frangipane or molasses gingerbread cake with mascarpone cream?

"I didn't mean we should change the menu," she said hurriedly. "I'm sure everything will be perfect."

"A traditional Christmas pudding soaked in brandy is an excellent idea." Digby nodded. "I don't know why I didn't think of it."

Pierre and Andreas said goodbye and Louisa gathered her purse. She was about to leave when Digby stopped her.

"I apologize for last night," he said. "My cat was hit by a bicycle and I had to take him to the vet."

"Your cat!" Louisa exclaimed. "I thought—"

"That I got a better invitation," he laughed. "That's the problem with being a celebrity, people assume the worst. I would never stand someone up without a good reason."

"I hope your cat is all right," Louisa offered.

"His name is Felix and he's fine. If he wasn't a bit shaken, I'd be furious at him. He forgets he's an indoor cat and roams around the pavement."

"We're getting wonderful footage of London." Louisa noticed the perfect half moons on his fingernails. "Today we filmed at St Paul's Cathedral and the Tower of London."

"Why don't we have afternoon tea?" Digby suggested. "Claridge's afternoon tea is the best in London. They've been serving it at the Foyer for 150 years."

Noah didn't have anything scheduled this afternoon, but he wasn't fond of Digby. He wouldn't be happy if he crossed the lobby and saw them eating cucumber sandwiches and sipping oolong tea. But that was silly. Meeting Digby was one of the reasons she came to London.

"You can't say no, it's a British tradition." He propelled her toward the entrance. "Everyone drinks tea from porcelain cups and eats raisin scones with Cornish clotted cream and Marco Polo jelly."

"In New York people just grab a Twix on the subway," Louisa laughed. She couldn't pass up the opportunity. Digby had so much to teach her. "I would love to have afternoon tea. I packed a picnic lunch and didn't have a moment to eat it."

The Foyer dining room was more impressive than the Plaza in New York or the Ritz in Paris. Marble floors were scattered with ivory rugs and a gold harp stood in the corner. Chairs were upholstered in gray silk and there were great urns of roses. A white Christmas tree was decorated with silver stars and twinkling lights.

Louisa had never seen so many cakes. Platters held lemon buttermilk cakes and dark chocolate sponge cake and white chocolate éclairs. And the sandwiches! Dorrington ham with whipped brown butter, and chicken with smoked tomato, and smoked salmon on soft white bread.

"Afternoon tea is all about the details," Digby said when the waiter had steeped Ceylon tea leaves in water that was heated to exactly 175 degrees. The waiter let it sit for three minutes and served it in striped cups.

"Claridge's uses bone china with a jade-and-white pattern. The cakes are served on a specially designed stand and the stemware is Waterford crystal." He picked up an egg mayonnaise sandwich. "Notice the bread on the sandwiches: it's sliced to the exact thickness of its filling so that it's pleasing to the eye."

"I remember when I read the Eloise books and wrinkled my nose at the sandwiches. How could any little girl choose watercress when she could have peanut butter and jelly?" Louisa laughed. "But these are wonderful. The flavors are delicious and the bread melts in my mouth."

"When did you know you wanted to be a pastry chef?" Digby asked.

Louisa tried to hide her surprise. Noah said Digby only liked to talk about himself. But he was genuinely interested in her. She was glad she came. She'd already learned so much: that you spread clotted cream on the scone before the jelly, and cucumber sandwiches were served on white bread because in the nineteenth century white bread was a delicacy.

"Ever since I was a child," she began. "But I knew for certain the summer after high school. I stayed at a bed-and-breakfast in Normandy and one afternoon there was a wedding in the garden. The bride wore a lace dress and carried a bouquet of calla lilies. I stood on my balcony and watched the ceremony, but it was when they cut the cake that I got a funny feeling. I could see my whole life in front of me as clearly as a sign on the highway.

"It was like a scene from *A Midsummer Night's Dream*: floral centerpieces and crystal champagne flutes and rose petals strewn across the lawn. The cake had its own table and was buttercream with royal icing and mimosa blossoms. The groom served the bride the first slice of cake and you could see the love in their eyes. All the guests clapped and I'd never seen two people so happy.

"I realized I wanted to create desserts that were beautiful and elegant and the best thing people have ever tasted. I tore up my application to NYU and applied to the Culinary Institute in Hyde Park." She sipped her tea. "I'm very lucky. Not many people get to do what they love."

Digby spread jelly on a scone and Louisa bit her lip. She should have said how Paul Bocuse had been her idol or she dreamed of receiving a Michelin star. Instead she babbled about love like a teenager.

"I quite agree," he said finally. "When you dine at the finest restaurants: Alain Ducasse at the Connaught or Per Se in New York, it's the little things you notice. A sprig of parsley on a milk-fed lamb or an edible golden apple on top of a cheesecake. The lamb would have tasted just as good without the parsley, and the golden apple probably ended up on the side of the plate. But the chef was in love with his creation. He could as soon send it out unadorned as he could appear in the dining room naked."

Louisa's cheeks burned and she had never been so happy. Someone understood her and she really was a chef!

"I hold a series of master classes at my flat in Mayfair." Digby finished his scone. "It's usually full with a waiting list, but I happen to have a cancellation." He looked at Louisa. "Would you like to come?"

"You want me to attend master classes taught by Digby Bunting?" she gasped.

"I should hope I teach my own course," he laughed. "The classes are on British puddings. The kitchen is state of the art and the other students are quite accomplished. At the end of each session, we sample the desserts accompanied by glasses of sherry."

Noah probably had the whole day planned. She could hardly say she wasn't available to visit the British Museum because Digby was going to teach her how to make chocolate ganache.

"It sounds wonderful, but my day is tightly scheduled." She fiddled with her napkin. "I'm supposed to tour London from the top of a double-decker bus."

"The first class is tonight at seven o'clock," Digby urged. "Surely you have an evening off."

"Tonight?" Louisa looked up.

Noah hadn't scheduled anything for tonight. She breathed a sigh of relief. She could attend Digby's master class without ruining Noah's plans!

"Here's my address." Digby took a card out of his pocket. "I'd be so pleased if you came."

"All right, I'll be there." She slipped the card in her purse.

"You're going to be a wonderful addition." He smiled and his eyes were the color of sapphires. "I'm glad you can come."

Louisa entered the living room of her suite and slipped off her pumps. She had three hours to take a bath and get ready for Digby's master class. Noah still hadn't returned and she was dying to tell him about her afternoon.

He would have been proud of the way she described her

croquembouche. And they were going to follow her suggestion and serve a Christmas pudding! She was part of *Christmas Dinner at Claridge's*, and it was going to be the event of the holiday season.

The silver cake server rested on the coffee table and she picked it up. What had Noah been about to ask her? It was probably nothing: Would she wear the red dress tomorrow or did she need more mascara? It couldn't have been anything important. After all, he said whatever she was doing was perfect; they shouldn't change a thing.

She was glad she hadn't asked Noah if he wanted to do something fun tonight. She would have to cancel; she couldn't miss Digby's master class. The pale light filtered through the drapes and she felt like a kid on Christmas morning. She was at Claridge's at Christmas and all her dreams were coming true.

Chapter Eight

KATE PEERED OUT THE WINDOW of the black cab and caught her breath. She and Trevor were on the way to Covent Garden and London glided past them like pages in a glossy coffee table book. They passed the Savoy Hotel with its striped canopies and Balthazar London with its picture windows and the Noël Coward Theatre. And the shops! She was dying to sample the fragrances at Jo Malone and stroke the supple leather goods at Aspinal. Just seeing the patterned silk blouses at Ted Baker was like reading a copy of *Vogue*.

Her hair was knotted in a loose chignon and she felt like Anne Hathaway in *The Princess Diaries*. A silver box had arrived at her suite while she was getting ready. Inside was a pair of long white gloves with a note from Trevor saying he was looking forward to their evening.

She couldn't possibly wear them with her black cocktail dress, so she made a quick trip to Harvey Nichols. She tried on a rose-colored Jenny Packham gown and teal strapless Alexander McQueen. She finally settled on a floral embroidered pink satin gown and paired it with silver pumps and diamond stud earrings.

Now the cab turned onto Bow Street and stopped in front of the Royal Opera House. It had Greek columns and marble steps covered with a plush red carpet. And the people! Women in gowns like bright shades of lipstick and men wearing cashmere overcoats.

"Remember when we were at St Andrews and I begged you to go to the Royal Opera House?" Kate peered out the window.

"We were studying *Romeo and Juliet* and the Royal Ballet was giving a performance," Trevor recalled. "Some students were driving to London for the weekend. They stayed in their parents' flat in Kew and returned with bottles of Rémy Martin filched from their parents' private collection."

"We could have gone," Kate said. "It wouldn't have cost you a thing."

"Sit in the back of some student's Range Rover for eight hours? I was only invited because you refused to go without me," he sniffed. "There was a perfectly good production at the Edinburgh Opera House. We took the bus and afterward ate fish and chips and toured the Scottish National Gallery."

"I couldn't go without you. We were study partners," she reminded him. "It would have been fun. The group went dancing at Annabel's and had brunch the next day at the Savoy."

"We're here now." His eyes softened. "You look beautiful, Kate. I'm glad you came."

"I couldn't refuse." She smiled. "Where else will I ever wear long white gloves?"

They entered a foyer with red velvet wallpaper and crystal chandeliers. Red sofas were scattered over Oriental rugs and there was a champagne bar with burgundy-upholstered chairs.

"I'm glad I didn't buy the red Halston," Kate laughed. "I would have clashed with the décor."

"You would only have made it more eye-catching," Trevor offered.

A woman in her early thirties approached them. She wore a peach organza gown and emerald earrings.

"Trevor!" she exclaimed. "What are you doing in London? I thought you'd be at Yardley Manor. I'm so disappointed Craig and I are missing Susannah's house party."

"I had business in town," Trevor said evasively. "I doubt I'll be missed, I always get in the way. I give away our hand in bridge and misread Susannah's prompts at charades. The house party will run smoothly without me."

"Nonsense," the woman laughed. "You know everything about math and taught us how to play chess." She turned to Kate. "I'm Jane Davies."

"I'm sorry I didn't introduce you," Trevor apologized. "Kate is an old friend from St Andrews."

"It's a pleasure to meet you." She held out her hand. "Susannah and Trevor give the best parties. That reminds me—" She turned to Trevor. "We're spending April in Cornwall and you and Susannah must come. We just redecorated the house."

"I'll put it on the calendar," Trevor said as the bell chimed. "It's time to go in."

"You look somehow familiar," Jane said to Kate. "Have we already met?"

"I don't think so." Kate shook her head. "I live in New York."

"I love New York," Jane mused. "Everyone is in a hurry and the skyline is spectacular. It was wonderful to see you, Trevor. Tell Susannah I'm devastated I'll miss her plum pudding."

Trevor led Kate to the box and she glanced eagerly at the stage. A white Christmas tree reached the ceiling and a pink rug was littered with wrapped boxes. Stockings hung from the stone fireplace and a round table held cakes and dried fruit.

The ballerina who played Clara was lovely and the Nutcracker was handsome and brave. In the second act the stage was transformed to the Land of Snow and Kate almost felt cold. Snowflakes covered the ground and trees were strung with icicles and the corps de ballet wore white tutus and white satin ballet slippers.

They entered the lobby and Trevor bought glasses of champagne.

"I love the ballet." Kate sipped her champagne. "When I was a girl, I played a mouse in the local production of *The Nutcracker.* The next year I was promoted to Mouse King because I was the tallest girl in the class," she laughed. "My ballet career didn't last long after that."

"I will miss having a box," Trevor mused. "Susannah will get it in the divorce, along with Yardley Manor and most of the people in our contacts." He sighed. "I have my club membership and the dogs. Though the dogs may not be happy. At Yardley Manor they get fed goose and sirloin tips."

"Susannah won't get all your friends. That woman, Jane, was eager to have you as a houseguest," she reminded him.

"Jane doesn't know we're getting a divorce." He shrugged. "Susannah wanted to keep it quiet until after the house party. It's easier to be festive when you're not discussing solicitors or who gets the didgeridoo Prince Harry gave us for our wedding."

"Did Prince Harry really give you a didgeridoo?" she laughed.

"He brought it back from Australia. At first I thought it was some kind of primitive weapon. But then Harry showed me how to play it, and I quite liked it."

A woman approached them and Kate recognized Jane.

"I hope I'm not interrupting, but I kept thinking about Kate during the ballet." Jane joined them. "I remember where we met."

"You do?" Kate wondered.

"It was at a Christmas house party in Scotland a dozen years ago," Jane answered. "It was at one of those huge estates that never runs out of bedrooms. There was sledding and an amateur production of a Noël Coward play." She fiddled with her earrings. "You were with Ian Cunningham. I remember the first time I saw you, in front of the fire in the drawing room. You had white-blond hair and a tan complexion.

"To be honest, we wanted Ian to date someone from our own circle," she continued. "But you were such a good sport during the snowball fight and taught everyone how to make American s'mores." She paused. "By the end of the week we were hoping you were a couple."

Kate glanced at Trevor and his cheeks were pale. He gripped his champagne flute so tightly she was afraid it might break.

"Ian and I didn't work out," Kate said quickly. "We broke up a long time ago."

"It's a pity," Jane said. "You would have made a wonderful addition to the group. Ian was clearly smitten with you."

Jane drifted away and Kate turned to Trevor. His brow was furrowed and there were lines around his mouth.

"This has been lovely, but I should go," she said. "I'll call a cab. You can stay and have a proper dinner."

"What are you talking about?" he asked.

"The past is all around us." She waved her hand. "At your private club and the Royal Opera House and at house parties in the British countryside. We can't pretend nothing happened and we're just going to get hurt." She tried to smile. "It's better if we become Facebook friends and send each other messages on our birthdays."

"You can't leave yet," he urged. "I want to show you something."

"What is it?" she wondered.

"It's a surprise," he answered. "You won't be disappointed."

Trevor flagged a cab and they drove to Hampstead. The taxi stopped in front of a stone building with an iron gate.

"Where are we?" she asked, stepping onto the pavement.

"Do you remember the night we first met and I took you to see the James Gregory Telescope? This is the Hampstead Observatory." He led her inside. "It was founded in 1898. It's the only observatory in London that's open to the public."

"We're going to stargaze wearing formal attire?" she laughed.

"It's like those nights at St Andrews when everyone got dressed up for a dance, and it was so boring they left early. They lounged around the quad in dinner jackets and evening gowns and saw who could toss cigarette butts the farthest."

"You never joined us," she recalled. "You sat at the desk in your room and looked down as if we were a group of thugs."

"I'm here now." He took her hand and led her up a circular staircase. "Wait until you see Orion and Pluto."

At the top of the staircase was a room with rounded windows. Kate peered through the telescope and gasped. The stars were so close they were like diamonds on some fabulous tiara.

"I haven't looked through a telescope in years." She stepped away. "Nobody stargazes in New York. There's so much to do, it's impossible to just stand and look at the sky."

"Nothing is impossible if you want it badly enough," Trevor murmured.

"Trevor," she said and felt a sudden uncertainty, like when she was ice-skating in Central Park and the ice was slightly cracked. She didn't know whether to keep skating or turn back.

"You're bright and beautiful and full of life," he whispered. "What I really want is to kiss you."

He moved closer and wrapped his arms around her. His kiss was warm and she tasted champagne and butter.

"Trevor, wait." She pulled away. "You're just separated and I'm leaving in a few days."

Trevor ran his hands through his hair and took a deep breath.

"You're right. I got carried away by the ballet and the champagne and the stars," he said.

"It is beautiful here." She moved to the window and gazed at the sky. "I'm glad we came."

He straightened his tie and a smile crossed his face. "Should we go? We don't want to get caught making out, like two students sneaking into a chemistry lab."

She walked over to him and kissed him lightly on the mouth. He kissed her back and she inhaled his musk aftershave.

"Now we can go." She nodded and started down the stairs.

Kate stood at the window of her suite and sipped a glass of sherry. It was almost midnight and a thick fog had settled over the sidewalk. Silver Rolls-Royces were shrouded in mist and she could see the faint outline of Hyde Park.

Kissing Trevor at the observatory had been wonderful, but it couldn't lead to anything. She had a busy career and Trevor was starting a divorce.

She had never been able to separate love and attraction. They were stuck together like the leads in a romantic movie: they always started out having a casual fling but ended up standing at the altar.

And she and Trevor could cause each other so much pain. Trevor's whole body tensed when the woman at the ballet mentioned Ian. Ian's name would keep popping up and it would be like living with an unexploded bomb.

She flashed on the house party Jane had mentioned. She had been stranded at St Andrews and Ian had rescued her.

Kate opened her textbook and fiddled with her pencil. It was finals week and Mitchells was crammed with students lugging heavy backpacks and drinking endless cups of coffee. Their eyes were rimmed and they wore baggy sweatpants and St Andrews sweatshirts.

She and Ian had had a lovely time at the Snowdrop Ball. He kept her champagne glass filled and was a wonderful dancer. But when they returned to the residence hall, his lips barely brushed her cheek.

She had only seen him a few times since, and he was usually in the middle of a group. Once he called her name while she was crossing the quad. When she turned around, he was flanked by two girls in sheepskin coats and fur boots like a rock star arriving at the airport.

Now Trevor walked toward her table, carrying a Styrofoam coffee cup. His hair fell over his forehead and his socks didn't match.

"How can you drink more coffee?" She shuddered. "It's only noon and it's your fourth cup. You need to eat something—a slice of shepherd's pie or a sausage roll."

"I can't afford coffee and food at the same time. The only

important thing is staying awake." He set the cup on the table. "I've even given up fighting with the dryer for a matching pair of socks. It's like a fire-breathing dragon. I wear whatever it spits out."

"Finals will be over in two days," Kate said with a sigh. "Then I'll be sitting on the beach in Santa Barbara. On Christmas Day all the surfers put on red hats and surf at Butterfly Beach. I wish you were coming. My parents would love to have you."

"I can barely afford my train ticket home and I don't have a valid passport." He shrugged. "I have bad news. Your Christmas isn't going to involve palm trees and surfboards."

"What do you mean?" she asked.

"There's an airline strike," he answered. "All the flights are grounded."

"That's impossible!" she exclaimed. "The strike has to end. I have to be in California for Christmas."

"You've never experienced a British transportation strike," he chuckled. "Heathrow will be more crowded than Wembley Stadium at a Rolling Stones concert. Once the flights resume, it will be impossible to get a seat. You could be waiting at the airport until New Year's."

"What am I supposed to do?" She bit her lip. "The dorms are closed and if there's a strike, all the hotels will be full."

"I wish you could come home with me, but there isn't any room. My aunt arrives with her four children," he explained. "We can stay here and bunk down in the Student Union. We'll have unlimited cups of coffee and packets of shortbread."

"You can't miss Christmas with your family." She collected her books and stood up. "I'll think of something."

"Where are you going?" he wondered.

"To call my parents and tell them they don't have to make my favorite gravy."

She hurried down North Street and bumped into a man wearing a wool coat. He bent down to pick up her books and she recognized Ian's blond hair.

"These textbooks weigh a ton." He gave them to her. "If one dropped on your foot, you could break it."

"It's finals week. Most students carry backpacks heavier than a stack of gold bullion." She eyed his empty hands. "Not all of us can pass our classes on our good looks and smile."

"I've been studying all week," he protested. "There's a very nice library assistant who keeps my books behind the counter. She even provides me with a Shetland wool blanket."

"Lucky you." She started walking. "Thank you for picking up my books. I'm in a hurry, I have to make a phone call."

"Are you always rude to people who are trying to be nice to you?" He followed her.

"What do you mean?" She turned around.

"Ever since the Snowdrop Ball, you've been avoiding me," he said. "I've seen you crossing the quad, and you never even wave in my direction."

"You're always busy." She flushed. "I didn't want to interrupt."

"I'm not busy now." He took her arm. "I'm going to the Student Union for hot apple cider. Why don't you come? You can tell me why you're putting innocent people at risk by barreling along the sidewalk."

They sat on low sofas in the Student Union and Ian ordered hot apple ciders and scones with strawberry butter.

"There's an airline strike and I can't get home for Christmas," she said, nibbling the warm scone. "The dorms are closed and all the hotels will be full. I'll be sleeping on a bench at Heathrow Airport."

Ian brushed crumbs from his plate. "I can't let that happen. You can come with me."

"Come with you where?" Kate asked warily.

"To Churchill Lodge," he said. "It's my uncle's shooting estate in Warwickshire. It was built in the seventeenth century. There's grouse hunting and on Christmas Eve the whole parish sings carols on the doorstep."

"If you think I'm going to go away with you when we hardly know each other . . ." Her cheeks flushed.

"I don't expect to share a bedroom," he chuckled. "Churchill Lodge has more bedrooms than the Ritz and just as many servants. There are scavenger hunts and charades, and on New Year's Eve there's a ball that makes the Snowdrop Ball look like a dance at the rec center."

"You really can just bring a guest unannounced?" Kate wondered.

"You would make a stunning addition to the dinner table and I'm sure you're good at games, all Americans are competitive," he said and Kate noticed his eyes were the color of blue topaz. "We'll even stop at Debenhams and pick you up some wellies. You don't want to get those gorgeous legs wet if you go fly-fishing."

"All right." Kate nodded and felt a frisson of excitement. "I'll go, thank you."

Kate sat at her desk and pored over a map of Scotland. There was a knock at her door and she answered it.

"I've been looking for you." Trevor entered the room. "I have good news."

"So do I." Kate beamed. "I'm going to spend Christmas at Churchill Lodge in Warwickshire. There will be sledding and a New Year's Eve ball. It's going to be like something out of a Jane Austen novel."

"I'm guessing one of your society members invited you. The food will be so rich you'll get a stomachache, and everyone will be hung over from drinking malt whiskey." He shuddered. "It sounds gruesome."

"I think it sounds wonderful. It has one of those huge kitchens you see in the movies and a hallway lined with antlers. Not that I want to meet a moose in a dark corridor when I'm on the way to get a midnight snack," she laughed. "But it will be a great experience. Ian said the dining-room table sits fifty and there's a forest with its own Christmas trees."

"Ian?" Trevor looked up.

"Ian Cunningham." She nodded. "I ran into him in front of the Student Union. It belongs to his uncle and I'm going as his guest."

"That's impossible." He ran his hands through his hair. "You can't go with Ian."

"What do you mean 'I can't'?" she demanded.

"He just wants to sleep with you," he started. "Ian Cunningham goes through women faster than other students consume Cadbury Flakes."

"Churchill Lodge is so big, we'll probably be staying in different wings." She bristled. "Anyway, I'm quite capable of taking care of myself."

"It's a bad idea," he insisted. "Why would he invite a girl he barely knows to a family Christmas unless he has designs on her?"

"Because he was being kind. You might think that anyone with a decent haircut and gold watch only thinks about himself, but you're wrong. Ian didn't even try to kiss me goodnight after the Snowdrop Ball." Her eyes flashed. "If you'll excuse me, I have to figure out what to wear to a Scottish Christmas."

"Kate, I'm sorry," Trevor said. "I'm a little disappointed."

"Disappointed?" she asked.

"I phoned my mother and she was going to borrow a rollaway," he explained. "It would have been in the living room and you would have been woken up too early on Christmas morning, but we could have spent the holidays together."

"I already said yes to Ian." She bit her lip. "It would be impolite to cancel."

"You're not missing anything. My mother can't cook a decent ham and no one has the courage to tell her." He walked to the door. "I have to go do my laundry. I'll see you later."

"Trevor, wait." Kate suddenly felt as if she was losing something important.

"Yes?" He turned around.

"Thank you, it was very nice of you to try. I'll come with you to the laundry." She joined him. "We wouldn't want the dryer eating up your last pair of socks."

Kate put the glass of sherry on the sideboard and unzipped her dress. Noah had the whole day scheduled tomorrow and she needed to get some sleep.

What would have happened if she had spent that first Christmas with Trevor's family instead of with Ian? It was like when you see a handsome man sitting five rows ahead of you on an airplane. You always wonder if everything would be different if you'd sat in seat 5B. But life wasn't like that. Many things went into shaping your future.

Her phone buzzed and she pressed Accept.

"What are you doing awake?" Trevor asked. "It's past midnight."

"I'm in London to work," she reminded him. "My inbox is lit up like a Christmas tree."

"I was wondering if you would like to have breakfast tomorrow morning," he offered. "We can go to the Foyer and have Scottish haddock omelets. You can even bring your laptop and I'll feed you eggs while you work."

Kate slipped off her earring and pressed the phone to her ear. "I had a wonderful time tonight, but I'm not sure we should see each other. I'll be gone in a few days and it will have been for nothing."

"We don't have to think about the future, we can just enjoy each other's company." He paused. "Never mind about breakfast. Tomorrow night I've been invited to a reception at Buckingham Palace. The Queen won't be there but it will be in the White Drawing Room."

"Buckingham Palace!" Kate gasped.

"Someone saw me at the club and sent me an invitation," he explained. "It's just a little Christmas gathering, but they give out lovely presents. It would be much more fun if you were there."

"You really have an invitation to Buckingham Palace?" she responded. "But won't people think it's odd that you're there without Susannah?"

"I'll just tell them she's stuck in the country. One of us had to attend and you're an old friend from college."

"You do know how to impress a woman," she laughed. "I've always been crazy about the royal family. I'd love to come."

"I'm glad. I'll pick you up at seven." He paused. "And Kate, would you do something for me and wear the white gloves? They make you look like a princess."

Kate hung up and slipped on her robe. She'd seen *The Nutcracker* at Covent Garden and tomorrow she was attending a reception at Buckingham Palace! She pulled back the satin sheets and climbed into bed. Christmas at Claridge's was better than she imagined.

Chapter Nine

LOUISA SAT ON THE SOFA in the suite's living room and took out her card to Chloe. It was barely 8:00 a.m. and she longed to be snuggled under Claridge's down comforter. She wished the curtains were closed and the central heating was on high and the sheets were pulled right up to her chin.

She had been so excited last night after she returned from Digby's first master class, she couldn't sleep. She sat at the desk in her suite and scribbled down everything Digby taught them: how to make the pastry for an eggnog cup and how much Madeira to use in a butterscotch and banana trifle.

She suddenly longed for a cup of black coffee from the coffeepot at the bakery on the Lower East Side. This morning she would have added two spoonfuls of beans to make the coffee extra strong.

Digby had asked her to accompany him to the Pimlico Farmers' Market to buy supplies for tomorrow afternoon's class. They were going to choose lemons for a panettone and figs for a holiday roll and pears for a kumquat pudding.

The market was tucked away in Orange Square. Only chefs

and locals shopped there, and the fresh produce was one of London's best-kept secrets.

It would have been nice if they could have gone a little later, when it wasn't so cold. A layer of ice covered Hyde Park and the guests entering Claridge's wore floor-length coats and leather boots.

But she had to meet Noah and board the double-decker bus at 11:00 a.m. Anyway, attending a farmers' market early was part of the charm. The rest of the city was still waking up but the market bustled with people and activity. Vendors offered you pastry samples and there was the scent of fresh bread and spices.

Last night, Noah's light hadn't been on when she returned from the master class. She had knocked on the door, but there was no answer. Maybe he had gone out for a late dinner or to a club. It really was none of her business; he could do whatever he liked.

Her phone buzzed and she pressed Accept.

"Louisa, it's Ellie," a female voice said over the line.

"What are you doing up so late?" Louisa exclaimed, wondering if anything was wrong. "It's 3:00 a.m. in New York."

"You know how busy the bakery is the week before Christmas, I'm too wound up to sleep. I thought I'd catch up on phone calls and see how you're doing. Chloe received your recipe card and she's beaming. I said she had to wait to make the Rudolph Shortbread until you come back, but she begged me to go out today and buy the pipe cleaners. It was such a sweet gesture, I really appreciate it."

"I still feel slightly guilty for running off the week before Christmas, even though I'm covered at the bakery," Louisa explained. "Plus, I love baking with Chloe. She has natural talent. I was just sitting down to write a new card." She turned over the embossed card. "We're going to make Snowdippers. They're like cake pops with dark chocolate and marshmallows and all white sprinkles. We'll wrap them in cellophane paper and she can give them to her friends as presents."

"It sounds wonderful. Now I want to hear all about you," Ellie prompted. "It's raining in Manhattan and I'm mired in bookkeeping. Tell me about Claridge's and Harrods and all the exciting things you're doing in London."

"Well, I'm going to the outdoor market with Digby Bunting this morning," Louisa admitted.

"Did you say Digby Bunting?" Ellie gasped. "He's the heartthrob of the culinary world."

"He's very nice in person and he's taken an interest in my baking," Louisa said warmly. "He asked me to attend his series of master classes, and now he's taking me shopping for ingredients."

"You're gone four days and you're already hobnobbing with baking royalty," Ellie laughed. "Next you'll be serving apple pie à la mode to the Queen."

"I doubt that, but I am having a good time," Louisa conceded. "Thank you for letting me go."

"You did something wonderful for me too. Bianca is going to mention the bakery on television," Ellie reminded her. "Send us some photos of you and Digby at the outdoor market. I'll pin them on the wall so our clients know that you're rubbing elbows with one of the hottest pastry chefs in the world."

Louisa hung up the phone and wrote out the recipe card for Chloe. She slipped it in an envelope and walked to the closet in her bedroom. She was meeting Digby soon and had to get dressed.

She was tempted to pull on a pair of jeans and her thickest sweater. But Digby was a celebrity. What if the paparazzi saw them and snapped a photo? Noah would be furious if her picture was splashed across *The Sun* and she wasn't dressed properly. As long as she was representing *Baking with Bianca,* she had to look her best.

She reached into the closet and selected a pair of camel-colored slacks and a scoop-neck sweater. She brushed her hair and applied her makeup and hurried into the hallway.

A man in a leather jacket stood at the elevator. A newspaper was folded under his arm and he held a coffee mug.

"Louisa!" Noah turned around. "What are you doing up so early? You've been so cranky in the mornings; I arranged the schedule so you could sleep in. I imagined you'd be lying in bed dreaming of sugar plum fairies."

"I started work at the bakery every morning at 5:00 a.m.," she reminded Noah. "And I wasn't cranky, I was jet-lagged. Cranky is a mood you can snap out of by inhaling a floral perfume. Jet lag feels like a disease. It drags your whole body down like quicksand. I'm much better now, I could run a marathon."

"You're not running a marathon in those shoes." He eyed her narrow heels. "Where are you going?"

Louisa gulped and suddenly wondered what Noah would say about Digby's master classes. If only she could have told him yesterday, before she went. But it wasn't her fault he had been gone all afternoon and evening.

"I haven't seen you since you disappeared to track down that camera," she said evasively. "I have so much to tell you."

"It was a scavenger hunt," he said and sighed. "The camera was at Gatwick instead of Heathrow, and on the way back the taxi got stuck in a traffic jam. The driver ended up sharing his packet of chips and ham sandwich because it took us four hours to get to

Claridge's. I didn't go to bed until midnight and now Kate wants me to buy props for our shoot. She thinks you should wear a red raincoat and hold an umbrella."

"It's not raining." She peered out the hallway window.

"She thinks it will set the mood. I wouldn't mind a little rain, it might warm things up." He shivered. "I had to go out earlier and it was as cold as a ski resort. I hope you're not going farther than the lobby, you're going to freeze without a proper coat and boots."

"That's what I've been trying to tell you," she blurted out. "I'm going to the Pimlico Farmers' Market with Digby Bunting."

"What did you say?" Noah's eyes flashed.

"People are waiting." She gestured to the open elevator. "Perhaps we should talk about it later."

"We'll talk about it now." He stepped into the elevator and pressed the button to send it down without them. He stepped out again and the door closed. "Why are you going to the farmers' market at the crack of dawn wearing a low-neck sweater and stilettos?"

"It's hardly the crack of dawn, and you have to go to the farmers' market early. The best fruits and vegetables are gone by 9:00 a.m.," she informed him. "And this is a scoop-neck sweater, you picked it yourself."

"For a cocktail party where the lights are dim and everyone's wearing holiday attire," he spluttered. "And those shoes belong on a runway model."

"I was only trying to make you happy. If anyone took a photo of Digby and me and I looked like I rolled out of bed, the paparazzi would go crazy." She realized what she just said and put her hand to her mouth.

Noah's cheeks paled and he stuffed his hands in his pockets.

"Maybe you should tell me everything I missed. Because if Kate finds out you spent the night with Digby Bunting, there will be a terrible scandal. She will be furious at me for hiring you, and I'll wish I was on the first flight to New York."

"Of course I didn't spend the night with him!" she exclaimed. "I left his flat at 10:00 p.m. And how dare you think I'd do anything to jeopardize *Christmas Dinner at Claridge's*. I was only there because he invited me to his master class." She sighed. "It was so thrilling. Six chefs gathered in a state-of-the-art Mayfair kitchen. I made a Bûche de Noël and Digby said it was the best he ever tasted. After class, he opened a bottle of sherry and we all ate each other's desserts."

"Digby invited you to a master class?"

"Yesterday after the meeting." She nodded. "We had afternoon tea at the Foyer. He holds a series of master classes that usually has a waiting list longer than a kid's letter to Santa Claus." She paused. "It's very selective, only skilled chefs are invited."

"Digby invited you to his master classes when he never sampled your pastries?" he asked suspiciously.

"What are you implying?" she demanded.

"Didn't you ever have a boy in high school who needed help with his algebra homework? You go to his house to study and his textbook is in his bedroom. The next thing you know, you're pushing him away and dashing down the stairs." He waved his hand. "Digby didn't invite you because of your crème fraîche icing; he invited you because he wanted to sleep with you!"

"That's an outrageous thing to say," she gasped. "There were five other chefs there. The only other room I saw was the powder room. And he knows I'm a serious chef, I'm part of *Christmas Dinner at Claridge's*."

"I know how guys like Digby operate," he insisted. "He may not have made his move last night, but he invited you for an early-morning rendezvous."

"To the farmers' market! He picks one student to help buy supplies before each class," she explained. "I'm going to learn how to choose the freshest eggs and the best type of ricotta for a cheese-cake."

He rubbed his brow. "I'll come with you."

"What did you say?" she looked at him.

"We'll film you and Digby eating sliced ham and sampling local cheeses. We can shoot a whole segment on Pimlico Road, there are some fabulous boutiques and galleries."

"I'm meeting him there in twenty minutes," she protested. "You don't have your camera operator."

"I'll shoot it with my iPhone." He took her arm and led her into the elevator. "I wouldn't ever want a camera operator to be out of work, but the camera quality on the iPhone is excellent."

Pimlico Road was lined with interior design stores and antiques shops and art galleries. Plate-glass windows were filled with old-fashioned sleigh beds and bone china. There was a haberdashery that sold handmade linens and a goldsmith that specialized in 18-karat gold jewelry.

"Pimlico Road doesn't have elegant boutiques like the King's Road but it has some of the best antiques stores in London," Louisa said, peering into a furniture store. "Someday, I'm going to buy a cottage in Upstate New York and furnish it with floral sofas and woven rugs. It will have a farmhouse kitchen and an attic that can be converted into a nursery."

"I thought all you want is your own restaurant," Noah said in surprise.

"That's all I want now, and I'll sacrifice anything to get it." She nodded. "Eventually I want a home and family. I don't want anything fancy. I could never be one of those women who has a living room where the cushions are always plumped and there isn't a smudge on the coffee table. But in ten years, I'd love to get married and have children."

"Ten years is a long time to wait," he offered. "What if you don't meet the right guy? Your biological clock will stop ticking and you'll never have a family."

"That's a gloomy prediction," she laughed. "I can't worry about it now. I'm so close to opening my own restaurant. This time next year I'll be serving cinnamon rolls and pecan pie to customers lining up at the door." She paused and her eyes sparkled. "I don't know how to thank you for bringing me to London. You are my Christmas guardian angel and I'm very grateful."

"There is something I was going to ask you . . ." Noah began.

"What is it?" She turned to Noah.

A man called to them from the other side of the street. He wore a cashmere overcoat and Burberry scarf.

"That's Digby," Noah said, looking up. "It will have to wait."

"What if he doesn't want to be filmed?" she said anxiously. "We should have asked him first."

"Digby lives for the camera." Noah shrugged. "He probably wishes there was a cameraman in the bathroom to see him flexing his muscles when he shaves."

Louisa turned to Noah and her good mood dissolved.

"That's a terrible thing to say! You have to be polite to Digby," she warned him. "I'm very lucky that he invited me to his master class."

"I'm only here to get footage for Kate," he assured her. "I'd never let my personal feelings get in the way of my job."

"There you are!" Digby joined them. "I'm sorry I'm late. I stopped and picked up two cappuccinos. It's so cold this morning, the only thing that warms me up is scalding-hot coffee."

"I'm exactly the same. Thank you." She accepted the cup and inhaled the sweet aroma. "This is Noah. If you don't mind, he's going to film our shopping expedition."

"Why should I mind?" He shook Noah's hand and Louisa noticed his palms were perfectly smooth.

They entered the farmers' market and Louisa sucked in her breath. There were stalls of Bramley apples and Comice pears. Glass cases were filled with cheeses with bright-red rinds and plump figs. Digby pointed out bronze and black Christmas turkeys, and sausages that smelled so good, Louisa was suddenly starving.

"This is so inspiring." She eyed jars of blackberry jelly. "Whenever I see the berries at the farmers' market in New York, I want to go straight to the bakery and bake a strawberry cream cake or blueberry tart."

"What are your aspirations?" Dibgy turned to her.

"My aspirations?" she repeated.

"Do you want to be the pastry chef at a grand hotel like the Ritz, Paris or the St. Regis in New York? Or would you rather be the head pastry chef of a Michelin-starred restaurant?"

Louisa noticed Noah trailing behind them and wished Noah could hear them. Digby thought she was talented enough to have her own kitchen!

"I'm going to open a restaurant in New York," she answered. "It will specialize in desserts: poached rhubarb in the spring and mint chocolate chip ice cream sandwiches in summer and maple cheesecakes in the fall. At Christmas I'll sell Scandinavian princess cakes with white and blue frosting, and eggnog mousse and croquembouche. The croquembouche will be so delicious, people won't mind sitting in the subway or being jostled on the midtown bus to pick one up for Christmas."

"I envy you," he admitted.

"What do you mean?" she wondered.

"I'd give anything to spend all my time whisking eggs for a custard tart or paring apples for an apple crumble," he explained. "Instead I'm approving merchandise deals and scheduling book tours. Last week *Hello* said my barber comes to my flat because I'm too spoiled to visit the hair salon. The truth is I don't have time for a haircut and shave. At home, I can read contracts while he's cutting my hair and my manager can go over my itinerary while I'm getting a shave."

"I don't understand." She frowned. "You're so successful, you can do whatever you want."

"There's always some wunderkind poised to take over," he answered. "The cooking world is as bad as acting. If your name isn't on social media or your face isn't on television, people forget about you."

"Why not give it all up and focus on your cooking?" she asked. "You must have enough money. Your last cookbook was on the *New York Times* best seller list for two years."

"My publisher has invested in me for ages, I can't let them down. And what would happen to everyone who works on my television specials?" he responded. "I can't turn my back on people that depend on me because I'd rather make tapioca pudding in an English manor."

Louisa looked up and saw Noah tapping his watch.

"It's almost 10:00 a.m.!" she exclaimed. "I should go."

"There's somewhere I want to show you first," Digby said and took her arm.

They turned onto Ebury Street and entered a shop with a red front door and striped awnings. R CHOCOLATE was scrawled in gold letters over the window and chocolate boxes were wrapped in pink tissue paper.

Digby opened the door and Louisa inhaled the heavenly scent of cocoa and nutmeg. Every surface was covered in chocolates! Fudge bars were stacked in pyramids and sea salt caramels were arranged like pieces on a chessboard, and there were glass cases of tiramisu and chocolate fondant.

It wasn't just the chocolate that took Louisa's breath away; it was the polished wood floor and marble-topped tables and old-fashioned cash register. There was an espresso machine and bottles of syrup and flavorings.

"It's just how I picture my restaurant," she breathed. "The walls will be eggshell yellow and there will be a huge mirror behind the counter. Round tables will be scattered around the store and glass cases will be filled with almond cakes and fruit tarts."

"I thought you'd like it." Digby beamed. "R Chocolate is one of the premier chocolatiers in London. The cocoa is imported from all over the world and they only use the finest ingredients. You can buy a single chocolate truffle or sit at a table and sample soufflés and éclairs."

"I can't imagine picking out just one chocolate," Louisa laughed.

"That's like standing in Tiffany's and being asked to choose only one diamond."

"Let me put together an assortment," Digby suggested.

He moved around the store and selected pralines and pastel-colored macarons. There were chocolate nougats and hazelnut rochers.

"You're not buying all these?" she asked in astonishment.

"We'll try some here, and you can take the ones you like best." He offered her a chocolate profiterole. "This is one of my favorites: a whipped cream filling coated with caramel and Peruvian dark chocolate."

Louisa took a bite and tasted butter and cream and the lightest touch of caramel.

"It's the best profiterole I ever tasted," she agreed.

"You have a spot of caramel on your cheek," he said and put his finger on her cheek. He wiped the caramel carefully and suddenly there was a crash.

"I'm sorry, I dropped my phone," Noah explained.

Noah bent down and knocked over a plate of chocolate marzipans. The marzipans tumbled to the ground and Noah reached down to pick them up. His jacket caught the side of a display table and a coconut chocolate cake teetered on its stand. He tried to steady it but the cake toppled and splattered all over the floor.

"God! I'm terribly sorry." Noah gulped, running his hands through his hair. "Why don't you two go ahead, and I'll clean the whole thing up."

"Don't be silly. I'll help." Digby bent down and gathered macarons. "It will go much faster if we do it together."

"Accidents happen." Louisa glowered at Noah. "I'll ask the salesgirl for a broom."

"What do you think you were doing?" Louisa seethed. Digby had left for an appointment and she and Noah were standing in Sloane Square.

"It was an accident, anyone can drop their phone." He peered down the road for a taxi. "I gave the girl behind the counter a one-hundred-pound tip. That should cover the ruined chocolate and leave a little extra for her."

"You were trying to make Digby uncomfortable," she insisted.

"Do you really think I'd create havoc in a chocolate shop because Digby put his thumb on your cheek?" he demanded.

"You did notice!" she gasped. "It was perfectly innocent. I got a little caramel on my cheek and he wiped it off. What if he takes back the invitation to his master class? He was probably so embarrassed, he doesn't want to see me."

"That's ridiculous," Noah scoffed. "If he really thinks you're a talented chef, a mishap at the chocolatier isn't going to change anything."

"That's what this is about!" she exclaimed. "You still think he only invited me because he wants to sleep with me. He asked me what my goals are. He thinks I could be the pastry chef at a luxury hotel or Michelin-starred restaurant."

"He thinks all that after tasting your Bûche de Noël?"

"This discussion isn't going anywhere." She strode down the sidewalk.

"Where are you going?" He raced after her.

"I'm supposed to be on that double-decker bus in twenty minutes, and I don't feel like sharing a taxi."

"You can't walk in those shoes." He waved at her pumps. "We're both overwrought. Let's talk about it on the way."

"No thank you," she said. "I'll get my own cab."

"We won't find two separate cabs at this hour," he implored. "We're lucky if we get one."

"Then I'll catch a bus to get to the double-decker bus." She turned and her eyes glistened. "You said I made the best cinnamon rolls and now you don't believe in me at all. Maybe you were the one who was lying. All you wanted was someone to wear the same color lipstick as Bianca and do something nice with her hair. Digby thinks I could be a great chef and so do I." She noticed a bus waiting at the bus stop and climbed on board.

"I'll see you at Claridge's," she called out the window. "Don't be late, we're on a tight schedule."

Louisa sat on top of the double-decker bus and rubbed her hands. She had been so excited about the sightseeing tour of London. Kate rented out the whole bus and they were going to stop at Madame Tussauds and the Parliament building and Big Ben.

But Louisa hadn't realized the bus didn't have a roof and she couldn't stop shivering. They visited the Sherlock Holmes Pub and she ordered a hot apple cider. It was so wonderful to sit in the warm pub she almost got left behind. She had to run after the bus and bang on the door before the driver realized he'd left without her.

Noah barely acknowledged her. He sat in the bottom of the bus and scribbled on his clipboard. When she asked if he liked the footage of her with Jack the Ripper, he said he'd check it later. She walked back upstairs and knew he wouldn't be happy. The wax figure had been so lifelike, she hadn't smiled for the camera.

If only they hadn't gotten into an argument. Noah accused Digby of hitting on her, when Digby had been completely professional. And what if Noah had been lying to her and didn't think she was a talented chef? But she remembered when they met at the bakery and he marveled at her cinnamon rolls. He offered her his leather jacket and car keys and said they were the best he ever tasted.

Noah had done so much for her: bringing her to London and making her part of *Christmas Dinner at Claridge's*. She shouldn't have said terrible things to him. Now she didn't know how to fix it.

The bus pulled up in front of Claridge's and Louisa entered the lobby. A fire crackled in the marble fireplace and the Christmas tree glinted like a jeweled brooch.

She passed the Map Room and admired the teal silk sofa and sideboard set with a crystal decanter. There was a shelf of leather-bound books and a walnut desk with an upholstered chair.

It looked so inviting with its plush red carpet and paneled walls. A woman flipped the pages of a coffee table book and she recognized Kate.

"Louisa! What are you doing here?" Kate looked up. "I didn't know you were back."

"I just arrived and I'm freezing," Louisa answered. "It looked so cozy in here, I thought I'd have a brandy."

"Is that what you were wearing on the bus?" Kate glanced at her scoop-neck sweater. "No wonder you were freezing."

"It's my fault." Louisa filled a glass with gold liqueur. "I didn't realize the bus didn't have a roof. It was like sitting on a chairlift when it's thirty degrees with a wind chill factor of minus ten."

"I've done that," Kate laughed. "All I wanted was to ride the lift back to the lodge and have a hot chocolate." She paused. "But surely Noah could have found you a jacket?"

Louisa couldn't tell Kate what happened. She didn't want Noah to get in trouble.

"Noah was preoccupied," she said evasively. "We had a full itinerary."

"I've been answering e-mails all morning." Kate nodded. "I love working in here. The butler serves tea and buttermilk scones and there are so many books. I'm going to a reception at Buckingham Palace and I was reading about the royal family."

"You're going to Buckingham Palace?" Louisa gasped.

"Trevor is related by marriage to the Queen," Kate explained. "We're going to nibble watercress sandwiches and drink champagne in the White Drawing Room. I've been practicing curtseying all morning."

"Is Trevor the man you had dinner with?" Louisa wondered. "You didn't say he was married."

"He's separated." Kate fiddled with her earrings. "He's staying at Claridge's until he finds a flat. Last night we saw *The Nutcracker* at Covent Garden."

"You said your love life was boring, but you've seen Trevor every night." Louisa sank onto the sofa. The brandy warmed her throat and it was nice to have someone to talk to.

"I did say that, didn't I?" Kate laughed. "There is something between us, but I'm leaving in a few days. And our past is complicated, one of us could get hurt."

"Sometimes I'm glad I don't have time for love." Louisa cradled her brandy snifter. "It's easier making vanilla custard layers for a Napoleon than it is to figure out men."

"I'm sure men say the same about us." Kate smiled. "The most important thing is friendship. If you're lucky enough to find a good friend, you do everything to keep him."

"I suppose you're right," Louisa agreed. "But even friends have silly arguments. How do you make things right when you've both been wrong?"

"Always be the first to apologize," Kate said emphatically. "It's hard to be angry with someone if they said they're sorry."

"That is good advice," Louisa mused.

"Every relationship has problems. Did you know the Duke and Duchess of Cambridge broke up during their courtship because the paparazzi wouldn't leave them alone?" Kate turned back to her book. "The press called her Waity Katie because Prince William took so long to propose."

"It would be terrible to have cameras flash in your face whenever you buy a carton of milk. Though she does live in a palace and has servants to do whatever she asks." Louisa gulped her brandy and shivered. "Right now I'd give anything if there was a hot bath waiting for me upstairs."

Louisa entered her suite and placed her purse on the end table. A bouquet of purple lilies stood in a crystal vase and silver bowls were filled with macadamia nuts. The light filtered onto the scarlet sofa and the wood furniture was freshly polished.

Digby's second master class was tomorrow afternoon and she wanted to be prepared. She was going to run a bath and read Digby's new cookbook. She wanted to know exactly how much ginger to add to a chocolate ginger cake in case Digby asked her in front of the other students.

There was a knock at the door and she opened it. Noah stood in the hallway. He wore a wool coat and his hands were stuffed in his pocket.

"Could I come in?" he asked.

"You may as well." Louisa walked back into the living room. "But if you came to tell me the footage in the London Dungeon was too dark, I told the cameraman to use a light. He said you always give him instructions, and you didn't say anything about it."

"All the footage came out wonderfully." Noah perched on a love seat. "Your sweater was a good choice, the turquoise looked lovely on film."

"I should have listened to you and worn a coat and boots. My cheeks are still numb and I can't feel my toes." She eyed Noah suspiciously. "Why are you here?"

"I want to take you somewhere," he said.

"I'm too cold. I'm not going outside until I've soaked in a hot bath." She shook her head.

"You don't have to go outside." He walked to the door and smiled. "Follow me, I promise it will be worth it."

They took the elevator to the first floor and walked through a maze of hallways. Noah pushed open a door and entered a small kitchen. There was a silver fridge and marble counter stacked with mixing bowls and measuring cups.

"This is the kitchen used for the private dining room," he said. "It's fully equipped and the pantry has every kind of spice."

"It's gorgeous." She admired the double ovens. "But why are we here?"

"I didn't beg you to come to London because your eyes look

even bigger on camera, I asked you because your cinnamon rolls were the best I ever tasted. I knew you could stand next to those chefs and prepare a dessert Kate and Bianca would be proud of." He paused. "I spoke to the head pastry chef. You're going to bake cinnamon rolls for Claridge's afternoon tea."

"You want me to bake cinnamon rolls that are going to be served at Claridge's?" she gasped.

"I already know they're the best in New York, now we'll know they are the finest in London." He pointed to the fridge. "The dough is already made because we don't have all afternoon. But I bought the ingredients for the icing. If I forgot anything, I can run down to the main kitchen."

Louisa walked to the sink so Noah couldn't see the tears in her eyes.

"I shouldn't have accused you of dropping your phone to make Digby uncomfortable." She turned around. "You would never jeopardize the show because of your feelings. It was wrong and I apologize."

"We both said things we shouldn't have, but we can't think about it now." He pulled out a stool. "I brought my computer so I can sit here while you work."

"You're going to wait while I bake cinnamon rolls?" she asked in astonishment.

"I have to." He opened his laptop. "Someone has to taste them before they're served at the most famous afternoon tea in London."

Louisa tied an apron around her waist and assembled cream cheese and confectioner's sugar. The pot simmered on the stove and she felt the familiar thrill of turning butter and milk into something rich and delicious.

The dough turned golden brown in the oven and she layered it with thick icing. The cinnamon rolls cooled and she washed mixing bowls and measuring spoons. Finally she arranged the rolls on a plate and handed one to Noah.

He ate it carefully and put it back on the plate. He brushed crumbs from his slacks and looked at Louisa. "The cream cheese gives the icing the right texture, and the hint of vanilla is perfect. It's delicious."

"You have a spot of icing on your chin." She leaned forward and wiped his chin.

Suddenly she had the urge to kiss him. She reached up and kissed him softly on the mouth. He kissed her back and his mouth tasted warm and sweet.

"I'm sorry, I don't know what got into me." She pulled away. "I have to go. I need to study some recipes for Digby's master class."

"Louisa, wait," Noah urged.

"Yes?" She turned around.

"It isn't just the cinnamon rolls that were perfect," he said and his eyes sparkled. "The kiss was great too."

Louisa raced down the hallway like Cinderella leaving the ball before the clock struck midnight. The corridors were so confusing; it took forever to reach the elevator. She was afraid Noah would follow her and it would be so awkward.

She hadn't meant to kiss him. It had been the glass of brandy and heady scent of cinnamon rolls.

She recalled what Kate said about finding a good friend. Noah was one of the kindest people she'd ever met. Even if she didn't have time for love, she couldn't spoil their friendship.

The elevator door opened and she stepped inside. She leaned against the paneling and remembered Noah's lips on her mouth. Noah was right. It was the best kiss she could remember.

Chapter Ten

KATE STOOD ON THE STEPS of Buckingham Palace and marveled at the wide columns and guards in red-and-black uniforms. The iron gates were inscribed with a gold insignia and even in winter, the gardens were more beautiful than she imagined.

She couldn't afford another trip to Harvey Nichols, so she wore the same floral satin gown she wore to *The Nutcracker*. Her hair was pulled into a loose chignon and she had splurged on a bottle of jasmine perfume.

Trevor was the last person who would comment on her dress; he used to wear the same blue shirt every day at St Andrews. Then why was she nervous, like when she brought her prom dress home and it looked different than at the department store?

Of course she was anxious: she was attending a reception at Buckingham Palace! She would see the rooms that seemed as make believe as illustrations in a children's book: the Music Room where the royal christenings were held and the Picture Gallery filled with paintings from the Royal Collection.

It was more than that. All day there was a fluttering in her stomach, as if the cream on her scone was slightly off. She kept checking her phone to see if Trevor called. When he texted and said he was detained and would meet her at Buckingham Palace, she was a little disappointed.

She couldn't have feelings for Trevor; they lived on different continents. But they had similar interests and he was so easy to talk to. And she couldn't ignore the new frisson between them; it was like an electric current.

It couldn't go further than a kiss. She meant what she said to Louisa: nothing was more important than friendship. If she and Trevor could repair their friendship after all this time, it would be foolish to jeopardize it.

A man strode toward her and she recognized Trevor's sandy-colored hair and broad shoulders. He wore a white dinner jacket and black slacks.

"There you are." Trevor approached her. "I was afraid you might have trouble getting through the gate."

"The cabdriver gave my name to the guard and I thought he'd send me away," Kate admitted. "But he waved me right in."

"Buckingham Palace is the royal family's personal residence, and they are allowed guests," he said. "The only difference is they have to be cleared by British intelligence."

"Was I really investigated by the MI-Five so I could attend a Christmas reception?" Kate laughed.

Trevor took her arm and smiled. "If you were, we'll never know."

A courtier led them down a red-carpeted hallway flanked by wide pillars. There were marble sculptures and a pair of Chinese vases that were a gift to King George V from the Emperor of China.

They passed a ballroom that was big enough to hold a concert and the Blue Drawing Room decorated with cobalt silk wallpaper. The Grand Staircase had gold filigree railings and portraits behind gilt frames.

"It's like the descriptions in a Russian novel," Kate breathed. "How can one place hold so many treasures?"

"The State Rooms were built in 1820 for King George IV," Trevor said. "There are nineteen rooms and they contain the most important pieces in the Royal Collection: marble busts by Canova and paintings by Holbein and Sèvres china from France."

"I wouldn't want to be a maid," Kate laughed. "What if you knock something over while you're dusting?"

The courtier opened double doors and Kate gasped. The White Drawing Room had Oriental carpets and gold candelabras and a low-hanging crystal chandelier. There was a rolltop desk and gilded piano. A pair of cabinets had panels depicting flowers and birds and a huge mirror stood above the marble fireplace.

"I can't go in," Kate said, suddenly panicked.

"Of course you can." Trevor took her arm. "The room looks imposing but everyone is friendly."

"You don't understand, I'm wearing the same dress I wore to *The Nutcracker*. I didn't bring any evening gowns in my suitcase and I couldn't afford to buy two," she implored. "What if someone saw me at the ballet?"

"You'll always be the most beautiful woman in the room," Trevor assured her. "And I have it on good authority that even the Queen wears the same dress twice."

Waiters in white dinner jackets carried trays of Welsh rarebit and Scottish salmon in a dill sauce. There were cups of leek and potato soup and a selection of champagnes.

Trevor introduced her to a couple with three last names who

were first cousins of Prince Charles. There was a dancer with the Royal Ballet and a member of Parliament.

"Trevor!" A young man approached them. "I haven't seen you since Balmoral."

"Kate, this is Lord Peter Balthazar." Trevor shook his hand. "Kate is an old university friend from St Andrews."

"Don't remind me that I'm a lord." Peter shuddered. "It makes me feel like one of the stocky men in the portraits above the fireplace. I'm always reluctant to come to these things. The men look like penguins and the women wear jewelry that's so heavy I'm afraid they'll faint and we'll have to call the paramedics."

"Don't frighten Kate," Trevor admonished him. "She's never attended a royal reception."

"You should come to Balmoral, it's more relaxed." Peter turned to Kate. "I once saw the Duchess of Cambridge in a dressing gown and slippers. She needed a cup of tea and there was no one to make it." He paused. "Last time I was there, I had a broken foot. Trevor and I played backgammon for two days and he even let me win."

"I didn't let you win," Trevor laughed. "You became quite good."

"And you listened to stories about my love life," Peter continued. "I'm very indebted."

"I hope it worked out with the scuba instructor from St. Croix." Trevor grinned.

"She went back to the Caribbean." He shrugged. "I don't blame her. You have to be madly in love to trade a white sand beach for London in July." He looked at Trevor and Kate. "Let me get you a drink."

"But we have champagne." Kate held up her glass.

"They give these bottles to the staff as Christmas presents."

Peter grabbed three glasses from the bar. "I know where they keep the good stuff, follow me."

He led them to a corner of the room and pressed on a gold panel. The wall fell away and they entered a dark hallway.

"The secret passageway was built so the royal family could sneak away during receptions. It's also where they hide the vintage wine." He reached behind a shelf and drew out a bottle of red wine. "This is a 1945 Château Mouton Rothschild and goes well with Yorkshire pudding."

"We're not going to drink wine from the Queen's personal collection?" Kate asked, horrified.

"Don't worry, the important wines are kept in a cellar that even the Germans couldn't touch," Peter laughed. "This bottle won't be missed."

They reentered the drawing room and Kate glanced at Trevor. His eyes shone and he and Peter were deep in conversation about trout fishing in Scotland.

"It was nice to meet you." Peter held out his hand to Kate. "I'm going to slip away before one of my great-aunts asks how to update her iPhone." He turned to Trevor. "We must have lunch at the club. You can let me win again at backgammon."

The waiters brought out trays of custards and bread and butter pudding. There were wedges of hard cheese and sliced pears. Kate sipped a dry sherry and talked about ice-skating at Hampton Court and the Christmas tree at Trafalgar Square.

Finally they said goodbye and walked back to the Ambassadors' Entrance.

"You looked completely at home in there," she mused. "Drinking wine and reminiscing with Lord Balthazar."

"What do you mean?" he asked.

"At St Andrews you wouldn't have anything to do with students who drove imported sports cars and wore Italian loafers," she said. "But you stood in a room with more treasures than the Taj Mahal and belonged."

"I worried that if I let down my guard, other students would get ahead of me. And with Susannah I often felt like a sore thumb attached to her hand." He paused. "But being here with you tonight, I realized if I'm with the right woman it's pleasant to drink a vintage wine with people with similar interests."

"Trevor—" she said warningly.

"There's no chance of a reconciliation with Susannah," he cut in. "I found a flat in Belgravia."

"Why are you telling me that?"

"I've enjoyed the last few days." He paused. "We live in different countries, but the world is a small place. I would like to keep seeing you."

"We're friends enjoying Christmas in London," Kate reminded him. "We can't be more than that."

"Kate." He touched her cheek. "We're adults, we can be whatever we like."

He leaned forward and kissed her. She kissed him back and his mouth was warm and sweet.

"I'm not sure," she said when they parted. She patted her hair and smoothed the creases in her gown.

Trevor stuffed his hands in his pocket and grinned. "That's a start."

Kate sat on the teal silk sofa in the Map Room and traced the rim of a brandy snifter. She'd told Trevor she had to catch up on e-mails and worked better in the quiet space with the sideboard set with teas and roast beef sandwiches.

Could they really start a relationship? In four days she'd be at Heathrow, answering Bianca's frantic e-mails and worrying about next week's show. The dinners with Trevor would become a fond memory whenever she opened her passport.

But they got along so well. They had always been like two trains traveling on parallel routes. And now there was a passion she couldn't ignore.

What if memories of Ian cropped up between them? It would be like planting a rose in a garden where the soil was barren. She sipped the brandy and remembered when Ian got between them the first time. It was the beginning of her second semester and she and Ian had just returned from Christmas at Churchill Lodge.

Kate sat on the single bed and zipped up her jacket. The space heater in her dorm room wasn't working and she had to put on her whole wardrobe to stay warm. She turned the page of her chemistry book and thought she really should study at the Student Union.

She didn't feel like running into Ian. It was better to wear two pairs of socks and hope the maintenance man arrived soon.

Everything about her dorm room seemed bleak after Christmas week at Churchill Lodge. It had been like something out of a PBS special with elaborate banquet halls and drawing rooms with roaring fireplaces.

Ian's uncle was averse to the cold, so the bedroom wing had the most delicious central heating. Even the bathroom floors were heated and every night there was a tray of steaming hot chocolate next to her bed.

They played charades and performed plays and ate grilled sole and raspberry trifle. She and Ian cut down their own Christmas tree and decorated it with tinsel.

She hadn't meant to become involved with Ian, but he was impossible to resist. They practiced a scene from *Romeo and Juliet* and the peck on the cheek turned into a real kiss. His mouth was soft and his hands were in her hair and she felt young and alive.

They took long walks in the snow and ate cauliflower cheese in the local pub. Ian asked her to teach him how to make s'mores and they snuck down to the kitchen at midnight. They roasted marshmallows and chocolate in the kitchen's vast fireplace and it was so romantic.

On New Year's Eve, there was a grand ball with platters of Scottish haddock and grilled asparagus. She wore a sequined dress and they danced and drank champagne. Then the music and bubbles gave her a headache, and she went upstairs to find some aspirin. When she returned, Ian's arms were wrapped around a brunette.

She highlighted her chemistry book and resolved not to think about Ian. She had already signed up for the A Capella Society and Foreign Affairs Society. And spring in St Andrews would be lovely! She would visit the Botanic Gardens and attend poetry festivals and outdoor readings.

There was a knock on the door and she answered it. Trevor stood in the hallway, clutching a paper sack.

"I was hoping you were the maintenance man." She shivered. "My heater stopped working over Christmas break and the room feels like an igloo. You could make ice cream by mixing cream and vanilla and sugar."

"It is freezing." Trevor entered the room. "My mother sent me back with an extra space heater. I can lend it to you."

"The maintenance man promised he'd be here this afternoon." She perched on the bed. "I've been studying for hours, but I keep daydreaming about mink coats and sheepskin boots."

"You didn't miss much at Christmas in York," Trevor mused. "On Christmas morning, my niece saw a mouse and refused to come down to the living room." He smiled. "It turned out to be a ball of wool but it delayed our present opening by two hours."

"It sounds lively," she laughed.

Trevor looked at Kate. "You haven't said a word about your holiday."

"There's nothing to tell." Kate's cheeks flushed.

"Before you left, you were raving about sleigh rides and indoor tennis." He frowned. "Did something happen?"

"What do you mean?" she asked.

"There's something different about you, and it's not the three sweaters you're wearing."

Kate fiddled with her pencil. Trevor was her best friend, she could tell him anything.

"Ian and I had a holiday romance," she admitted.

"You're making a terrible mistake," Trevor protested. "Ian will shower you with gifts, but he has no loyalty. He'll trade you in like an old pair of skis."

"I know that now." She paused. "On New Year's Eve, I found him kissing another girl."

"What a jerk!" Trevor jumped up.

"This isn't the eighteenth century and you don't have to

challenge him to a duel," she laughed. "I told him I never want to talk to him again."

"Are you sure you don't want me to do something?" he asked.

"It was a silly interlude." She shrugged. "I wouldn't mind if you bring that space heater. I can hear my teeth chattering."

"I almost forgot, this is for you." He handed her the paper bag. "I brought it from York."

She opened it and took out a linzer torte. "You said your mother was a terrible cook."

"I wanted to give you something for Christmas," he said and a smile crossed his face. "My aunt made it, and it's delicious."

Kate stood at the counter of the Student Union and rubbed her hands. Trevor had to attend a tutorial and suddenly she longed for a warm raisin scone with strawberry butter.

She turned and saw Ian sitting in a booth. He wore a ski sweater and his blond hair brushed his forehead.

"Make that two raisin scones and a tall latte." Ian approached the counter. "Put it on my tab."

"What do you think you're doing?" she demanded.

"I'm ordering you a hot drink," he explained. "You look like you need thawing out."

"I'm fine." She took her scone and sat at a table. "The space heater in my room isn't working and I got chilly."

"I wasn't talking about that, though I don't want those lovely lips turning blue." He followed her. "I meant you're ignoring me. You didn't talk to me on the drive back to school and you haven't taken my calls."

"You were kissing another girl," she reminded him.

"It was New Year's Eve and you disappeared."

"If I'm that easily replaced, you'll have no trouble finding someone else to take sledding." She opened her chemistry workbook. "If you'll excuse me, I have to do a chemistry lab."

"You're not serious?" he demanded. "I thought you just wanted me to try harder: take you to dinner at the Adamson or bring you a bouquet of lilacs."

"There are plenty of girls who don't mind being another number on your speed dial," she said. "Thank you for taking me to Churchill Lodge, I'll send your uncle a thank-you note."

"You're smart and lovely and we have a great time." He touched her arm. "How can I change your mind?"

"Underneath that ski sweater there's a decent guy," she said slowly. "But I can't date someone I don't trust."

Ian ate the last bite of scone and stood up. "I'll see you tonight at the debate."

"You're a member of the Debate Society?" she wondered.

"I'm not just a member." He grinned. "I'm in tonight's debate."

Kate slipped into the Barron Theatre and took a seat in the back. She'd spent too long on her chemistry homework and was almost late to the debate.

"Good evening." A young man wearing a blazer and tie approached the podium. "Following the rules of the Debate Society, the scheduled debate topic can be changed to address current events. Tonight's topic will no longer be the lasting effects of holiday tours on the salmon population." He consulted his notes. "It will be whether Kate Crawford should give Ian Cunningham another chance. Mr. Cunningham will take the podium."

Kate gasped and was tempted to run back to the residence hall. But Ian crossed the stage and took the podium. His eyes met hers and his smile could have lit up a concert hall.

"Fellow students and guests of the Debate Society," he began. "In my experience we all put labels on each other. Johnny is a champion rower, and Emily is the star of our student productions and James wishes he was Harry Potter." He waved at students in the front row. "Putting labels on fellow students makes sense, because we are often too busy to get to know each other.

"The problem is we come to believe the labels ourselves. Most of you see me as the guy with film-star good looks who always has a piece of eye candy on his arm. That's not a bad gig," he laughed. "After all, we didn't come to university just to study physics.

"But along comes a girl who sees past the shiny surface and thinks there's a guy she could hang out with: a guy who is decent and can truly care for someone." He cleared his throat. "How do you convince her that the boy under the ski sweater would do anything for her? Fellow debaters, support me in promoting my cause." He paused and his eyes were bright. "Kate Crawford must give Ian Cunningham another chance."

Kate hurried across the playing fields and climbed the steps of the residence hall. She looked up and saw Ian standing at the door.

"What are you doing here?" she demanded. "You hijacked the debate and embarrassed me in front of everyone. How will I show my face again?"

"I didn't mean to embarrass you," he insisted.

"Then I don't know what the theatrics were for." She fiddled with her key. "You should go. I'm sure there are a group of adoring girls waiting at the Student Union."

"I meant every word," he assured her. "If you give me another chance, I will never look at another girl."

"I don't believe you," she scoffed. "That's like expecting an ostrich to fly."

"I might look, but it will never go further than that," he urged. "Please, Kate. You're everything I dreamed about, I promise I'll never hurt you."

Kate looked up and wished his eyes weren't so blue and he didn't have chiseled cheekbones.

"One chance," she whispered.

He wrapped his arms around her and kissed her. She kissed him back and her whole body quivered.

She finally pulled away and entered the residence hall. Trevor's light was on and she wondered if he had seen them. A pit formed in her stomach and she knew Trevor would be furious.

Kate sipped her brandy and paced around the Map Room. It was almost midnight and she should go upstairs to her suite. But she still had e-mails to answer and notes to approve.

Would she have given Ian a chance if she knew Trevor was in love with her? Had Trevor been in love with her then, or did that come later? It was so long ago, she could hardly remember.

Her phone buzzed and she picked it up.

"I'm calling to see if you're still awake." Trevor's voice came over the line.

"I told you I had work to do," Kate chuckled. "I'm not in London on holiday."

"I had a wonderful time tonight." His voice softened. "I can't wait to see you again."

She squeezed the phone and remembered his mouth on her lips. She took a deep breath and murmured, "Neither can I."

Chapter Eleven

LOUISA GLANCED AT THE ROOM service tray of porridge with brown sugar. There was a raisin scone with clotted cream and grapefruit in a porcelain cup.

Christmas was in three days and Claridge's felt like the set of a holiday movie. A horse-drawn carriage idled at the entrance and carolers sang in the lobby. They served plum pudding in the French Salon and Brandy Alexanders in Claridge's bar. She even received a wrapped ornament with her breakfast tray and a note thanking her for spending Christmas at Claridge's.

Noah had sent a text saying filming was canceled because of bad weather. It made sense; she couldn't risk getting sick. But she had been looking forward to visiting Westminster Abbey. The boys' choir was going to sing and she could see the church where the Duke and Duchess of Cambridge were married.

She ate a bite of scone and wondered if the snow was the real reason Noah gave her the day off. They would have driven to the abbey in a taxi and she would have hardly been outside at all. Maybe he was embarrassed by the kiss and didn't want to see her.

She wished again she hadn't kissed him; it was like adding nuts to a chocolate chip cookie. Any additions got in the way of enjoying the gooey chocolate and fresh-baked cookie.

Maybe she'd buy him a packet of English toffees from Harrods with a note saying she had been a little tipsy and hadn't meant to kiss him. But that would be worse, like girls in high school who ignored the boys they liked. She was so confused; she didn't know what she wanted.

It didn't matter anyway. When they returned to New York, they would both be so busy. They'd meet for coffee once a month and eventually lose touch. The past week would become a sweet memory like old Christmas cards she kept in a drawer.

She couldn't think about Noah now. First she had to write Chloe's card and then she had to prepare for Digby's master class. The only good thing about Noah canceling their plans was that she had all morning to study the recipe for sticky marmalade roll. It seemed simple, but holiday rolls were tricky. If she left it in the oven too long, it would be as tasteless as second-day bread at the supermarket checkout.

There was a knock at the door and she opened it. Noah stood in the hallway, clutching a sheath of papers.

"It smells wonderful in here." He entered the suite. "Kate said I could order room service for breakfast. But there's something too personal about a butler showing up when I'm wearing boxers."

"You're welcome to my breakfast." She waved at the bowl of porridge. "It's delicious but I can't eat another bite. I was just writing my recipe card for Chloe, thank you for making sure the concierge sends them overnight. Ellie called and said Chloe already got the first one, it was very kind of you."

"Christmas is all about children," he answered and smiled. "You're doing something wonderful."

"It's not much but I like to help Ellie and Chloe when I can. Ellie has been so good to me." Louisa flipped through the magazine on the coffee table. "We're going to bake Melting Snowman Biscuits, it's such a fun recipe. The snowman has jellybeans for eyes and chocolate drops for a nose and arms made of pretzel sticks. Then you put the marshmallow snowman on top of a gingerbread cookie and melt the whole thing in the oven."

"Now you've made me even hungrier," he said, sprinkling brown sugar on her porridge. "I brought your schedule for Christmas Eve." He gave her the papers. "I've allowed plenty of time for hair and makeup. Bianca spends ages in the makeup chair before a show. You can't have a shiny forehead or a stray hair when three cameras will be trained on you baking your croquembouche."

"You could have e-mailed it to me." Louisa placed the papers on the coffee table.

"I don't trust e-mails. One click and ten hours of work disappears." He noticed the open recipe book. "Did Digby give you a signed copy of his cookbook?"

"He gives one to every member of the master class," she explained. "Last night was so exciting. He said my apple crumble was the best in the class. It was quite difficult: if you bake it too long, the gingerbread crumbs become burnt toast." She paused. "He wants me to appear on his television special. It doesn't shoot until next spring and I'd have to fly back to London. But it's wonderful that he asked, there are five other chefs in the class."

"What do these other chefs look like?" Noah wondered.

"What do you mean?"

"Are they middle-aged women with lacquered hair and more powder on their cheeks than you'd use in a mortuary?"

"I hadn't noticed," Louisa responded.

"It must be a small kitchen and you all work together," he prodded. "It's like my high school chemistry lab partner. No matter how I tried, I couldn't ignore the ring around his collar or that he wore the same shirt two days in a row."

"Three of the chefs are men. Edith is in her early sixties and Hannah owns a restaurant in Bath. It's very exclusive, it just earned a Michelin star."

"How old is Hannah?" he asked.

"She's in her fifties," she admitted. "She was in the tech industry and it's her second career."

"I see." Noah ate another bite of porridge.

"I know what you're implying and you're wrong." She flushed. "Digby's praise has nothing to do with the fact that I'm the only female under thirty. Why can't you believe he just appreciates my baking?"

"He signed your cookbook with a heart." Noah pointed to the page.

"Now you're being childish," she declared. "People text heart emojis all the time. It doesn't mean anything."

"The first time you met Digby at the reception at the Fumoir, you were wearing a red cocktail dress. At the meeting to go over the menu, you had on that striking Alexander McQueen sweater and slacks. You curled your hair yourself and were wearing a new lipstick."

"You bought all the clothes at Harrods," she reminded him. "You insisted I dress well when I'm representing *Baking with Bianca*."

"What were you wearing to his class last night?" he wondered.

"I wore a pink wool dress and leather pumps."

"You wore a wool dress to bake?" Noah asked, horrified.

"I put on an apron," she corrected. "It's the softest merino wool and fits me like a second skin."

"When I saw you at the bakery, you had on a knee-length apron and worn moccasins. Your hair kept falling in your eyes and you didn't wear any makeup."

"If you have a point you should hurry up and make it," she snapped. "This afternoon is Digby's second master class. I still have a lot of recipes to study and then I have to take a bath and get ready."

Noah stood up and walked to the bedroom. The closet was open and he rifled through the sweaters.

"What do you think you're doing?" She scooped up a bra and pair of cotton panties.

"You can wear these." He handed her sweatpants and an over-sized Dartmouth sweatshirt.

"These are my gym clothes," she said. "The sweatshirt belonged to my first boyfriend after high school. He dumped me for a female lacrosse player but let me keep his sweatshirt."

"Put your hair in a ponytail and don't use any makeup," he continued. "You can wear lip gloss. Kate would get angry if your lips got chapped."

"I'm not going to show up for Digby Bunting's master class as if I'm going to a spin class at the YMCA." She shuddered.

"Tell him there was a leak in the ceiling of your suite and your entire wardrobe was ruined," he suggested. "You wore the only things you could salvage. If Digby only cares about your baking, he won't care if you show up in flannel pajamas."

"I don't own pajamas." She noticed a chiffon nightie on the closet floor. "I wear a nightie to bed."

"You're certainly not wearing that." He eyed the sheer fabric. "I didn't think you're the kind of woman who sleeps in chiffon."

"It's none of your business what I sleep in." She snatched it up. "I'll do it, if it means you will believe me. Digby Bunting is a complete professional and only cares about the consistency of my raspberry blancmange."

"I hope you prove me wrong." Noah walked back to the living room. "I have to check on the ingredients for your croquembouche, I'll see you later."

Louisa waited until Noah left and then sat on the sofa. Neither of them had mentioned the kiss. But Noah sent dozens of e-mails a day; why had he dropped off the schedule in person? And why was he so sensitive about Digby? He acted like a little boy fighting over a tricycle on the playground.

She finished the card to Chloe and sealed the envelope. Then she placed the bowl of porridge on the tray and opened the cookbook. She would worry about Noah later. First she had to prove that Digby Bunting didn't care if she showed up in a felt robe and slippers, that he only cared about her marmalade roll.

Louisa rang the doorbell of Digby's flat and wished she hadn't listened to Noah. Wearing a sweatshirt and no makeup was a terrible idea. The building's doorman asked if she was making a delivery and pointed to the service entrance. And the woman in the elevator clutched her Harrods shopping bag as if Louisa might run away with it.

She heard footsteps and Digby answered the door. He wore a blue blazer and twill slacks and looked like he was attending a film premiere.

"Louisa?" he asked. "Are you all right? I hope you're not coming down with the flu."

"I'm perfectly fine. There was a leak in my closet." She crossed her fingers behind her back. "I hope you don't mind me dressing like this. These are the only clothes I could find."

"Of course not." He walked toward the kitchen. "Follow me, everyone is here."

Why hadn't Digby kissed her on the cheek like he did last night? He had been so polite, offering her a glass of wine and showing her his new cookbook. She was being silly. She was late and he had a million things to do.

She entered the kitchen and admired the ivory plaster walls and speckled marble floor. Low-hanging lights illuminated granite counters and there was a stainless-steel fridge and double oven.

The other chefs nibbled macadamia nuts and clinked wineglasses and it was like some glamorous cocktail party. She was suddenly so angry with Noah she couldn't breathe. She'd prove she was right and then she'd never talk to him again.

"I've been studying the recipe for sticky marmalade rolls." She turned to Digby. "I even stopped at Harrods and bought a jar of Oxford marmalade. I'm ready to demonstrate it to the class."

"Demonstrate it?" Digby looked at her absently.

"Last night you said we'd teach the lesson together," she reminded him. "You were so excited by my apple crumble, you couldn't wait to taste my marmalade roll."

"Did I say that? I hope you don't mind, but I should probably have another student assist me." He rubbed his chin. "Why don't you join Graham?" He waved at a man with horn-rimmed glasses. "He's making rice pudding."

"You want me to make rice pudding?" Louisa was puzzled.

Rice pudding was the simplest recipe in the world. You stirred milk and butter and sugar and added nutmeg. She'd learned it during her first month at culinary school and it didn't take any skill at all.

"All the ingredients you need are on the counter." He pointed at the butter and sugar and vanilla bean. "I'll check on it later."

Louisa took the rice pudding out of the oven and admired the golden nutmeg and dusting of cinnamon. She inhaled the scent of vanilla and had never smelled anything so wonderful.

She was being silly. Of course Digby had to give the other students a chance. And rice pudding was a popular dessert; it was even on the menu at Claridge's.

"The rice pudding is done." She handed Digby a ceramic bowl. "I used a dollop of raspberry jam. It gives it a delicious flavor."

"The flavor is good, but it's a little lumpy," he announced.

"Lumpy?" Louisa repeated in horror.

"Next time use more cream," Digby suggested before he moved on. "It creates a smoother texture."

Louisa folded her apron and smoothed her hair. She wanted to say goodbye to Digby, but he had disappeared. She walked through the hallway and found him in the library. The room had leather sofas and an oak desk piled with hardback books.

"Louisa! I'm sorry that I snuck away." Digby looked up. "My publisher dropped off copies of my new cookbook. These all need to be signed and delivered to Harrods this evening."

"I thought about the offer you made yesterday, and I'd love to appear on your television special," she began. "It will give me an excuse to return to London. It will be nice to see Hyde Park with blossoms on the trees instead of a layer of ice."

"I was going to tell you. I'm afraid I had a call from my producer," he answered. "They're changing the format of the show."

"They're changing the format?" she repeated and felt a little unsteady.

"They only want celebrity guests: Victoria Beckham baking Bavarian cream with caramel sauce and Gwyneth Paltrow making a mango sorbet." He paused. "I'm terribly sorry. But you know television, it's all about the ratings."

"I understand." Louisa nodded and turned to the door. "Thank you for including me in the master class. I'm having a wonderful time."

"Louisa, wait," Digby called.

Louisa turned around. Digby was going to apologize. He didn't really think her pudding was lumpy; he was just concerned about the other students. If he praised all her desserts, they might get jealous.

"Do you mind taking a few cookbooks to Claridge's?" he asked. "The concierge wanted to display some in the lobby and I'm too busy to leave my flat."

"Of course." She grabbed a stack from the desk. She carried them to the door and nudged open the handle. "I'll see you later."

Louisa gazed out the window of her suite at the white expanse of Hyde Park. All of London seemed like it was wrapped in a cashmere blanket. The Parliament building was covered in snow and

Big Ben was a white outline and she could see the blurred spires of St Paul's Cathedral.

She remembered when she met Digby at the reception at the Fumoir. He was so friendly. He wanted to know how to make s'mores and what type of apples she used in an apple pie.

Meeting Digby was one of the reasons she came to London and when she was around him she felt like a serious chef. Had he really only complimented her apple crumble because she wore a pink dress and lipstick?

The cookbook was open on the coffee table and she noticed the recipe for rice pudding. Suddenly she froze. She always used milk in rice pudding, but Digby only had cream in his kitchen. Of course it had been lumpy! Cream was thick and delicious but you needed to add more to give the rice pudding a silky texture.

She had been so anxious, she forgot to taste the pudding herself. But she could hardly knock on Digby's door and ask if she could make another batch. Suddenly she had an idea. She walked into the hall and pressed the button on the elevator.

The elevator stopped on the first floor and she strode down the hallway. She opened a door and discovered the kitchen where she and Noah made cinnamon rolls. The cinnamon rolls had been a great success; the pastry chef at the Foyer was going to permanently add them to the afternoon tea menu.

She checked the pantry and found nutmeg and sugar. The fridge held butter and milk and cream. She turned on the oven and a thrill ran down her spine. She was a pastry chef and she was going to make the best rice pudding in the world.

Louisa rinsed mixing bowls and checked her phone. She'd texted Noah twenty minutes ago and he hadn't replied. She wanted to take the pudding to Digby, but first she had to be certain it was perfect.

"I got your texts. What are you doing in here and what's the emergency?" Noah burst into the kitchen. "Don't tell me you hurt yourself! There must be a first-aid kit around here somewhere."

"It's nothing like that," Louisa assured him. "I need you to sample my rice pudding."

"You sent me a text saying you had an emergency because you wanted me to try a dessert?" He raised his eyebrow.

"It is an emergency. My whole future depends on it." She waved at the bowls on the counter. "I want you to tell me which rice pudding is better."

"Why does your whole future depend on two bowls of rice pudding?" he inquired.

"That's none of your business," she retorted. "I conducted your silly experiment of wearing sweatpants to Digby's master class. You can do this for me."

"This does have something to do with Digby!" Noah exclaimed.

"I may have made a slight miscalculation in my recipe," she offered. "But I fixed it."

"All right, I'll try them." Noah nodded. "But afterward you have to tell me what happened. If Digby said anything mean, I'm going to have a word with him."

Louisa handed him a bowl and Noah took a small bite. He tasted the other pudding and placed the bowl on the counter.

"The first pudding is quite good but the texture is lumpy." He nodded. "It stuck to the roof of my mouth."

"And the second one?" she asked and held her breath.

"The second one is like a fine cognac," he mused. "It's rich and smooth and melts in your throat. It's the best rice pudding I ever tasted."

"For a moment I thought you were right, and I wasn't a good chef at all." She beamed. "I just used the wrong amount of cream, it could happen to anyone."

"I never said you weren't a good chef. I said Digby was too busy admiring your legs in a miniskirt to recognize it," he corrected. "Of course you look gorgeous in a cocktail dress and stilettos. But it's when you're passionate about your baking that you become beautiful."

"You think I'm beautiful?" Louisa asked in surprise.

"I noticed it the first time we met." He nodded. "You were explaining how you used molasses in your cinnamon rolls. Your cheeks were flushed and your eyes sparkled, and you were lovelier than a movie star."

"Why didn't you tell me before?" she wondered. "You insisted I get a haircut and have my makeup done and buy a whole new wardrobe."

"You need those things for television. I did think about it the first day when you were out of sorts." He grinned. "But it would have gone to your head and you would have been impossible to work with."

"Well, you're wrong. I'm not beautiful, my hair is too thin and my eyebrows aren't even. But I am a good chef." Louisa finished clearing spices and smoothed her apron.

"I was about to go and see the Christmas tree at Trafalgar Square," Noah said. "Why don't you join me?"

"I can't go now." She shook her head. "I have to take the pudding to Digby."

"Leave the pudding in the fridge," he urged. "The snow almost stopped and Trafalgar Square will be like a winter wonderland."

"But I'm not even wearing a jacket." She wavered.

She was tired from making the rice pudding; it would be nice to get some fresh air. And Digby said he was terribly busy, it might be better to take it to him later.

"You can wear mine." He handed her his jacket. "It won't take long. You'll be glad you went."

The taxi pulled up in front of Trafalgar Square and Louisa gasped. The Christmas tree was more than sixty feet tall and decorated with blue and silver lights.

"Every year, Norway sends a Christmas tree to thank England for its support during World War II," Noah explained. "Thousands of people gather for the tree-lighting ceremony and there's ice-skating and caroling."

"It's spectacular," she breathed. The lights were the most beautiful she had seen: bright and luminescent like strands of pearls.

"Do you remember when you kissed me yesterday?" he asked suddenly.

"It was an accident." She flushed. "I had a glass of brandy and was excited about the cinnamon rolls. It didn't mean anything."

"You looked so pretty, all I could think about was kissing you." He paused. "But I knew it would be a mistake."

"A mistake?" she wondered.

"We'll go back to New York and you'll be working long hours and I'll spend every minute studying for law school," he began.

"Even if we find time to see each other, we can't afford to go to dinner or the movies."

"I thought exactly the same thing." Louisa nodded vigorously.

"It would be the worst time in our lives to have feelings for each other, so it's better to stop before we begin."

Louisa gulped and it was as if the world froze. The lights on the Christmas tree stopped flickering and the ice-skaters stood still, and even the light snow falling on the ground seemed to pause.

"You have feelings for me?" she whispered.

"Why else would I want to kiss you?" he wondered.

He wrapped his arms around her and kissed her. She kissed him back and inhaled the scent of vanilla and nutmeg.

"What do we do now?" she asked when they pulled apart.

"We go to a pub and get hot apple cider." He rubbed his hands. "You're wearing my jacket and I'm freezing."

Louisa curled up on the sofa in her suite and tucked her feet under her. It had started snowing again and she decided to take Digby the rice pudding in the morning.

The whole night had been wonderful. She and Noah wandered around Trafalgar Square and sampled mulled wine and hot chocolate. He took her hand when the boys' choir sang "Silent Night" and she felt festive and happy.

Christmas in London was like being trapped in a fabulous snow globe. But what would happen when they returned to New York? Noah said they would be too busy to see each other, and she wouldn't let anything get in the way of opening her restaurant.

She couldn't think about that now. Christmas Eve Dinner was

in two days and she had to make sure her croquembouche was perfect. She closed her eyes and tried to picture the golden pastry puffs wrapped in spun sugar. But all she saw was the blue and silver lights on the Christmas tree, and all she could think about was Noah's lips on her mouth.

Chapter Twelve

KATE SAT AT A TABLE in Claridge's Reading Room and sipped a cup of Earl Grey tea. It was early evening and the restaurant hummed with activity. Waiters carried platters of rock oysters and couples sipped Bellinis. It felt so festive.

She had been relieved when it started snowing and the day's filming was canceled. She could relax in her suite and catch up on her e-mails. But the central heating made her sleepy, and her bed was so perfectly made, she'd feel guilty if she took a nap. She finally closed her laptop and took the elevator to the Reading Room.

Trevor hadn't called all day and she wondered if last night was a mistake. They were two people alone in London at Christmas. Just because they enjoyed each other's company didn't mean they should start a relationship.

She recalled all the times she'd called Trevor at St Andrews: at midnight when she couldn't figure out an algorithm, and at 5:00 a.m. to remind him he had an early-morning chemistry lab, and when her cat died and she needed someone to talk to.

But if she called Trevor now she would be getting herself in deeper. It would be better to treat last night like a pleasant interlude. They had been at Buckingham Palace! It was easy to feel romantic when they passed State Rooms where Prince Philip courted Queen Elizabeth and Charles and Diana gave fabulous balls.

A waiter approached her. He wore a white dinner jacket and carried a phone on a silver tray.

"Miss Crawford, I have a phone call for you."

"A phone call?" She looked up.

"It's a gentleman." He nodded. "He said you were already acquainted."

She took the phone and wondered if someone at the network was calling from New York.

"Hello?" she said into the receiver.

"You're harder to track down than a CIA agent." Trevor's voice came over the line. "Your phone didn't answer and the butler knocked on your suite but you weren't there. I finally asked the concierge to search the hotel for a beautiful blonde with green eyes."

"I must have left my phone upstairs," Kate laughed. "I'm drinking tea and contemplating ordering something very British for dinner. I only have two more full days and I haven't tried the venison Wellington with wilted leaf spinach."

"Wilted leaf spinach tastes as bad as it sounds. I'd leave the country to avoid eating it," he warned her. "I hoped we could have dinner together."

"Where did you have in mind?" she asked.

"It's snowing so hard it's impossible to get a cab, and I don't feel like being surrounded by tourists in Claridge's dining room." He paused. "Why don't we order room service in my suite?"

"That's not a good idea." Kate hesitated.

"It's an innocent invitation," he persisted. "I can ask the butler to stay, and I promise to behave like a gentleman."

"If the butler stays I'll feel like a schoolgirl being watched by the lunch monitor," she laughed. "All right, I'll come."

"I'll see you at seven." He paused. "I promise it will be a lovely evening."

Kate rang the doorbell of Trevor's suite and smoothed her skirt. She wore a black cocktail dress and silver pumps.

"Kate." Trevor opened the door. "You see, this was a good idea. I don't have to take your coat and there isn't any snow in your hair."

She gazed around the living room and her nervousness was replaced by a girlish delight. It was like an illustration in an Eloise book with rounded windows and striped drapes and a baby grand piano. Yellow silk sofas were scattered with pastel cushions and there was a leopard skin rug.

"Goodness!" she exclaimed. "This is nothing like my suite."

"It's the Prince Alexander suite, it's meant for someone with more extravagant tastes," he said with a sigh. "I keep telling the maids they should take the flowers home but they just smile and bring me more."

"It's like the bachelor pads you see in movies," she said. "The male lead gets divorced and finds himself in a suite at the Plaza with a four-poster bed and mirrored bar."

"Tell me about your apartment." He handed her a gin and tonic.

"You want me to describe my apartment?" She frowned.

"I know everything about the Kate from ten years ago, I want to know more about Kate who lives in New York," he prodded.

"It's a studio on the Upper East Side," she said. "The kitchen is the size of the galley kitchens you see on airplanes, and I'm lucky

I don't have time to entertain because there are only two chairs. But it's three blocks from Central Park and there's a wonderful coffee roastery on the corner."

"Kate, I—" Trevor was interrupted by the doorbell. "That must be our dinner. I hope you don't mind, I ordered for both of us."

The table was set with green-and-white-striped china. There was a basket of fresh bread and whipped butter. And the food! Platters of Cornish lobster risotto and Parmesan gnocchi. Claridge's chicken pie with quail's eggs as the main course with sides of truffle macaroni and cauliflower cheese.

"Do we need all this?" she asked, glancing at the warm apple crumble and crème fraîche cheesecake.

"I didn't know what you'd like, so I asked them to send a selection," he admitted. "We can send it all back and just order fish and chips."

Trevor fiddled with his collar and Kate's tension disappeared. They might be in a suite with a baby grand piano and view of Hyde Park, but Trevor was still the boy who was completely uninterested in food and could happily exist on a box of crackers.

"It looks delicious." She smiled. "I'm starving, I can't wait to start."

They ate roasted tomato and basil soup and talked about St Andrews and London and New York.

"Do you remember when I'd knock on your door with sausage rolls and Yorkshire pudding?" she asked. "You'd be sitting at your desk with a half-eaten packet of crisps. You wouldn't even look up, I'd have to threaten to feed you like a preschooler."

"Eating took up too much time, it was more important to study trigonometry," he recalled.

"Once I said there was a gas leak to get you to dine in the residence hall," she said. "I was afraid you'd get scurvy if you didn't eat some cooked vegetables."

"That was worse." He shuddered. "All the other students talking about their summer plans and the internships their parents got them in the city. I was much happier eating a bowl of instant porridge in my room."

"You didn't give it a chance," she insisted. "Everyone was friendly and there were students from all over the world."

Trevor put down his fork and looked at Kate.

"There were so many things I didn't know then: that enjoying a thick steak didn't diminish my desire to succeed, that taking a week's holiday didn't mean I wasn't serious about my work." He stopped. "But even then I realized there was nothing more important than being with the person who made me happy."

Kate reached for her wineglass and her sleeve got stuck in her necklace. She tried to loosen it, but it wouldn't budge.

"Let me help," he offered.

His fingers brushed her neck and she sucked in her breath. Her sleeve came free and he turned her face toward him. His lips were soft and she tasted butter and wine.

"Kate," he whispered. "I want you so much."

"I want you too, but it's not a good idea." She pulled away. "It's better if we stop now."

"I've always listened to you: when you insisted I go home for my parents' twenty-fifth anniversary a week before finals, and when you said I couldn't meet the recruiter from Credit Suisse without wearing a tie." He gulped his wine. "But I'm looking at the girl with the blond ponytail and golden tan I fell in love with and we're finally together." He waved at the bedroom. "Why shouldn't we take advantage of a king-sized bed with fitted Frette sheets?"

"I was looking out for your best interests. Your parents would have been devastated if you missed their anniversary, and I took notes for you in class. And the recruiter from Credit Suisse might have offered you a job, you couldn't show up in a T-shirt and jeans." She fiddled with her pearls. "What if it doesn't work out and we lose everything we gained?"

"You are the girl who flew five thousand miles to attend university on a different continent. You moved to New York without knowing a soul and got a job in television." He touched her cheek. "You taught me the most important thing: sometimes you have to be brave and take a chance."

Music drifted over the stereo and Kate couldn't think of a single reason not to kiss him.

She reached up and kissed him on the mouth. His hands stroked her dress and every nerve in her body tingled.

"You have to see the bedroom." He took her hand and led her down a short hallway.

The bedroom had a canopied bed and striped wallpaper and love seats upholstered in red velvet. There were Tiffany lamps and an art deco mirror. A painting in a gold frame hung over the fireplace and there was a terrace overlooking Hyde Park.

"We can't make love here," she laughed, feeling young and giddy. "It would be like having sex on a movie set. Someone is going to yell 'cut' and the whole place will disappear."

"It's completely real." Trevor grinned. "You can test out the bed."

"If I try the bed do you promise to behave yourself?" She slipped off her pumps and climbed onto the bed.

Trevor sat beside her and whispered, "I definitely don't promise to behave myself."

He unzipped her dress and pulled it over her head. His mouth traveled over her body and the pleasure welled up inside her.

"Are you sure?" he murmured.

"I'm sure now." She nodded and lay on the quilted bedspread.

He lay beside her and stroked her breasts. His fingers made circles on her nipples and she turned and kissed him slowly on the mouth. He kissed her deeply and their bodies intertwined.

God, it felt wonderful! She wanted to stay that way forever. Then he pressed against her and she longed to have him inside her. Trevor rolled on top of her and covered her body with his. He pushed in deeper and the warm glow became a liquid center. Her body opened and the luxurious waves started.

She gripped his shoulders and he wrapped his arms around her. Suddenly he groaned and fell against her breasts. The throbbing was so intense; she closed her eyes and wanted it to last forever.

Kate padded to the bathroom and poured a glass of water. She felt a new excitement, like a child attending a birthday party. Was she really falling in love and did Trevor feel the same? She peered out the window and the snow in Hyde Park resembled the softest mink coat. She placed the glass on the marble counter and climbed back into bed.

Kate sat in the living room of her suite and fiddled with a teacup. It was almost midnight and she didn't really feel like tea. But brandy might give her a headache, and if she drank coffee, she'd never fall asleep.

She'd told Trevor she had an early-morning meeting and returned to her suite. It had all been so perfect: the room service dinner of tender chicken and red wine and then making love in the canopied bed. She didn't want anything to spoil it.

God, she had forgotten the pleasure of sex! But she was leaving London in three days and Trevor wasn't even divorced. She couldn't pine for him like a girl who had nothing to do except write letters to a boy she met at summer camp.

That was the problem with sex: it heightened everything. Fruit tasted sweeter and the sky seemed bluer and you thought you were the luckiest person in the world.

She finally settled on having tea and poured it into the cup. She stirred in honey and remembered the beginning of her last semester at St Andrews. She and Ian were wildly in love. The sex was wonderful and she thought she would be happy forever.

Kate sat at a table at Mitchells and ate a bite of scone. She spent Christmas break in Santa Barbara and had missed the Scottish breakfasts of black pudding and scones layered with jam and cream.

It was her last semester at St Andrews and she couldn't believe she and Ian had been together for three years. The first year of their relationship, she treated it like a new sweater she was afraid to take out of its box. Any day she would discover a loose thread and have to return it to the store.

But Ian kept his promise and barely flirted with other girls. They cheered at rugby matches and he taught her how to play cricket. On weekends they explored seventeenth-century castles in Aberdeen or stayed in bed and made love and ate cheese and fruit.

And the holidays! They were invited to go skiing in St. Moritz and sailing in the Canary Islands. One summer she only went home to Santa Barbara for a week because she and Ian flitted between Majorca and the south of France.

At first Trevor couldn't understand why she was going out with Ian. But Ian sent Kate flowers and brought her chicken soup when she had the flu. The flock of girls that had surrounded him disappeared, and Trevor admitted Ian was a good boyfriend.

Kate looked up from her scone and saw a familiar-looking boy enter the café. His sandy blond hair was cut short and he wore a V-neck sweater.

"Trevor? I haven't seen you since I got back," she greeted him. "What did you do to your hair and what are you wearing?"

"I took your advice and got a haircut and some new clothes," he said. "Recruiters will be on campus soon and I won't get a job if I look like Bob Dylan."

"You look positively handsome." She beamed. "There's something else. Your wrists don't look like they belong on a giant bird and your chest is thicker."

"My mother turned the cooking over to my father this Christmas, it turns out he's an excellent chef." He grinned. "We ate Cornish game hens and new potatoes every night I was home."

"Ian had to stay on campus." She ate her scone. "He was terribly jealous that I was in California. He kept sending me weather reports and begging me to come back."

"I imagined he'd spend Christmas at his uncle's castle in Scotland or his parents' flat in London."

"He's head of the Ibsen Society and they spent all break preparing for the student production," she explained. "Tonight is opening night. You should come."

"No thank you." He shuddered. "I'd rather memorize Chinese verbs than watch students mangle *Hedda Gabler.*"

"You're missing out." She sipped her coffee. "There's going to be specialty cocktails and desserts."

"You can bring me a bowl of sticky pudding." He grinned. "I have to go do my microbiology homework."

Kate nibbled shepherd's pie and hoped Ian would arrive soon. The play had been a success and afterward everyone moved to Sandy's Bar. There were platters of smoked haddock and fried scallops. A bartender made black tartans with whiskey and Kahlua and there was a dessert table of crumbles and custards.

"You should try the haggis," a girl said beside her. "It's delicious."

"I can't eat another bite; I'm waiting for Ian." Kate held out her hand. "I'm Kate, it's a pleasure to meet you."

"I'm Jasper," she replied.

"You're Jasper?" Kate asked in surprise. Ian and Jasper had stayed on campus during winter break to prepare for opening night. It never occurred to her that Jasper was a slim brunette with long eyelashes.

"I always get that reaction; it's a family name." Jasper smiled. "It's good of you to come. Most ex-girlfriends would stay home."

Kate clutched the sideboard and thought the room was spinning.

"What did you say?" she gasped.

"It's nice of you to support Ian. It must be awkward to meet his new girlfriend."

"Who is his new girlfriend?" she asked and tried to keep her voice steady.

"I thought he would have told you by now." Jasper looked at

her and her eyes were wide. "I am. We haven't known each other long, but we're madly in love."

Kate was tempted to race back to her residence hall. But she wasn't some freshman girl who would burst into tears and think of reasons to forgive him. Ian owed her an explanation and he was going to give it to her.

"I've shaken so many hands I might need you to write my history essay." Ian joined her as everyone was leaving.

"I'm going home," she said icily. "I have a paper to write."

"I'll walk with you." He followed her outside. "We can stop in my room for a nightcap. I received a bottle of gin for Christmas and learned how to make gin and jams."

"Did Jasper teach you?" she asked. "Or were you too busy falling in love to mix a cocktail."

"What did you say?" Ian froze.

"I met Jasper at the reception." She strode along the sidewalk. Usually the walk was so beautiful. The ancient buildings were dusted with snow and the playing fields were white and the streetlamps glowed like embers in a fireplace. But now she was shivering and longed to reach her room.

"What did she tell you?" he asked and she could hear the fear in his voice.

"That you haven't known each other long but you're in love." She turned to him. "Apparently she's your new girlfriend."

He ran his hands through his hair and looked at Kate. "We were practically alone on campus for two weeks. We ate together and spent hours going over scripts," he began uncomfortably. "I suspected she had a crush on me, but I thought of her as a kid sister. Then one night there was a snowstorm and we were stuck in the Student Union. We were practicing a romantic scene in the play and—"

"And what?" Kate cut in.

"She kissed me," he said slowly. "At first I thought she was just playing the part, but then she put down the script and kissed me again." He looked at Kate. "I kissed her back, I don't know what I was thinking." His forehead creased. "I didn't mean to, and I swear nothing has happened since."

"You kissed her!" Kate tried to stop shaking.

"She kissed me first," he protested. "I regretted it the minute it happened. Of course she's not my girlfriend." He touched her hand. "I'm in love with you."

"You should have thought of that before you kissed her!" Kate raged.

"You're not going to storm off because of a few silly kisses," he begged. "For three years I've never even glanced at another woman. I'm in love with you! I made a stupid error but that doesn't change anything to do with us."

Kate looked at Ian and wondered if he was telling the truth. It didn't matter if he was in love with her. There would always be another Jasper and she would never feel safe.

"It changes everything!" she retorted, turning and hurrying along the pavement. "I was a fool to have trusted you. I'll never do it again."

"Let me walk with you. It's snowing." He put his hand on her arm. "You might slip and no one will see you."

Ian wore a camel-colored coat and wool slacks and he had never looked so handsome. But she studied his blue eyes and her heart hardened like the icicles on the fir trees.

"I can take care of myself." She kept walking. "Have a nice semester."

Kate sat at the desk in her room and thumbed through her copy of *The Great Gatsby*. It had been three weeks since she broke up with Ian and she felt like she was recovering from the flu. Her legs were wobbly and she could never eat more than half a lamb cutlet at meals.

Sometimes she wondered if there had been other girls. But then she'd shake herself and think about something else. Dwelling on their relationship was like mulling over a bad grade on a trigonometry test. It was over and she had to move on.

Trevor let her stay in her room for a week and then threatened to call her mother unless Kate started going out. Every afternoon he burst into her room and insisted she put on her coat. They took long walks on the Old Course and hiked on the Fife Coastal Path.

Kate admired the galleries on North Street and remembered everything she loved about St Andrews. Then she would see a group of students lounging in front of Rector's Café and wonder if Ian was at the center. She would quickly cross the street before she was tempted to find out.

There was a knock at the door and Trevor walked inside. He carried a paper bag and his backpack was slung over his shoulder.

"I brought you a chicken pot pie, my mother sent it to me." He handed her the bag. "My father made it and it's delicious."

"For three years you wouldn't eat anything but crisps and an occasional apple, and now you keep bringing me food." She smiled.

"I didn't know what good food tasted like, I only ate my

mother's cooking." He perched on the bed. "Put on a sweater. We're going to see the Picasso exhibit and eat smoked haddock and truffle chips. Your cheeks are as thin as the models in your fashion magazines."

A card fell on the floor and he picked it up.

"You were invited to the Societies Dinner at the Adamson." He handed it to her.

"I'm not going." She tossed it on the desk.

"Even I know this is a prestigious invitation." He looked at Kate. "I'm disappointed in you."

"Disappointed in me?" she asked.

"You're behaving like that groundhog you Americans have that tests the weather and then scurries underground," he said. "You can't spend your last semester at St Andrews like a monk in a monastery. You came here to meet students from all over the world, and the only people you've talked to in the last three weeks are me and the janitor."

"The janitor wanted my advice on whether his daughter is old enough to read Harry Potter." She smiled. "This isn't about Ian. It's a formal dinner and I don't have a date."

Trevor ran his hands through his hair and looked at Kate. "I'll take you."

"That's very kind, but you would hate it." She shook her head. "The guys dress in tuxedos and the girls wear evening gowns and they talk about who will host the best graduation parties."

"I'm not asking you because I feel sorry for you," he corrected. "I'm asking you on a date."

"You want to go on a date?" She looked up.

"I've been wanting to ask you on a date since you left your homework on the table and I corrected it for you freshman year.

But we became friends and I didn't know how to turn an excursion to St Andrews Castle into a romantic dinner. Then you got involved with Ian and I couldn't interfere with your happiness." He paused. "Ian is gone and I'm not going to miss my chance." He read the invitation and grinned. "Besides it's a free dinner. I could never afford to feed you rock oysters and roasted duck."

Kate's heart beat a little faster. Did Trevor really have feelings for her and how did she feel about him? He looked so handsome with his short hair and broad shoulders. And they always had a good time together; they never ran out of things to say.

"All right." She nodded. "I'll go."

"Excellent." Trevor walked to the door. "I'll see you later."

"We were going to the art exhibit," she reminded him.

"First I have to borrow a tuxedo." He turned and smiled. "If I'm going to be your date to a society dinner, I have to look the part."

Kate placed her teacup on the coffee table and gazed around the living room of her suite. It was so elegant with its eggshell yellow walls and navy silk sofas and thick wool rug. A fire ebbed in the fireplace and there was a vase of white orchids.

She had earned this all herself. Could she disrupt her life for a man? That was the problem with sex; it made it impossible to think. Going to bed with Trevor might have been a terrible mistake or it might be the best thing she had done.

She stood up and walked to the bedroom. Pillows were scattered over the quilted headboard and there was a glass of cognac on the bedside table. She stroked the satin sheets and knew exactly what she wanted. She wanted Trevor to be sleeping beside her.

Chapter Thirteen

LOUISA PULLED BACK THE SILK drapes in her suite and couldn't imagine a more perfect day. Yesterday's clouds and snow had been replaced by a clear blue sky and bright sun. Snow melted on the striped awnings and the cars on the pavement gleamed as if they had been through a car wash.

Tomorrow was Christmas Eve and today was the last day of filming around London. They were going to visit Royal Albert Hall and St James's Palace where the royal family actually lived, and take a private tour of the Royal Mews.

She felt a bit guilty that she had explored Buckingham Palace by herself on the day they arrived. She should have known they would film there; it was one of the most important landmarks in London! Instead she missed her makeup session and arrived half an hour before the reception at the Fumoir and Noah had been furious.

Did Noah really think she was beautiful and why hadn't he told her? She turned to the mirror on her dressing table and thought he was wrong. She didn't have Bianca's smoldering brown eyes and pouty lips, or Kate's blond hair and long legs. But she never cared much about her looks. What was important was knowing how to make the meringue in a Baked Alaska melt in your mouth and how long to let the fruit soak in anisette in a chocolate cream trifle.

Then why did she spend an extra half hour this morning choosing her outfit and deciding on a lipstick? She tried to tell herself it was to look good for the camera and make Kate happy. The real reason was she wanted to see the look on Noah's face when she appeared on the hotel steps.

Last night had been magical: the kiss under the Christmas tree at Trafalgar Square and holding hands and listening to the boys' choir. She and Noah drank hot chocolate and talked about everything and she never wanted the moment to end.

She picked up a bottle of perfume and put it down. She recalled in high school when her friend Beth stopped taking Louisa's phone calls because Beth fell in love with the cross-country star. She didn't study enough for the ACTs because she attended all his meets and was rejected by her top colleges.

That wasn't going to happen to her; she had always put her career goals first. Look at everything she had achieved! Tomorrow she was appearing on *Christmas Dinner at Claridge's,* and in a few months she would open her own restaurant.

To be fair, it was because of Noah she was going to be on television. But it had nothing to do with his feelings for her. The only reason she was in London was because she made the best cinnamon rolls he ever tasted.

She couldn't think about her future with Noah; it was like checking her Pinterest when she had a molasses spice cake in the oven. It only took a minute to click on a recipe for buttercream icing. But it was so easy to get distracted and then the molasses hardened and the spice cake was ruined. It was better not to have the phone in the kitchen at all.

They really should remain friends for now. But how could she tell Noah without hurting his feelings? If Noah said he couldn't see her because he was too busy with law school she would be disappointed. Relationships were like a Magic 8 Ball. Every time you put it down, it came up with a different answer.

And she had so much to do! Kate wanted to go over details for tomorrow, and she had to take the rice pudding to Digby. Noah and the camera crew were meeting her in front of Claridge's at eleven and they were going to board a double-decker bus.

First she had to write her recipe card for Chloe. She sat at the rolltop desk and opened the ivory card. She couldn't believe that in just a few days she'd be back in New York, baking shortbread with Chloe in the bakery's kitchen. *Christmas Dinner at Claridge's* would be over and it would all feel like some wonderful dream.

Her phone rang and Ellie's number appeared on the screen.

"It's 3:00 a.m. in New York, you really need to get some sleep," Louisa said playfully. "Stir a cup of warm milk with brandy. It works for me every time."

"I'll sleep when Christmas week is over." Ellie's voice came over the phone. "Chloe wanted me to call and say the Gingerbread Sweaters recipe is her favorite so far. She wants to bake a whole sheet to take to her teachers after the holidays."

"That's a wonderful idea," Louisa agreed. "I'm just writing out a recipe for Christmas Pudding Rice Krispie Cakes. Chloe will love them: Rice Krispies Treats topped with warm chocolate pudding and buttercream icing. We'll dye the icing green and red, and add peppermint sprinkles."

"It sounds delicious. To be honest there's another reason for my call. I'm dying to know how things are going with Digby Bunting," Ellie continued. "I saw him on a television talk show last night and he is so handsome. Maybe you can convince him to come to New York after the show."

"I doubt that's possible. He has a new book coming out and his publisher keeps him busy with appearances." Louisa fiddled with her pen. "Besides, I'll be swamped when I get home. I need to put in long hours at the bakery, and bake with Chloe, and then there's Noah . . ."

"Who's Noah?" Ellie asked.

Louisa was tempted to tell Ellie everything: that she and Noah shared a wonderful kiss and were developing feelings for each other. That she was worried spending time with Noah would interfere with opening her own restaurant. But she couldn't expect Ellie to solve her problems over an international phone line. It would be better to wait and discuss it over hot chocolate in Ellie's office.

"Noah is the assistant to the producer of *Baking with Bianca*," she said. "He's just a friend but he's been very kind to me."

"Well, see if you can convince Digby to come to New York. If Digby Bunting showed up at the bakery and bought a bag of cinnamon rolls our sales would go through the roof," Ellie chuckled. "I should go, I have a mountain of paperwork. Chloe sends her love. She can't wait to show you the apron her grandmother gave her as an early Christmas present."

Louisa hung up and finished writing her recipe card. She slipped it into the envelope and grabbed her purse. Then she entered the hallway and knocked on Kate's door.

"Louisa!" Kate opened the door. "I'm glad you're here, I want to go over a few things. It seems simple to crack eggs into a mixing bowl on the set, but I've even seen Martha Stewart freeze up when the director is barking at her."

"I can't imagine Martha Stewart ever freezing up," Louisa laughed. "She's like an impossibly sleek sports car that never leaves the showroom. But Noah said it's easy." She was suddenly nervous. "All I have to do is stand on the X and smile into the camera."

"It is easy as long as you don't let anyone distract you." Kate poured a glass of orange juice and handed it to Louisa. "You are a wonderful chef and you're going to make a delicious croquembouche."

"I promise I won't let you down." Louisa felt a thrill of excitement. "I'm going to practice my smile until I look like the models in magazines who have never had bad news. I'll go to sleep dreaming of spun sugar and pastry puffs, and tomorrow I'll stay in bed until the show so nothing terrible can happen: slipping on the bathroom floor and twisting my ankle or getting run over by a motorcycle."

"You don't have to go to extremes," Kate laughed. "Just do what I do before a show. Take deep breaths and imagine the thing that makes you happy."

"The thing that makes me happy?" Louisa wondered if Kate knew about her and Noah. It would be terribly unprofessional and Noah might get fired.

"A movie that you love or dress you saw in the window at Saks," Kate continued. "Then the smile on your face will be natural."

"I hadn't thought of that," Louisa said with relief. She noticed a vase of two dozen peach-colored roses and gasped. "I've never seen such beautiful roses."

"McQueens delivered them this morning." Kate followed her

glance. "They were grown in a hothouse and transported in a temperature-controlled truck. I was shocked when they arrived, but they are lovely."

"You don't seem very excited." Louisa looked at Kate. "I know we don't know each other well, but do you want to talk about it? Sometimes it helps to tell someone what's wrong. I'm a good listener."

"The flowers are just unexpected." Kate sat opposite her. "Trevor and I were going to remain friends and now it's developed into something more."

"That isn't what you want?" Louisa prodded.

"Producing the show is a twelve-hour-a-day job. I can't flit off to London for a few days or spend whole weekends with him if he comes to New York."

"You said you didn't want to be alone forever," Louisa reminded her.

"I don't, but this might not be the right time," Kate answered.

"Then tell him to wait," Louisa said confidently. "If you've been apart for ten years, you won't change how you feel about each other."

"That's the thing about love." Kate fiddled with her earring. "Once you give yourself over to it, nothing is the same. You want to be with that person all the time, and it's the most important thing in the world."

"I'm not even going to consider falling in love until I own my restaurant." Louisa remembered Noah's kiss and had a funny feeling in her chest. "Now tell me all your other suggestions. I want *Christmas Dinner at Claridge's* to be the best show you've ever produced."

Louisa rang Digby's doorbell and had to smile. This time the doorman welcomed her profusely and offered to escort her to Digby's flat. The woman she shared the elevator with complimented Louisa's rose-colored cashmere dress and asked where she got her pumps. She even made Louisa write down the name of her perfume so should could buy a bottle for her daughter.

"Louisa." Digby opened the door. He wore a striped robe and blue velvet slippers. "This is a surprise, please come inside."

"I hope I'm not intruding." Louisa entered the flat. "I tried calling but you didn't answer your phone."

"I never check my phone before 10:00 a.m., it can ruin my whole day," Digby said. "Why don't you wait in the living room? I'll get dressed and make some coffee."

Louisa had never been in the living room before; she always walked straight to the kitchen. The sun streamed onto the parquet floor and it looked like a photo in *Architectural Digest*. Leather sofas were arranged around a glass coffee table and there were white bookshelves. A bronze statue stood in the corner and bay windows overlooked a garden.

She perched on an armchair and suddenly wondered if this was a bad idea. Noah wouldn't approve of Digby answering the door in a robe and slippers. But it was Noah's fault the rest of her day was tightly scheduled, and Digby had to try her rice pudding.

"I'm glad you're here," Digby said, entering the room. "I must apologize for my behavior yesterday, I was quite rude. My publisher insisted I sign all those cookbooks and I was in a hurry. I hope it wasn't inconvenient for you taking the books to Claridge's."

"Of course not, it has nothing to do with that." Louisa flushed. "It's about the rice pudding. You thought it was lumpy."

"Did I say that?" he wondered. "The master classes can be overwhelming. My palate can't handle too many chocolate fondants or linzer tortes before they all taste the same. You're a talented chef, I'm sure it was delicious."

"You were right, it was lumpy. But I made another batch and it's perfect." She handed him the bowl. "You don't need to try it right away, one doesn't eat rice pudding for breakfast. I'll leave it here and you can tell me what you think tomorrow at Claridge's."

"Nonsense, if you went to all this trouble I'll try it now," he insisted. "I'll get two spoons and you can join me."

Digby disappeared and Louisa walked to the bookshelf. The spines on the cookbooks were printed with the names of her idols: Anthony Bourdain and Paul Bucose and Alice Water. There was a signed cookbook by Alain Ducasse and a whole shelf devoted to Julia Child.

"Here we are." Digby returned, holding two spoons. "You are the chef, you take the first bite."

Louisa ate a spoonful of pudding and it tasted even better than she remembered. She waited for Digby to try it and had never been so anxious.

"The flavor is delicious," Digby said finally.

"And the texture?" She sucked in her breath.

"The texture is like a fine brandy," he mused. "It sits on your tongue for a moment, and then dissolves in your throat."

Louisa's heart lifted and she remembered her first class at the Culinary Institute. She baked a raspberry cheesecake and was terrified the raspberries were tart or the date on the cream cheese expired. The instructor ate a whole slice and asked if he could serve it at a dinner party. Louisa was so happy; she couldn't stop smiling.

"Do you really think so?" She exhaled. "I hoped you'd like it."

"In fact, it would be an excellent addition to the Christmas lunch I'm preparing tomorrow," he said suddenly. "You should join me."

"But tomorrow is *Christmas Dinner at Claridge's,*" she reminded him.

"I've been asked to prepare Christmas lunch at a country house about two hours from London," he explained. "The kitchen has every gadget you can imagine, and *Town & Country* is doing a four-page photo spread."

"*Town & Country!*" Louisa gasped. "But how will you prepare lunch and get back in time to do *Claridge's?*"

"I'm going to bake the puddings and leave them in the fridge. I couldn't turn it down, members of the royal family will be there." He smiled. "It will go much more smoothly if you assist me, and you'll have your photo in *Town & Country*. I promise we'll return in time."

Could she really drive two hours out of London the morning of *Christmas Dinner at Claridge's?* She told Kate she wouldn't do anything all day, but surely Kate wouldn't mind. And Louisa didn't have any other commitments besides getting her hair and makeup done in the afternoon.

Noah wouldn't be happy that she was assisting Digby. But he would have to understand; after all, his job was important to him too. He practically begged her to come to London because he was afraid he'd get fired if he didn't have a replacement for Bianca.

The sun made patterns on the bookshelves and she couldn't pass up the opportunity.

"I'd love to." She turned to Digby. "What time will we leave?"

"I'll pick you up at 10:00 a.m. We can buy the ingredients on the way." He looked at Louisa. "Why don't you wear that dress? The color will look wonderful in the photo spread."

She and Digby flipped through cookbooks and talked about Gordon Ramsay's recipe for Christmas bombe with cherry-flavored syrup. They were both fans of Thomas Keller's white cake encrusted with coconut and thought Jamie Oliver's chestnut torte with honeycomb was delicious.

Louisa noticed the time and said she would see him tomorrow. She hurried down Brook Street and hoped she wasn't late to meet Noah.

"There you are." Noah stood on the steps of Claridge's. "I knocked on your suite but you weren't there. I thought something happened."

"The best thing happened," she announced. "I took Digby my rice pudding and he said it was delicious. You see, it had nothing to do with what I was wearing. Yesterday's rice pudding was lumpy, but this time it was perfect."

"Did he really say that?" Noah asked, eyeing her red dress and leather pumps.

"I see the way you're looking at me," she snapped. "I had to dress nicely this morning for the show. You said the rice pudding was the best thing you ever tasted. Why shouldn't I believe that Digby felt the same?"

"It was excellent," he relented.

"And there's more," she said excitedly. "He made the most amazing offer."

Noah glanced at his watch and took her arm.

"You'll have to tell me about it on the way. We have an appointment at the Royal Mews and we can't keep Buckingham Palace waiting."

Noah stopped in front of a carriage with black leather seats and red spoke wheels. The driver wore a liveried uniform and two black horses were outfitted with elaborate reins.

"What are you doing?" she wondered. "I thought we were taking a tour bus."

"You were freezing on the bus and I was afraid you'd twist your ankle running up and down the stairs," he explained. "The carriage has a blanket and the driver well help you in and out."

"We're going to sightsee in a horse and buggy?" Louisa turned to Noah and her eyes were bright.

"I can't think of a better way to see London." He smiled. "Let's go, we can't be late."

Louisa felt like she was in a movie where every scene is so gorgeous, you can't take your eyes off the screen. Belgravia Square was filled with elegant boutiques, and St James's Palace was surrounded by a wide park and iron gates. The London Eye was the biggest Ferris wheel she had ever seen and Westminster Palace took up an entire city block.

They toured the Royal Mews and she posed in front of gold carriages and silver Rolls-Royces. And the horses! There were Windsor Greys and Cleveland Bays and Belgium Blacks. Louisa fed a horse a sugar cube and felt like a schoolgirl who snuck into the stables in Central Park.

She tried to tell Noah about Digby's offer, but the clip-clopping of the carriage made it impossible to talk. It would have to wait until they finished sightseeing.

The carriage turned onto Oxford Street and stopped in front of Selfridges department store. It was like some impossibly huge wedding cake with white pillars and revolving doors. The windows were filled with rocking horses and teddy bears and gold boxes piled like an Egyptian pyramid.

"I've been smiling so much my cheeks belong on a chipmunk." Louisa grimaced. "If we come back later, I promise I'll sample a Christmas hamper or pretend to pop Christmas crackers. Right now I need to sit down and have a cup of coffee."

"We're not going to do any of those things." Noah helped her out of the carriage. "I sent the cameramen home."

"Then why are we here?" she wondered.

Noah looked at her and his eyes danced. "To buy you a Christmas present."

"What did you say?" she asked.

"We fly back to New York on Christmas night and won't have a proper Christmas at all," he began. "If I was home, I'd spend Christmas reading law books. But you didn't tell me how you celebrate Christmas. For all I know, you're giving up a family Christmas with a ten-foot tree and giant turkey."

"I'm usually too exhausted to do anything." Louisa sighed. "Last year my friends wanted me to attend a dinner party and go caroling. I stayed in my apartment and ate deli turkey sandwiches and red velvet Christmas torte."

"I asked Kate if I could put a gift on the expense account." He pushed open the glass doors. "Choose anything you like. I'll have it wrapped up and delivered to you on Christmas morning."

They entered the store and Louisa caught her breath. A white Christmas tree was decorated with miniature music boxes and blue Wedgwood teacups. Salesgirls wore bright wool dresses and glass cases were filled with scarves and jewelry.

"You want me to choose anything?" Louisa turned to Noah.

"I already offered you my leather jacket, and you turned down the keys to my car." He grinned. "Pick something that will make you happy every time you look at it."

Louisa gulped and suddenly wanted Noah to kiss her. But so many wonderful things were happening: she was part of *Christmas Dinner at Claridge's,* and she was going to be featured in *Town & Country* with Digby. She didn't have time to fall in love.

"I can't remember the last time I shopped for anything besides a measuring cup," she said and laughed. "I don't know where to start."

"Start wherever you like," Noah replied. "There are five floors and we have all afternoon."

She sampled Jo Malone lotions and scribbled with a Mont Blanc pen and admired a pair of Burberry rain boots. There was a White Company duvet that would have been heavenly on her bed, and mimosa-scented candles.

"Why would anyone want an eighteen-karat cell phone case, that's an invitation to get robbed," she wondered. "And these pink slippers are warm but the pompoms make them look like mice."

"This is Selfridges. They have to sell things that are out of the ordinary," he said. "No one wants a can opener or garden hose for Christmas."

Louisa noticed a glass case filled with Christmas ornaments. There was a Christmas angel and a crystal snowflake. She admired pewter bells and a polar bear wearing a bow tie.

"This is what I want." She pointed to a red phone booth with a gold hook.

"You could have a bracelet or earrings and you want a Christmas ornament of a phone booth?"

"You said I should choose something that makes me happy."

Louisa turned to Noah. "We don't have classic phone booths in New York anymore. I'll hang it in my kitchen. Every time I look at it, I'll remember Christmas in London."

Noah leaned forward and kissed her. His mouth was soft and her whole body tingled.

"It's a perfect gift," he agreed. "I'll tell the salesgirl to wrap it up."

They sat in Selfridges Kitchen restaurant on the fourth floor and shared a warm goat cheese salad. Shoppers ate buttered scones and there was an electric feeling in the air of desperately wanting Christmas to arrive but not wanting the holidays to end.

"We don't have to be at Claridge's kitchen until 7:00 p.m. tomorrow, so I thought we could start the day at Balthazar. You need one proper British breakfast of fried eggs and sausage." Noah stopped and smiled. "Though I won't make you eat grilled tomato. There is nothing worse than a cooked vegetable in the morning.

"I got tickets to a Christmas pantomime," he continued. "It's not Christmas unless you're surrounded by children, and the pantomimes are some of the best theater in London. We can ice-skate at Hampton Court and attend early services at Westminster Abbey. We'll be back to Claridge's with plenty of time for hair and makeup."

Louisa gulped her coffee so quickly it burned the back of her throat.

"It sounds wonderful, Noah. But I'm afraid I can't," she announced. "I'm busy all day."

"What do you mean you're busy? You can't be taking another master class," he said teasingly. "It's Christmas Eve. You don't want to spend it making gingerbread cookies in Digby Bunting's kitchen."

"It's something much more exciting," Louisa said. "Digby has been asked to prepare Christmas lunch at an estate in the country. It's for a very important client and *Town & Country* is going to do a four-page spread." She took a deep breath. "He asked me to assist him."

"You and Digby want to run off to the British countryside on the day of *Christmas Dinner at Claridge's*," Noah said quietly.

"You make it sound like we're doing something wrong," she countered. "We're just going to prepare the puddings and leave them in the fridge. We'll be back in plenty of time."

"I'm afraid it's not a good idea." Noah shook his head. "What if his car breaks down or you burn your hand on the stove? I'd rather you didn't go anywhere without me."

"Digby drives a late-model Range Rover and I've never burned myself cooking," she assured him. "My rice pudding is going to be on the menu and the guest list includes members of the royal family."

"It wouldn't make a difference if the Queen herself shows up," he begged. "We've worked too hard to have the show derailed by a pompous chef who thinks he's a cross between George Clooney and Michelangelo."

"This is always about Digby!" she gasped. "I don't know what you have against him. He has been nothing but kind and this is a golden opportunity. When people see my photo in *Town & Country,* they will flock to my new restaurant."

"People will come to your restaurant because the pastries will be delicious," Noah persisted. "You don't need Digby Bunting."

"You dragged me to London and said being on *Baking with Bianca* will be good for my career," she reminded him. "Now you're trying to stop me from doing something just as important."

"I thought you wanted to spend time together on our morning off. We were starting to be important to each other," he said slowly. "It seems I was wrong."

The wrapped ornament twinkled under the lights and she sucked in her breath. A few minutes ago Noah kissed her, and now they were getting into a fight.

"I am having a wonderful time, and I appreciate everything you've done," she urged. "But this is a great opportunity and it doesn't interfere with the show. I don't see why I have to choose."

"Sometimes you just do." He picked up the package. "Never mind. It seems you already have."

"Where are you going?" she asked.

"I'm going back to Claridge's," he said. "I'll call a taxi. You can keep the horse and carriage."

Louisa fiddled with her key and opened the door of her suite. How dare Noah tell her she couldn't assist Digby! It was like asking a tennis player not to play at Wimbledon or a pianist not to perform at Carnegie Hall.

Noah said he had feelings for her, but his distaste for Digby was more important to him than her success. She was lucky they only had one kiss; they weren't ready for a relationship.

She entered the living room and gasped. A white Christmas tree stood next to the fireplace. It was strung with blue and silver lights and topped with a gold Christmas angel. Candles flickered on the side table and silver tinsel was littered over the rug.

There was an envelope with her name propped against the mantel. She took out the card and read out loud.

"Dear Louisa, tomorrow is Christmas Eve and you don't have

your own Christmas tree. I couldn't trek through the lobby with a fir tree, so I asked the concierge to deliver one.

"You've given me the best gift I can imagine this year. Since I met you life is more than just surviving each day without dropping from exhaustion. It's about enjoying each other's company and being excited for the future. I'm very glad you agreed to come to London. Merry Christmas. Love, Noah."

The late-afternoon sun filtered through the satin drapes and there was a pewter teapot on the sideboard. A fire flickered in the fireplace and the whole room was bathed in a silvery light.

Noah must have had it delivered while they were sightseeing. He was so thoughtful and she hadn't even gotten him a gift.

It still didn't excuse his behavior at Selfridges. If he really cared for her, he would have been thrilled about Digby's invitation. But it was a beautiful Christmas tree and the card was lovely. Maybe she should forgive him.

Tears pricked her eyes as she thought about Noah storming out of Selfridges. It didn't matter how she felt. Noah was furious and everything was ruined.

Chapter Fourteen

KATE TURNED ONTO BOND STREET and thought it was even more elegant than Fifth Avenue in New York. Flags flew over the storefronts and windows were filled with diamond necklaces that looked so expensive, she couldn't imagine wearing them in public.

Tomorrow was Christmas Eve and she had been so busy, she hadn't explored Mayfair at all. There was so much to see. Grosvenor Square was like a snowy white handkerchief, and Bruton Street had smart cafés and there was Piccadilly Circus and Park Lane. She could have spent hours in the lobby of the Langham Hotel and admiring the paintings at the Halcyon Gallery.

And the shops! She stroked crimson-colored sweaters in Mulberry and admired suede loafers in Hermès and spent a few minutes in Bulgari. She was dying to try on ruby butterfly earrings, but she was afraid the salesgirl would coax her into buying something she couldn't afford.

William & Son beckoned to her from the corner and she took a deep breath. She had only been there once, to buy Ian a twenty-first-birthday present. It was still terribly imposing. Glass cases were filled with navy silk ties and the air smelled of leather goods and men's cologne.

"Can I help you?" A saleswoman approached her.

"I need a gift," Kate replied.

"Is it for someone special?" the woman asked. "A husband or boyfriend?"

"I'm not married, but it is for a man," Kate answered. "I haven't gotten him a present before, it's all brand new."

"I understand," the woman said knowingly. "You aren't comfortable enough in the relationship to just get him a sweater or nice tie. You want something that when he opens it, he can't imagine having lived without it."

"That's it exactly!" Kate exclaimed. "I just don't know what to get."

"What does he like?" she asked.

"He loves astronomy and anything to do with mathematics. He hates romantic poetry and isn't a fan of Shakespeare and refuses to read *Don Quixote*. He's not interested in sports and doesn't like loud concerts. He's good at backgammon and is crazy about his dogs."

"I thought you said it was a new relationship?" The woman raised her eyebrow. "I've been married for twenty years and don't know half those things about my husband."

"It is a new relationship," Kate said and suddenly it all seemed so simple. "But we've been best friends for years."

The woman showed her silver martini shakers and silk pocket squares and pearl dress studs. There were leather driving gloves and the softest cashmere slippers.

"What about these?" She snapped opened a black velvet box. "Every man needs a pair of cuff links."

Kate remembered when she asked Trevor to the Snowdrop Ball freshman year and he refused. Now he dined at private clubs and wore tailored suits.

"It's perfect." Kate handed her a credit card. "Please wrap it up."

Her phone buzzed as she left the store and she pressed Accept.

"Kate." Trevor's voice came over the line. "I'm sorry I haven't called, I've been tied up all day."

"Your ears must be ringing, I was just thinking about you," she laughed.

"There's something I want to talk about," he answered. "How about dinner tonight at the Dorchester?"

"The Dorchester!" Kate exclaimed.

The Dorchester was one of London's most exclusive hotels with a three-star Michelin restaurant and suites overlooking Park Lane. "Will and Kate," as she had begun to think of them, were frequent visitors and it was the London haunt of movie stars and celebrities.

"You're spoiling me." She smiled. "I'm happy eating fish and chips at a corner pub."

"Tonight it has to be the Dorchester," Trevor insisted. "I'll meet you at 7:00 p.m. And Kate, there's a small box waiting for you in your suite. Open it before you leave."

Kate hung up and strode down Bond Street. It was late afternoon and the air smelled of pine needles and perfume. Christmas lights were strung across the pavement and it looked like a holiday postcard.

Maybe Trevor was going to ask her to move to London. She was a respected television producer; it wouldn't be hard to get a job. But she'd worked so hard and she would be starting at the beginning.

And she loved so many things about New York: the eclectic

restaurants and billboards in Times Square. New Yorkers complained about the humidity in the summer and slush in the winter, but they were living in the most exciting city in the world.

London had arts and history. Mayfair was impossibly elegant and Notting Hill had outdoor flower markets and used bookshops. The fashions were stunning and there was Buckingham Palace and the royal family!

Perhaps Trevor was considering moving to New York. He could be a guest lecturer at Columbia and they would get an apartment in Morningside Heights. On the weekends they would drive upstate and it would be like when they explored the countryside around St Andrews.

She told Louisa falling in love made you want to be with the person all the time. That didn't have to be a bad thing. It could make life exciting and full of possibilities.

She passed Agent Provocateur and stopped in front of the window. It had been so long since she entered a lingerie shop. But she was going to dinner at the Dorchester with Trevor. It might be fun to wear a silk camisole underneath her dress.

She tucked her present to Trevor under her arm and felt a thrill of anticipation. The door swung open and she walked inside.

Kate entered the lobby of the Dorchester and instinctively smoothed her hair. It was like something out of the 1930s with paneled walls and Oriental carpets and mahogany furniture. A Christmas tree was decorated with colored ornaments and a grand piano stood in the corner.

"Kate, you're here." Trevor approached her. He wore a dark suit and carried a bouquet of roses.

"I was afraid you'd be wearing a tuxedo and I'd have to go home because I'm hopelessly underdressed," she laughed, kissing him on the cheek.

"You could never be underdressed." He handed her the flowers.

"You sent me those gorgeous roses and then you left me a gift, and now you're giving me more roses." She inhaled the sweet scent. "I haven't received this many presents since I was a child."

"I've never had anyone to buy Christmas presents for," he said, taking her hand.

"Didn't you buy Susannah gifts?"

"Susannah bought her own Christmas presents and put my name on the card." He shrugged. "She was afraid my taste wouldn't match her wardrobe."

"You have wonderful taste." She touched her ears. "The earrings are beautiful. But you shouldn't have, it's not even Christmas."

"I'm being selfish. You're leaving on Christmas night, and I wanted to see you wear them."

"Then I'm very lucky," she said and laughed. "They're gorgeous and I adore them."

They entered the Grill and it was even more glamorous than Kate imagined. The floors were polished parquet and the booths were butterscotch-colored leather and a glass chandelier hung from the ceiling. A huge mirror stood behind the bar and there were potted palm trees.

"I feel like I'm in a James Bond movie." She slipped into a booth. "Any minute men in tuxedos will chase each other across the tables."

"I doubt that will happen," Trevor laughed. "Though Ian

Fleming used to dine here. The bartender invented a drink for him. It's called the Vesper martini and it's Tanqueray and vodka, shaken not stirred."

"How do you know these things?" she asked suddenly. "At St Andrews all you cared about was algorithms. Now you're an expert on cocktails and popular culture."

"I've grown to appreciate the good things in life." He shrugged. "Like having a drink with a beautiful woman two days before Christmas."

The waiter appeared and they ordered Angus prime rib and scotch sours with lemon juice and sugar.

"The Dorchester makes the smoothest martinis." Trevor sipped his drink. "I could use two of these. I've been on the phone with Susannah."

"With Susannah?" Kate asked and felt a pinprick of worry.

"I'm coordinating how to pick up the dogs," he explained. "I don't know how people handle divorce with children. She doesn't want me to collect them until after the holidays because they add to the ambience. They do look wonderful lounging under the Christmas tree."

"Aren't the guests wondering why the man of the house is out and about in London while his wife is at Yardley Manor?" she asked curiously.

"Susannah told everyone I had to give an important lecture." He waved his hand. "They might give it a moment's thought and then they'll go back to their backgammon tournaments and Christmas buffets."

"Do you miss Christmas at Yardley Manor?" she wondered.

"The kitchen is full of delicious scents and every room is decorated with wreaths and mistletoe. But there are too many people and too much food and too many games. It's like having a three-day pass to Disneyland and not being able to leave." He looked at Kate. "Do you wish you were in New York for Christmas?"

"I love Christmas in New York." She nodded. "The windows on Fifth Avenue are spectacular and no one minds the miserable weather and endless lines for taxis. But this afternoon I walked around Mayfair and it's like a small village," she said slowly. "I could fall in love with London."

"When I woke up this morning, you were gone. I was afraid you thought last night was a mistake," Trevor said abruptly. "I sent the roses to tell you how much I enjoyed it."

"I should have left a note, but I didn't know what to say." She fiddled with her earring. "But I went to buy you a Christmas present and realized I knew you better than anyone in the world." She took a deep breath. "I'm having a wonderful time and don't want it to end."

He leaned forward and kissed her. She kissed him back and tasted lemon and sugar.

"We have two more days, we'll figure it out." He touched her hand.

They ate mushroom risotto and talked about Christmas and theater and books. Trevor's hand brushed her sleeve and she felt a tingle of desire mixed with the wonderful feeling of being home.

"I thought this trip was going to be a disaster," she said as the waiter replaced their plates with bowls of Peach Melba. "We lost our star chef and I was worried about Noah's replacement. But Louisa is lovely, and then you turned up at Claridge's. I wasn't even that surprised, we always seemed to find each other."

"I had just driven from Sussex and all I wanted was a brandy."

Trevor nodded. "You were sitting by yourself and you were so beautiful."

"You said you wanted to talk about something," she remembered.

"I'd rather talk in private. Let's wait until we get to Claridge's." He squeezed her hand. "I'll pay the bill and call a taxi."

They crossed the lobby and stood on the hotel steps. A man stepped out of a black cab and Kate had a sudden premonition. Like when they filmed a segment of *Baking with Bianca* in the Hamptons last summer. The weather report predicted clear skies but Kate noticed a single cloud in the morning. By noon it was pouring and the outdoor kitchen was ruined.

"Good god, I can't believe it!" a man with a British accent said. "Trevor Skyler and Kate Crawford at the Dorchester. I wouldn't be more surprised if I ran into the president of the United States and our own prime minister."

"Hello, Ian." Trevor held out his hand. "It's nice to see you."

"Trevor and I ran into each other a few months ago in Spain." Ian turned to Kate. "But Kate, has it really been ten years? You look the same as the last day at St Andrews. That blond hair and those long legs and that iridescent smile. It's imprinted on my memory like stamps on my passport."

Kate gasped and wished she could run back into the Dorchester. Ian's hair was thinner and his belt was tighter, but he had the same blue eyes and smile that could light up New York.

"I'm in London for work," she answered quickly. "Trevor said you were married."

"We're in London so my son can meet his grandparents." He nodded. "There's nothing better than coming home for Christmas.

The Yorkshire pudding is better than anything in Spain, and you run into all the best people."

"We have to go," Trevor said shortly. "Our cab is waiting."

"You mustn't rush off, we have so much to catch up on," Ian suggested. "Why don't we stop in at the bar and have a cognac?"

"I don't think so." Trevor shook his head. "Maybe another time."

"Well, in that case at least I should get a kiss." He turned to Kate. "I don't know when I'll see you again."

Before she could stop him, he leaned forward and kissed her. It was only a quick kiss but her cheeks flushed and she felt unsettled.

"It really was good to see you both," Ian said and his face broke into a smile. "I'll have to return to London more often."

Kate sat in Claridge's bar and fiddled with her glass. How could they have run into Ian? But it wasn't that unlikely; his parents owned a flat in Mayfair. Where else would he stay except the Dorchester or Claridge's?

Trevor was completely silent in the cab. When they arrived at Claridge's, he said he had to make an important phone call and would see her later. Kate couldn't bear being alone in her suite and inhaling the scent of Trevor's roses. She entered the bar and ordered a scotch.

Ian was married with a child. She had no interest in him and it didn't change a thing. But it was as if the clock turned back and they were all students at St Andrews again. She remembered the day of graduation. The June sun glinted on the ancient buildings and she was overcome with nostalgia and excitement for the future.

Kate stood under the tent erected in St Salvator's Quad and nibbled a smoked salmon sandwich. She really must go back to her room before tonight's Graduation Ball or she'd be too tired to finish arranging the centerpieces.

But the tent looked so beautiful with its pink tablecloths and pastel-colored balloons. If she left, it might feel like an ordinary afternoon instead of her graduation day from St Andrews.

The whole day had been thrilling. She woke early and attended the chancellor's breakfast. She remembered when she arrived four years ago and he was so terrifying in his black robes. Now he shook her hand and gave her a quick hug.

The ceremony in Younger Hall seemed to last forever. Her pumps were too tight and she had to keep poking Trevor so he didn't scribble equations on his program. Then the students paraded down North Street and tossed their caps in the air and she was so happy and sad at the same time.

It had been a wonderful semester. After the society dinner in January, she and Trevor cautiously started dating. They were like trapeze artists who didn't want a fear of heights to interfere with their act. Neither of them wanted to hurt their friendship, but the attraction between them made them bright and happy.

They did all their normal things: spent long hours in the library and studied too late in their rooms. But she would bring him a sticky toffee pudding or he would surprise her with a bouquet of flowers and they both had that giddy feeling of knowing someone cared.

She accepted an internship at a network in New York and Trevor was starting a postgraduate degree at the University of

London, and they didn't know when they would see each other. They avoided the subject like pilots navigating around a dangerous storm. Once they were walking down South Street and Kate noticed Trevor was far behind her. When she asked why he stopped, he said he wanted to know what it would be like to be without her.

"There you are." Trevor approached her. "I couldn't drag my mother away from the chancellor. She was so thrilled that he stopped to talk to her, she asked him about his golf game and the names of his favorite restaurants. I didn't have the heart to tell her he doesn't play golf and eats all his meals in his residence."

"Of course he talked to her." Kate smiled. "You practically won every prize."

"You did well yourself: the Entrepreneur Award and Howe Prize for debate."

Kate clutched her champagne glass and flinched. She and Ian had tied for first place and collected their awards together. She tried to avoid him all semester. Whenever he saw her he hinted how much he missed her, like a fisherman dangling bait. She always coolly dismissed him, but the next time he tried again.

"My internship pays less than the desk person at the YMCA and has longer hours than an investment banker." She sighed. "You're going to study at one of the most prestigious universities in the world and become a famous mathematician."

"Or fail miserably and teach high school math in York." Trevor grinned. "My mother is still upset I'm not coming home. She expected me to unpack my suitcases and move back in to my bedroom."

Trevor looked so handsome in his cap and gown. His hair was cut short and he wore a white shirt and yellow tie.

"I'm proud of you." She kissed him. "When you win the Nobel Prize, I'll tell my friends you once corrected my calculus homework."

Trevor squeezed her hand and looked up. "My mother is walking toward us. We have to leave or she'll ask me to take more photos with the chancellor and it will be so embarrassing."

They stepped out of the tent and crossed the lawn. The sky was pale blue and the grass was emerald green and the sun glinted on the tall spires.

"Don't you think it's not fair that the university looks so beautiful in summer?" she commented. "I remember when I came in September and thought the sea would always be the color of sapphires and the Old Course would resemble something out of *The Wizard of Oz*. Then November arrived and I had never been so cold."

"It will be cold in New York," he reminded her.

"But the office buildings are properly heated and you can ride the subway instead of a bicycle," she answered. "You'll have to send me some sausage rolls. The best way to warm my hands is rubbing them on the packaging."

"I was thinking about hand delivering them," Trevor said slowly.

"What did you say?" Kate stopped and turned around.

"I've been doing a little research and Columbia has an excellent master's program," he continued. "It wouldn't be until next year because I've already been accepted at the University of London."

"You're thinking of moving to New York?" she repeated.

"We've never talked about the future, and frankly I can't imagine living in a city where the skyscrapers are so tall you have to crane your neck to see them. But I'm willing to give it a try."

"But you've never been to New York." Kate frowned. "You might hate it. It's hopelessly overcrowded and you can't get a packet of fish and chips or Cadbury Flake bar."

Trevor reached into his pocket and took out a black box.

"This isn't an engagement ring, we're both twenty-two and don't know the first thing about marriage," he began. "I suppose one calls it a promise ring, but then I feel like I'm sixteen and infatuated with the girl who agreed to go with me to the dance.

"Even if I get accepted at Columbia, I wouldn't start until next year and you might be engaged to some hedge fund manager with a summer cottage in the Hamptons. But I've felt about you the same I did when we met, and I'll never feel this way about anyone else."

Trevor opened it and took out a silver ring. Kate felt like a skydiver who was suddenly afraid to jump. It all looked so beautiful: the dazzling sky and ground laid out like a tapestry. But what if she couldn't open her chute?

"I'm just asking you to wait for me," he finished. "So we can figure out if we want to be together."

"It's beautiful, and I can't imagine being with anyone else," she stumbled. "But I hadn't thought about the future. I'm just worried about finding a decent apartment and learning how to use the subway."

"You don't have to give me your answer now." He pressed the ring into her hand. "Keep it and tell me tomorrow."

She slipped it into her purse and felt a little relieved. The clock struck four o'clock and she jumped. "I have to change and prepare for the Graduation Ball. I'm head of the setup committee. If I'm not there, the other members might drink all the champagne and eat the best hors d'oeuvres before everyone arrives."

"I would go with you, but I promised my parents I'd take them to the Adamson for dinner," Trevor said.

"I won't stay late," she replied. "I'll make sure everything is going smoothly and come join you."

"If I survive until then." He kissed her. "My mother will have drunk too much wine and be telling the waiter he could get a real job if he just got a haircut."

Kate stood in the corner of the ballroom and thought it really did look lovely. A black-and-white dance floor was strung with twinkling lights and there was an ice sculpture and glass bar. Vases were filled with yellow sunflowers and a dessert table held blueberry cheesecakes and chocolate-covered strawberries.

Kate decided not to leave before the band started and now she was glad she stayed. She worked so hard on the decorations; she had to see what they looked like with the lights dimmed and candles flickering on the tables. And it was her last ball at St Andrews. She wanted to watch the guys in white dinner jackets and girls in bright evening gowns twirl across the dance floor.

A man approached her and she recognized Ian's blond hair.

"You look beautiful tonight," he commented. "That's the loveliest gown in the ballroom."

"I had to dress up for the ball." She smoothed the skirt of her yellow organza gown. "I'm on the committee. But I'm not staying long, I just wanted to see the decorations."

"Why are you alone?" he stood beside her. "Don't tell me Trevor jilted you. I never trusted him; no one is that nice. He's like one of your American Boy Scouts with a backpack."

"Trevor is having dinner with his parents." She turned away. "If you'll excuse me, I have to join them."

"Don't go yet," he suggested. "Let me get you a glass of champagne."

"No thank you, I'm not thirsty," she said. "I only stayed to see the decorations."

"Do you remember the Snowdrop Ball?" he asked suddenly. "You wore that ivory gown and you were the most beautiful girl there."

Kate recalled Ian in a black tuxedo. When he walked her home, all she wanted was for him to kiss her.

"It was years ago, I can't remember what I wore." She turned to the exit. "It was nice seeing you, I'll see you later."

She stepped outside and a male voice called after her.

"Kate, wait!" Ian appeared, waving something in the air. "You left your purse on the table."

He handed her the purse and touched her arm.

"Sit with me for a few minutes," he urged. "It's so beautiful outside. You don't want to sit in a stuffy restaurant when you can enjoy a Scottish summer night."

It was beautiful. The sky was as wide as a football field and the air smelled of dew and flowers. And it was her last night at St Andrews. She wanted to sit and gaze at the brick buildings forever.

"I'll stay for a few minutes," she conceded, settling her wide skirt on the stone steps.

"Here, have my glass of champagne." He handed it to her. "So tell me what Kate Crawford is doing after graduation."

"I have an internship at a network in New York," she answered.

"I knew you'd take the television world by storm." He nodded.

"I'm going to open a nightclub in London with a friend. Before you make some comment that it's an excellent way to pick up girls, it's strictly a business venture. I want to do something with my trust fund besides watch it grow while I play croquet."

"I hope it will be a success." Kate sipped the champagne and thought she really should leave.

"I know I made a mistake with Jasper," he said slowly. "I've regretted it from the moment it happened. But I swear it was just a few kisses, there was never anything more."

"A few kisses are much more than nothing. Anyway, that's ancient history." She stood up. "I really have to go."

"You and I were in love for three years and might not see each other again," he insisted. "You can give me five minutes."

Ian's cheekbones glinted under the stars and he looked like a lead in a romantic movie.

"All right." She nodded and sat down.

"I was faithful the whole time we were together. Not because I was afraid you'd find out, but because I wasn't interested in anyone else," he began. "For three years I was that guy you saw underneath the ski sweater. Then I was alone with Jasper on winter break and made a stupid error." He looked up and his eyes were dark. "You don't know how many times I wished I could take it back."

Kate remembered the debate where Ian begged her to give him another chance.

"It's not important," she said quietly. "We've both moved on."

He handed her a crumpled piece of paper. "Read this."

"What is it?" She turned it over.

"It's a receipt for this." He reached into his pocket and drew out a blue velvet box. He opened it and displayed a diamond engagement ring. "Look at the date on the receipt. I bought it over winter break."

"You bought an engagement ring?" Kate sucked in her breath.

"I wasn't going to give it to you right away," he said. "I was going to wait until your birthday."

"Why is it in your pocket?" she asked and felt like she couldn't swallow.

"I carry it all the time. I hoped there might be a time when I could give it to you." He got down on his knee. "I've missed being together and I don't want to miss it anymore." He paused. "I love you, Kate, and I'll spend the rest of my life trying to make you happy."

He pressed the ring into her palm and Kate gasped.

"You can't ask me to marry you," she whispered.

"I could open a nightclub in New York or you could get an internship in London," he continued. "We'd travel the world and have everything we want."

"It's our last night at St Andrews and we're both nostalgic." She held the ring gingerly. "Please take it back."

"Just think about it," Ian begged and his eyes were the color of cornflowers. "You can give me your answer in the morning."

Kate entered the residence hall and ran up the stairs to her room. How could she have talked to Ian and why did he propose? They hadn't spoken to each other in months and now he asked her to marry him.

And she and Trevor were young and had so much ahead of them. Was she ready to give him a promise when they had only been together for a few months?

It was supposed to be the most wonderful night with laughter and tears and toasts to the future. Now all she wanted was to climb into bed.

Her purse lay on the coffee table and she opened it. Ian's

diamond ring was snuggled next to Trevor's black box. She held them in her hand and her heart raced and she felt almost dizzy. She slipped them back into her purse and blinked back tears.

Kate sat in the booth in Claridge's bar and sipped her scotch. How dare Trevor storm off because they saw Ian. It wasn't her fault that Ian kissed her; Trevor was acting like a child. She picked up her phone and dialed Trevor's number.

"It's Kate," she said when he answered the phone. "I'm sitting at the bar and I had to talk to you. You were the one who said we should make a fresh start, but then Ian appeared on the steps of the Dorchester and you stormed off."

"It was a shock to see him," Trevor admitted. "But I really did have an important phone call, I wouldn't lie to you."

"You were so quiet in the taxi and you barely said goodnight," she continued. "We had a beautiful evening and you ruined it."

"He kissed you in front of me," Trevor returned. "What was I supposed to do?"

"Ian is married with a child," Kate reminded him. "It was just a kiss between old friends."

"It's late and I have a throbbing headache," he answered. "Do you mind if we discuss this in the morning?"

"I suppose so," Kate relented. "I'll see you tomorrow."

She paid her check and walked into the lobby. The chandeliers glinted on the Christmas tree and giant wreaths hung from the fireplace and it all looked so festive. Tomorrow was Christmas Eve and they would drink eggnog and forget all about their argument. She pressed the button on the elevator and hoped she was right.

Chapter Fifteen

LOUISA SIPPED PINK GRAPEFRUIT JUICE and thought the Foyer had never looked so inviting. It was the morning of Christmas Eve and the buffet table overflowed with English muffins and *pain au chocolat*. There was a selection of mueslis with mixed berries. And the omelets! Smoked salmon with poached eggs, and Dorrington ham with truffles, and Scottish haddock in a Mornay sauce. She asked the chef to prepare his favorite because she couldn't possibly choose.

Less than a week ago she had been standing in the bakery, jiggling the stove to turn it on and drinking endless cups of coffee. Her feet had been freezing and there was a small leak in the bakery window. Now she was about to climb into a Range Rover and drive to a country estate outside London. She would serve rice pudding to members of the royal family and have her photo in *Town & Country*.

If only she and Noah hadn't gotten into a terrible fight, everything would be perfect. She tossed and turned all night, replaying the scene in Selfridges like a YouTube video you watched too many times because it was so easy to hit Play.

She typed out a dozen texts to apologize but deleted every one.

There was no reason why she shouldn't assist Digby. She had done nothing wrong and Noah was acting like a child.

She did miss Noah. She wished she could ask him what to wear for the *Town & Country* shoot, and if you had to curtsey when you met a duchess. She didn't want to make a mistake.

The grapefruit juice prickled the back of her throat and she missed more than Noah's advice on how to smile for the camera without it looking forced. She missed his warmth and the way his eyes lit up when he saw her. And their kisses! On the Ferris wheel at Winter Wonderland and in the kitchen at Claridge's and under the tree at Trafalgar Square. How could they end everything because of one silly argument?

But she couldn't let her emotions cloud reality. Noah didn't support her and he couldn't interfere with the most important day of her career.

And she had so much else to think about. She had to stop by the gift shop and buy a decorative box for Chloe. She was going to ask the pastry chef of the Foyer to write down a few of their children's Christmas recipes: White Chocolate Unicorn Bark made with white chocolate and mini-marshmallows and Snow-Capped Fairy Cakes with coconut icing. Then she would put them in a pretty box and give them to Chloe as a late Christmas present. She pictured Chloe's wide green eyes when she unwrapped the ribbon and already felt better.

A man entered the dining room and she recognized Noah's leather jacket. She looked down and poured Mornay sauce on her omelet.

"Can I join you?" he asked.

"I'm not sure if I'm ready to sit together yet after last night," she said. "There are plenty of empty tables."

"I don't want to sit by myself," he urged. "I would like to sit with you."

"If this is about assisting Digby, I told Kate my plans and she said it was a wonderful idea." She looked up. "So if you're here to give me another lecture, please save it for later. Digby is picking me up soon and I'm already so nervous I put on two pairs of panty hose and almost brushed my hair with my toothbrush."

"You are wearing two pairs of panty hose?" Noah glanced at her legs.

"I took one pair off." She flushed.

"I'm here to apologize and it's embarrassing enough doing it in the Foyer." He glanced at waiters carrying silver trays. "At least let me sit down."

"I don't believe you," she said suspiciously. "You're going to start apologizing and then say something mean about Digby, and it will start all over again."

"Cross my heart." Noah put his hand over his chest and grinned. "Now can I please sit down? I haven't eaten a thing and the smell of those eggs is making me faint."

Louisa nodded reluctantly and Noah pulled out a chair. He took an English muffin out of the bread basket and covered it with jam.

"I said some awful things yesterday and I was wrong," he began. "Of course you should assist Digby. It's a wonderful opportunity."

"Do you think so?" she asked.

"Digby is a huge name and any connection with him is good for your career. And anyone would kill to be in *Town & Country.*" He ate a bite of muffin. "I am concerned about you getting back on time, but I trust you won't let the show down."

"Then why were you so upset?" She remembered Noah storming out of Selfridges. "You were like a boy who broke his favorite train set and wanted to blame someone else."

"Digby is handsome and charismatic. Women flock to him like shoppers to a Saks after-Christmas sale." He stopped and looked at Louisa. "I'm falling in love with you and I was afraid he would sweep you off your feet."

"You're falling in love with me?" Her fork froze in midair.

"I told you I had feelings for you," he reminded her gently.

"Having feelings for someone can mean lots of things," she mused. "That you like spending time together, or are hopelessly attracted or think about the person when you're apart." She hesitated. "But falling in love is different."

"I do like being together, and I want to do more than just kiss you, and I think about you all the time." He nodded. "But you're right, falling in love is different. It gets in the way of your work and keeps you awake at night, and sometimes makes you say things you regret. But I don't want to fight it, unless you think I should."

"Should what?" She felt like she was back on the carousel at Hyde Park. All Noah's words were delightful but when he stopped talking she felt dizzy.

"Falling in love might be inconvenient. But I'm not going to fight it if there's a chance you feel the same."

Louisa cut her omelet as if she was a surgeon performing a delicate operation. She swallowed a piece and her heart hammered in her chest.

"Yes," she breathed. "There is certainly a chance."

"Good," he said and ate another bite of muffin. "Because if there wasn't, I don't know what I'd do."

They shared the omelet and talked about *Christmas Dinner at Claridge's* and Louisa's croquembouche. She buttered toast and felt like she'd stepped into a storybook. The strawberry jam tasted sweeter and the sounds of rustling newspapers and clinking silverware seemed like a symphony.

"I don't know what shade of lipstick to wear for the photo shoot." She opened her purse. She placed a velvet box on the table-cloth and searched for two tubes of lipstick.

"What's that?" Noah pointed to the box.

"Digby sent me a pair of earrings, but I'm going to return them." She shrugged.

"Digby gave you earrings," he repeated.

"The card said he thought they were perfect for the photo shoot, but he did say I could keep them," she said uncomfortably.

Noah snapped the box open and gasped. There were diamond stud earrings with platinum backs.

"Digby gave you diamond earrings?" Noah looked at her incredulously. "These must cost a fortune!"

"He didn't show up with them at my suite, he had them delivered," she corrected. "And it's not a gift. It's a prop for the photo shoot."

"I'm sure he meant it as a gift." He pointed to the box. "The box is from Harry Winston and it's tied with a red bow."

"It's for the shoot for *Town & Country*," she said. "You wanted me to wear an Asprey watch on the show. I don't see any difference."

"Why don't you tell him that you appreciate it, but you'd rather wear earrings of your own?"

"I said I was going to return them, I would never accept such an expensive gift." She snatched up the box. "But there is nothing wrong with wearing them on the shoot. It would be rude to return them for no reason."

"Don't you see, it's as clear as that ice sculpture?" he urged, waving at an ice sculpture of a fish. "Digby plans on seducing you! Maybe he's not preparing a Christmas lunch at all. He reserved a room at some picturesque inn and he's going to ply you with champagne and caviar."

"Of course he's preparing a Christmas lunch, he sent me the menu." She bristled. "But what would it matter if he wanted to sleep with me?"

"What do you mean?" Noah was shocked.

"I just said I'm falling in love with you," she said slowly. "Now you're saying you don't trust me to be alone with another man."

"Of course I trust you." He ran his hands through his hair. "But it's Digby Bunting. He's the Pied Piper of pastry."

"I don't care if he's Chris Hemsworth! If you had Chrissy Teigen on the show I wouldn't mind." Her voice rose.

"I don't even know who Chris Hemsworth is. And Chrissy Teigen is married with a child," he said and stopped. "You're missing the point. Digby Bunting is an attractive available man and you're a beautiful young woman. I'd be a fool to let you traipse across the English countryside with him."

"I don't remember asking your permission." She gathered her purse and stood up. "Put the omelet on your own expense account, I just lost my appetite."

Louisa ran through the lobby and down Claridge's steps. She'd rather wait in the cold for Digby than sit and listen to Noah. How dare Noah say he loved her and then didn't trust her? Trust was one of the most important things about love; it's what set it apart.

A navy Range Rover pulled up and a blond man wearing sunglasses and a ribbed sweater stepped out. He must be a movie star: Leonardo DiCaprio or Ryan Gosling. He took off his sunglasses and she realized it was Digby.

"Louisa!" he called. "I'm afraid I'm early. I was going to come inside and wait for you."

"You don't have to," she answered. "I'm ready."

"Shall we go?" he asked.

Digby helped her into the passenger seat and closed the door. She pictured Noah finishing her omelet and turned to Digby.

"Yes," she said and her mouth trembled. "I've never been more excited."

They had so much to talk about on the drive; Louisa barely noticed the quaint British villages with their thatched houses. Digby shared his favorite pudding recipes: Colchester pudding with pink meringue and tapioca; strawberry-and-cream sandwich sponge which was named for Queen Victoria and made with double cream and vanilla. His fried Cox apples with cinnamon sugar sounded so good she wanted to ask if she could use the recipe at her restaurant, and his frozen blueberry cheesecake made her long for summer.

The car pulled up in front of iron gates and there was a stone house perched on top of a hill. It was three stories with slanted roofs and tall chimneys.

"Oh, it's gorgeous!" Louisa peered out the window at the snow-covered fields. There was a pond and pine trees decorated with colored lights.

"The house was built in the eighteenth century," Digby said. "It sits on the hill so the owner could keep an eye on all his land."

"It's like something out of a Jane Austen novel. I expect to see a man in a morning coat gallop across the fields on horseback," she breathed. "That sounds silly. I'm sure you're invited to estates like this all the time."

"On the contrary, your enthusiasm is infectious." He pulled into the circular driveway. "Why don't I give you a tour?"

"We can't just walk through someone else's house." She hesitated.

"I'm friends with the hostess." He jumped out and opened her door. "And the whole house party is attending Christmas Eve services at Chichester Cathedral. We have the place to ourselves."

The foyer had polished wood floors and gold leaf end tables and ivory pillars. There were drawing rooms with damask wallpaper and patterned rugs and heavy walnut furniture. And the fireplaces! She tried to count them on her hands but ran out of fingers.

A dining room had a marble-topped dining table and high-backed velvet chairs and portraits behind gilt frames. The music room reminded her of a State Room at Buckingham Palace with a grand piano and gold harpsichord. The rolltop desk was filled with sheet music.

The kitchen was down a flight of stairs and had stone floors and granite counters. Pots and pans hung from wood beams and French doors opened onto a frozen vegetable garden.

The camera crew set up lights and Louisa relaxed. She had been posing for the camera all week; this wouldn't be difficult at all. And it would be thrilling to make her rice pudding with the stainless-steel mixing bowls and whisks that came in three sizes.

"I wanted to thank you." She turned to Digby. "We just met and you've been so kind. I'm very grateful."

"We all need a helping hand when we're starting out." He

stood in front of the fridge and touched up his hair. "Besides, I told you my life can be very mundane. It's nice to have someone to share it with, even if it's only for a little while."

"To share it with?" Louisa repeated.

"The piles of cookbooks at Waterstones and Digby Bunting aprons at Harrods don't mean anything unless I have someone to come home to. Don't you agree?"

Louisa felt a little faint and wondered if the furnace was on high. She tried to think of something to say but Digby kept talking.

"You are talented and pretty. You must have a boyfriend in New York," he continued. "Next time you're in London, I'll give you both a tour of the kitchen at Kensington Gardens. I know one of the queen's chefs and it's quite impressive."

Digby thought she had a boyfriend, he wasn't talking about her at all! She wished Noah were here so he could see once and for all that Digby didn't want to seduce her. But it didn't matter. If Noah didn't trust her, she didn't want anything to do with him.

They littered the counters with cartons of eggs and bottles of whole cream. Digby was making viennetta parfait so there was butterscotch and chocolate caramel and puffed pastry. The stylist arranged bowls of fruit and a miniature Christmas tree hung with oranges and lemons.

"You aren't wearing the earrings," Digby noticed. "Don't tell me they didn't arrive."

"They're right here." She opened her purse and took out the velvet box.

"Why didn't you put them on?" he asked.

Louisa couldn't tell him she didn't want to wear them in front of the camera crew, it would be terribly rude. And why shouldn't she wear them? They were gorgeous and Digby was wearing a

Patek Philippe watch. After the shoot, she would thank Digby and say she couldn't keep them.

"I must have forgotten." She opened the box.

"Would you like me to help you?" he offered.

"No, thank you." She fastened the earring on her ear. "I can manage."

Louisa wiped the counter and put the measuring cup in the sink. The photo session had gone perfectly. Her rice pudding with blackberry jam was delicious; Digby even asked if he could include her recipe in his cookbook. He showed her how to make the crust on a Cambridge burnt cream, and laughed when she tasted his lemon ripple tart and it was too sour.

Now he was loading up the Range Rover and they were returning to London. It was early afternoon and she even had time for a bath. Digby had been a perfect gentleman and all Noah's worries were for nothing. She turned on the hot water and had to stop thinking about Noah.

"I have some bad news." Digby entered the kitchen. "The starter on the Range Rover froze. The car won't turn on."

"What do you mean it won't turn on?" she asked. "It's a brand-new car!"

"The interior of a Range Rover is like the most luxurious living room but the engine can be finicky." He shrugged. "I've had it for six months and it's been in the shop three times."

"Call the mechanic," she urged. "There must be something he can do."

"It's Christmas Eve," he reminded her. "Even if I could get hold of him, I doubt he'd trek out to Chichester to work on my car."

"There must be a mechanic around here," Louisa insisted. "Maybe there's a phone book upstairs."

"I already checked." He shook his head. "It wouldn't do any good, anyway. There's no cell phone reception."

"What about the house phone?" she asked and her heart beat a little faster.

"I found one but it doesn't seem to be working," he said.

"But we can't be stranded." Louisa suddenly felt as if she'd entered the walk-in freezer and the door closed behind her. "We have to be at Claridge's in a few hours."

"I'm terribly sorry." He rubbed his brow. "Everyone will be back from Chichester Cathedral soon and someone will give us a jump. We still have plenty of time."

Louisa let out a sigh of relief. Of course, someone would help them! It was an unfortunate blip but these things happened. And Digby was very apologetic; it wasn't his fault.

"I'm sure everything will be fine," she said and tried to keep her voice steady.

"Why don't we move into the drawing room? There's a nice fire and I'll find a couple of brandy snifters," he said and smiled. "We could both use a drink."

Louisa followed him up the stairs into a room with high ceilings and velvet sofas scattered over a patterned carpet. There was a giant Christmas tree and stone fireplace hung with stockings. French doors opened onto a wide porch and there were pots of geraniums.

Digby poured her a glass of brandy and she perched on an armchair. She took a small sip and then put it down. A shiver ran down her spine and she would have given anything to be sitting in the Foyer with Noah, furious with him for not wanting her to go to the countryside with Digby.

Chapter Sixteen

KATE PAID THE TAXI DRIVER and stepped onto Trafalgar Square. It was Christmas Eve and this evening was *Christmas Dinner at Claridge's*. It was only noon, but she had been working for hours, confirming with the stylist and double-checking the kitchen had all the ingredients. The day of a show was like preparing for a rocket launch. No matter how well you anticipated every detail, something could always go wrong on the launchpad.

Louisa had called and asked if she could spend the morning assisting Digby Bunting. Kate couldn't say no; Louisa was so easy to work with and it wouldn't conflict with the schedule. But she would be happy when Louisa returned to Claridge's. And Noah was strangely out of sorts. He was quite short with her when she asked him to pick up some aprons at Harrods. She couldn't blame him; he still felt responsible for Louisa and worried it would be his fault if the show weren't a success.

The small conflicts distracted her from thinking about Trevor. Maybe she should have knocked on his door last night after she hung up the phone. If they were together, he would realize seeing Ian was a slight inconvenience, like getting a cold when you arrived at a holiday destination. It put a damper on the first day's activities, but you couldn't let it spoil your vacation. Of course, Ian shouldn't have kissed her, but it only lasted a few seconds. And Ian was married! The whole thing was ridiculous.

This morning Trevor called and asked her to meet him at the National Gallery. She loved looking at paintings, but it was Christmas Eve. Perhaps she would suggest they attend the Christmas Concert at Royal Albert Hall or browse in the Christmas markets.

She suddenly wished it was her first day at Claridge's and she was sitting in the Reading Room. What would have happened if she left before Trevor sat down? Now she'd have that electrifying feeling she got before a show, when adrenaline coursed through her veins like the finest coffee. Instead, she was acting like a teenage girl who wasn't sure if her boyfriend was going to break up with her.

But she thought of all the things she said to Louisa: that she didn't want to grow old and only have memories of Bianca's shades of lipstick, that when you fell in love you wanted to be with that person all the time.

Perhaps Trevor just wanted to show her a favorite painting. They'd go back to his suite and make love and eat room service lobster bisque. She'd take a nap and wake up refreshed and energized for tonight's show.

The gallery was imposing with thick marble pillars and a domed ceiling. She recognized a Caravaggio in a gilt frame and a Degas of dancers in white tutus. Trevor stood in front of a painting by Rubens of a voluptuous woman draped in red velvet.

"Here you are; I haven't been to a gallery in ages." She approached him. "When I moved to New York, I visited the Met and Guggenheim all the time. But I started working such long hours, all I wanted to do on the weekends was curl up with *The New York Times* or catch up on my sleep."

"Do you remember when we were at St Andrews and visited the National Gallery in Edinburgh?" Trevor asked. "They had well-known artists: Raphael and Monet and Picasso. But there were some we never heard of: Uccello and Velázquez."

"Afterward we'd sit in a pub and think we were so cosmopolitan," she remembered with a smile. "Two college students exploring one of the greatest art collections in Europe."

"I'm sorry about last night," Trevor said. "I overreacted and ruined a lovely evening."

Kate looked up and let out her breath. Trevor wasn't upset about Ian; he just wanted to be together. She worried about nothing and everything was going to be all right.

"Seeing Ian was a shock, we were both rattled." Kate nodded. "And he shouldn't have kissed me. That was wrong."

"I want to show you something." He took her hand. They drifted through spaces filled with Van Dycks and Turners. Kate made him stop in front of Van Gogh's *Sunflowers*. She'd read about it so often and now she was seeing it in person.

They entered a room with a parquet floor and orange walls. It had a wood bench and windows overlooking a garden.

"When I arrived in London from St Andrews, I used to come here all the time," he began. "I always ended up in this room. I didn't even like the painting; it's a Bellini and quite drab. But no one came in here and I could sit alone for hours."

Kate noticed a new tone in his voice and looked up. His eyes dimmed and there were lines on his forehead.

"I was studying at the University of London and the National Gallery was free," he said. "After my classes, I'd wander through the rooms until my eyes burned and there were holes in my shoes." He stopped and looked at Kate. "It was the only way to stop thinking about you.

"Then one weekend I read there was a new exhibit," he continued. "It was ten years ago, I can't even remember the name of the artist. But I milled around with tourists and schoolchildren and realized something as thrilling as any Rembrandt. I was at the gallery because I wanted to see a painting, not because I wanted to forget about you."

"It was bad luck that we ran into Ian," she cut in. "But he'll go back to Spain and we won't see him again. His kiss was for old times' sake, it didn't mean anything."

"I'm more sorry than you can imagine, Kate," Trevor began. "But I don't think I can carry on."

"What do you mean?" she asked. "You are the one who said we wouldn't talk about the past, we were two adults alone in London at Christmas. I just wanted to stay friends and you said that even though you weren't divorced you were ready for a new relationship."

"I've loved everything about this week: showing you The Arts Club and *The Nutcracker* at Covent Garden and dinner in my suite." He shook his head. "But I can't go back to being the boy who spent all his time in an art gallery to avoid thinking about a girl."

"I was quite content before you showed up," she continued hotly. "But you couldn't be without me. Now you're saying you don't want a future because Ian Cunningham pulled up in a taxi? How dare you! We made love, doesn't that count for anything?"

"I thought it would be easy: dinners and conversation with a sophisticated, beautiful woman," he said slowly. "But you broke my heart and there are some things I can't forget. I can't risk it happening again. I am sorry, Kate."

"I see." Kate glanced down at her wool jacket and wondered why she felt so cold. She was a successful producer with everything ahead of her. She wasn't going to ask Trevor to change his mind.

"We're both so busy for the next two days, I'm sure we won't run into each other." She smoothed her hair. "Maybe you'll watch the show when it airs. Louisa's croquembouche will be superb."

"I'll look for it." He nodded. "Would you like me to call you a cab?"

"You go back to Claridge's. I'll stay and look at the paintings," she said and her eyes were bright. "I don't know when I'll be back in London, and I don't want to miss seeing the Holbeins."

Kate waited until Trevor left and sat on the wood bench. Trevor was right, the painting by Bellini was all browns and grays. But she didn't feel like jostling the crowds and she wasn't ready to go back to Claridge's.

She pulled her jacket around her and tried to make her heart stop racing. It had been foolish getting involved with Trevor. It was so complicated; how could it have ended differently?

But Trevor had been so confident about their future; she was swept along as if a genie offered her a ride on a magic carpet. And it had been wonderful exploring London together! She was so lucky to fall in love with her best friend.

Perhaps if they had talked about the past, they would have had a chance. You couldn't lock away certain events and hope they wouldn't resurface. It was like living on a fault line and being surprised by an earthquake. It was bound to happen so it was better to be prepared.

She tried to remember the day after graduation. It was all so long ago and she had been young and inexperienced. How could she know that waiting a few hours could decide her whole future?

Kate pulled back the curtains of her room and the sun streamed onto the wood floor. It was the day after graduation and already the campus looked different. It was like the last day of summer camp when the cabins were invaded by parents carrying cardboard boxes. All the things that had belonged to them for six weeks: the lockers where they kept care packages of Ritz crackers, the desks filled with writing paper and markers, were being emptied for a new batch of campers.

Last night she had been so upset, she never joined Trevor and his parents for dinner. She ate instant porridge in her room and tried to figure out what to do. Of course, she couldn't marry Ian. It was flattering that he asked, and she still felt a pinprick of attraction, like a gorgeous evening dress she passed in a store window. It was too expensive and it wasn't the kind of thing she'd wear, but it was still lovely to look at.

But she wasn't going to give up her future to become Mrs. Ian Cunningham. Even if she could trust him, they were too young and she wanted a career. And he would never change. If Ian went too long without being adored by women, he withered like a rose during winter.

Trevor was her best friend and she loved spending every minute with him. They could hike the Old Course without saying a word, or sit on the fire escape and talk for so long, they forgot the time and had to stay up late finishing an essay.

But Trevor coming to New York was completely different. She would be responsible for his happiness and she wasn't even sure of her own. What if she failed and ended up working at a local television station in Santa Barbara? Then Trevor would have changed his whole life and it would be her fault.

Trevor said she was courageous, attending university on another continent without knowing a soul. Why shouldn't Trevor do the same? If he wanted to come to New York, she shouldn't stop him.

And wasn't love the most important thing? If she said no, they would drift apart and she might not see him again. One day she would notice a photo of Trevor in an alumni magazine and wish she'd given it a chance.

Now she peered out the window and saw students climbing into station wagons. Guys carried boxes and girls hugged each other and scribbled down addresses. Parents waited patiently, thrilled that they got to spend a few hours with their grown children.

Why had she picked today to oversleep! She missed the postgraduation brunch and she couldn't even remember when Trevor was leaving. She had to go to his parents' hotel and tell him she wanted to give them a chance. But first she had to see Ian. She put the two rings in her purse and raced down the staircase and across the playing field.

The door to Ian's room was ajar and there was a pile of Ian's blazers on the bed. The leather shaving kit she gave him last Christmas was tossed on the floor, and there was a stack of old magazines.

"If it isn't Sleeping Beauty. You're still dressed for the ball." Ian appeared at the door, taking in her yellow organza gown and silver sandals. "I thought I was going to have to come over and kiss you to rouse you from your deep sleep."

"I couldn't fall asleep last night. I finally dozed off sitting in an armchair and then I overslept." She flushed, gazing down at her dress. "I didn't have time to change this morning, I wanted to see you as soon as possible."

"I hope it's with good news." He ushered her inside. "You're going to say yes to my proposal."

She glanced in the mirror and wished she had at least fixed her hair and reapplied her makeup. But she had been in such a hurry; the most important thing was saying no to Ian and then finding Trevor.

"I can't marry you, Ian." She shook her head. "I don't love you."

"That's not how you sounded last night," he muttered. His shoulders sagged and there was disappointment in his eyes. "You were quite nostalgic about our time together."

"I had too much champagne and nothing to eat," she admitted. "I apologize if I led you on. I didn't mean to."

"I promised to spend the rest of my life making you happy." He paced around the room. "I've been waiting all morning for your answer."

"I did love you once, but I don't anymore." She fished the ring out of her purse. "You want me most when you can't quite have me, and that's no way to have a relationship."

"Are you sure?" He looked at Kate and his eyes were bluer than the summer sky. "We had the best time fishing in Scotland and sailing on the French Riviera. You'll never have so much fun again."

"Perfectly sure." She handed him the ring. "Good luck with everything. I have to go."

"It's too bad you missed the postgraduation brunch. Everyone was asking about you," he said suddenly. "I told them I asked you to marry me and you had my ring."

"You did what?" she gasped.

"I could tell you loved me last night. I was certain you would say yes," he explained. "And you did have my ring. I gave it to you and you kept it."

"You wouldn't let me return it!" she exclaimed. "You'll have to tell them you were wrong. Anyway, we're all leaving. Your friends won't notice when you arrive at a summer house party with a different blonde."

"Trevor was there with his parents," he admitted. "They seem like nice people, he introduced me."

"Trevor was at the brunch?" She suddenly felt uneasy. "You didn't tell him I had your ring."

"Not directly." Ian shrugged. "But I can't be sure what he overheard."

Kate walked to the door. She had to find Trevor and tell him she gave Ian back his ring.

"You are making a big mistake, Kate." Ian stopped her. "Trevor is from a different world, you'll never be happy. We belong together. I'll give you everything you ever wanted."

"All I want is to be able to trust someone." She turned the door handle. "Goodbye, Ian. I hope you have a safe trip home."

She strode out the door and clattered down the staircase. There was a man entering the lobby of the dorm. Trevor wore a polo shirt and khakis and his mouth was set in a thin line. He looked up at Kate and suddenly froze.

Kate clutched the bannister and felt dizzy. Trevor took in the organza gown she wore to the dance and her quilted evening purse. Her hair was unbrushed and her face still had traces of last night's makeup.

"Trevor, wait!" Kate called.

Trevor's eyes were cold and his skin was the color of putty. He turned and raced out the door. Kate rushed after him but he sprinted across the playing fields. Her sandals slipped on the grass and she sank onto the lawn. By the time she brushed herself off and stood up, he was already gone.

Kate walked down North Street, past Mitchells with its graduation cakes in the windows and the newsagent selling postcards of St Andrews. Her gown was crumpled and her ankle hurt from where she fell and she wanted to take a bath.

If only Trevor hadn't appeared at Ian's dorm. What if Trevor thought she spent the night in Ian's room? She had to find him and tell him it had been perfectly innocent.

She entered a hotel lobby with a vinyl sofa and coffee table scattered with brochures. There was a reception desk and watercolor on the wall.

"I'm looking for Trevor Skyler." She approached the desk. "The reservation would be under his parents' name."

"Mr. and Mrs. Thomas Skyler?" He looked up. "I'm afraid they checked out."

"Checked out?" Kate repeated and a chill ran down her spine.

"About half an hour ago," the man said.

"They can't have," she insisted. "They weren't supposed to leave until this afternoon."

"They did seem in a hurry," he offered. "Maybe there was an emergency at home."

Kate felt the air leave her lungs. She sank onto the sofa and longed for a glass of water.

"I see this happen all the time," he said kindly. "Graduation day is supposed to be so joyful, but it can be the hardest day of the year. All those friendships torn apart like confetti at a summer picnic. But I've been here twenty years, and real friendships last forever. Whoever you were anxious to see must feel the same."

"Yes, of course." Kate thought about the velvet box in her purse. Tears pricked her eyes and she gulped. "I'm sure he feels exactly the same."

Kate gazed at the Bellini on the gallery wall and fiddled with her earrings. She had called Trevor at his parents' house all summer, but he never returned her calls.

Then Trevor started at the University of London. She was busy with her internship in New York, and had a relationship with a stockbroker that didn't amount to anything. Eventually she tucked her feelings away with the tartan blanket that didn't match her décor and the chipped coffee mug from Mitchells.

She had been perfectly content until she looked up from her tomato and Parmesan salad at Claridge's and Trevor was standing in front of her. Now she might never be happy again.

She strode through the gallery and pushed open the glass doors. There was the feeling of snow in the air and people carried shopping bags from Liberty and Harvey Nichols. She flagged a taxi and decided she couldn't think about Trevor. This evening was *Christmas Dinner at Claridge's* and she had so much to do.

Chapter Seventeen

LOUISA STOOD IN THE LIBRARY of the country house and thought she had never seen so many books except at the New York Public Library. An end table was littered with glossy coffee table books and paperback books with orange spines reached the ceiling. It really was the coziest room: mustard-colored leather chairs like something in a Sherlock Holmes novel and a fireplace big enough to fit Santa's sled, and a window seat overlooking frozen fields. If she weren't about to miss the most important event of her career, she would be perfectly happy to curl up with an Agatha Christie novel.

In the movies when the heroine was shipwrecked on a desert island or stranded in a rowboat in shark-infested waters, she closed her eyes and imagined being somewhere wonderful. Miraculously a helicopter appeared and she climbed the ladder to safety. She was whisked away to some luxurious hospital that seemed more like a hotel and fed waffles and fresh fruit until she felt better.

But Louisa was stranded at a country estate outside London. In the last two hours there hadn't even been the sound of a car in the driveway. Her cell phone didn't get reception and the house phone still wasn't working, and she had no idea when someone would come back to save them.

Digby was in the drawing room nursing his third scotch, but Louisa was too anxious to sit still. What if he drank too much and wasn't able to drive? She had never driven on the left side of the road in her life. Navigating holiday traffic on the A23 was as terrifying as Noah's anger when they returned to London.

She thought about Noah and shuddered. The only good thing about not having cell phone reception was that she wasn't tempted to call him. He would offer to come get them, of course. But she'd rather hitchhike in a snowstorm than have to hear Noah say she should have listened to him and never left Claridge's.

Digby would get them back in time. His whole reputation was at stake. She was just overwrought from the shot of brandy and the central heating that was turned on too high. A brisk walk around the grounds would clear her head.

But she was wearing a dress and pumps. If she went outside she could catch pneumonia or slip on the ice. Then she wouldn't be able to do the show and Noah would never forgive her. She wished she were back at the bakery on the Lower East Side with cinnamon rolls in the oven and rain pounding on the window. At least then she couldn't disappoint anyone.

Kate had been so good to her: giving her Bianca's suite at Claridge's and letting her have an expense account and telling Noah to buy her clothes and a Christmas gift. What had she done in return? Flitted off to a photo shoot with Digby Bunting on Christmas Eve morning.

A clock chimed two o'clock and she thought she was overreacting. Even if Digby drank the whole bottle of scotch, someone could drive them. They were only two hours outside of

London; it wasn't as if they were stuck on a remote moor in Scotland.

She turned and Digby stood in the doorway. He held a glass and looked as relaxed as if they were waiting for a massage at some fancy spa.

"You disappeared from the drawing room. I had to finish that lovely scotch by myself." He entered the library. "Don't worry, I switched to water. Drinking too much alcohol in the afternoon gives me a headache."

"I wasn't worried." Louisa concealed her relief. "I am a little concerned about getting back to London. Everyone is counting on me and I can't let them down."

"Our hostess probably decided to do some last-minute Christmas shopping in Chichester," he assured her. "They'll be back soon and we'll be on the road in no time."

Digby was right; she wasn't achieving anything by worrying. And everyone did last-minute shopping the day before Christmas. Last Christmas Eve, she left her apartment in New York for a croissant and returned with lipsticks from Duane Reade and a book she saw in the window at Barnes & Noble.

"It is a gorgeous house," she relented. "I've always wanted a library where the books are stacked so high you need a ladder to reach the ones on top. And the kitchen is like a movie set. It has the biggest walk-in freezer I've ever seen and the pantry is stocked with more spices than Harrods. I just know the rice pudding is the best I ever made."

"I was never allowed in our kitchen when I was growing up." Digby rubbed the rim of his glass. "My mother was a serious hostess and was afraid I would smudge the silverware."

"How odd, I imagined you were always tinkering with recipes," she mused. "I made my first pancakes when I was seven. The middle was a little soft and it was almost burnt around the edges. But the blueberry and whipped cream topping was delicious."

"The first time I really used a kitchen was when I worked at Gordon Ramsay's restaurant at the Connaught," he began. "I was nineteen and not interested in attending university. My father was friends with Gordon and arranged an interview."

"Gordon Ramsay is one of the most famous chefs in the world!" she breathed. "He must have recognized your talent right away."

"I never baked for him, but we are both big football fans." Digby shrugged. "We root for the same team."

"Gordon Ramsay gave you a job because you both liked football?" she asked doubtfully.

"At first I was against it," he remembered. "I'd rather go to the nightclubs. But I liked the camaraderie in the kitchen, and the waitresses were very pretty."

"Is that where you created your chocolate and salted caramel cake?" she asked. "It was in your first cookbook and it's one of my favorite recipes. The chocolate ganache filling is delicious and the white chocolate shavings are the perfect topping."

"The closest I came to baking at the Connaught was wrapping a potato in aluminum foil and sticking it in the oven," he laughed. "Though I did meet Alan, my publisher. He came in every afternoon and ordered John Dory and a gin and tonic."

"What a wonderful story!" She hugged her arms around her chest. "I can just imagine it: the struggling sous chef prepares a dessert at home and brings it to the publisher of England's most successful cookbooks. It's like James Dean being discovered pumping gas, or Lana Turner being noticed behind the counter at the soda fountain."

"That's not how it happened. One day Alan dropped his gin and tonic and I swept up the glass," he said. "He asked what he should order from the dessert menu and I suggested the chocolate hazelnut plume with praline cream. A waitress saved me a slice and it was excellent. A few days later, Alan returned and asked if I wanted to write a cookbook."

"Alan Matheson asked if you wanted to write a cookbook when you never baked anything?" she wondered.

"The publishing houses had just started putting out those glossy coffee table cookbooks. They sold them at Harrods next to the Ralph Lauren aprons." He ruffled his hair. "Alan thought my photo would look good on the back cover."

Louisa's hands were clammy and she thought she might faint. She opened her mouth but Digby kept talking.

"*Desserts with Digby* was a huge success and I was in demand on talk shows and at charity events," he continued. "Alan didn't want me to make a fool of myself so he signed me up for a few baking courses. I know how to bake simple things like pound cake and chocolate mousse."

"But you're the king of British puddings," she interrupted. "Your recipes for raspberry blancmange and butterscotch trifle are renowned. And you said you'd rather be in the kitchen than attending book signings and appearing on television."

Louisa remembered when she was a girl and discovered Santa Claus wasn't real. If she told her mother everything she knew about him—his wife was named Mrs. Claus and he lived in the North Pole and his workshop was run by elves—her mother would say Louisa was right, he was real all along.

"Alan writes most of the recipes." Digby shrugged. "And I do enjoy working in a kitchen. It's satisfying and quite mindless. After all, anyone can follow directions in a cookbook."

Louisa's cheeks were pale and she was having trouble focusing. "Are you all right?" he inquired. "You look a little ill."

"It's the central heating," she said quickly. "If you'll excuse me, I'm going to get a glass of water."

She hurried through the hallway and down the steps to the kitchen. She poured a glass of water and leaned against the sink.

Lots of famous people came to their success from odd beginnings. You heard stories about an actor who started as a driver for a big producer and ended up a movie star. Or an author who wrote greeting cards and his entire novel was scribbled on the backs of sympathy cards. But Digby hadn't done anything at all. His only contribution to his own success was the way he wore a blazer.

Her eyes pricked with tears. Maybe Noah was right and Digby didn't care about her apple crumble or rice pudding. The only reason he was interested in her was because she had a fashionable hairstyle and her eyes looked big with her new mascara.

She opened the fridge and took out cream cheese and butter and milk. She searched the pantry and found cinnamon and vanilla and powdered sugar. She was going to make cinnamon rolls and give them to Noah with a note. She was terribly sorry she didn't listen to him, and he was right about everything.

She looked up and Digby was standing in the doorway.

"What are you doing?" he asked. "You went to get a glass of water and didn't come back."

"I thought I'd bake cinnamon rolls until they return." She kept her voice steady. "I always make them on Christmas Eve, they're my favorite dessert."

"I can think of a more enjoyable way to pass the time," he said casually. "I found a guestroom that's not in use. I chilled a bottle of champagne and there's an en suite bath with a Jacuzzi tub."

"What are you talking about?" she asked, tying an apron around her waist.

"It's really much better this way," he continued. "I thought we'd have to grab a few moments in the powder room, or the backseat of the Range Rover. But now we have all afternoon and evening. Alan will fill in for me on the show; he's done it before. And that producer of yours can take your spot. She's very attractive with her blond hair and long legs."

"I don't know what you mean." Louisa wished she could close her eyes and be somewhere else.

"Of course you do." Digby selected a green apple from a bowl. "Why else would you have signed up for my master class? You don't need me to teach you how to make chocolate mousse. You brought me rice pudding when I was wearing a robe and slippers, and you accepted my diamond earrings." His lips curled in a smile. "I've known it since we had afternoon tea at Claridge's. You're attracted to me, and want to go to bed together as much as I do."

"I don't want to sleep with you! I signed up for your master class because you are a renowned pastry chef," she stammered. "I brought you the rice pudding because I wanted to show you it wasn't lumpy. And the earrings weren't a gift, they were a prop for the photo shoot." She took the velvet box out of her purse. "I was going to return them but didn't want to offend you."

"Keep the earrings." He waved at the box. "They were given to me by the manager at Harry Winston."

"I don't want the earrings." She placed them on the counter. "All I wanted was to be taken seriously as a pastry chef. I learned so much from you: why an Eton mess has a funny name, and how to make the berries keep their shape in a blackberry fool. When we were together I felt like I could achieve all my goals: open a restaurant with gorgeous décor like the chocolate shop on Pimlico Road, and write a cookbook as good as the ones on your book-shelf." Her mouth trembled. "I liked being around you because you made me feel like a proper chef. If I worked hard, I could get everything I wanted."

"I'm not interested in any of that, I get recipes in the mail every day. Aspiring chefs leave marmalade cake and strawberry meringue on my doorstep. Somebody once climbed a tree and left a key lime pie on the ledge outside my bedroom window." He moved closer. "What I am interested in is a lovely American with eyes like a young deer and a waist I can wrap my hands around."

"Please don't come closer." Louisa stepped back. "I'm sorry if you misunderstood, there can't be anything between us. I'm see-ing someone."

"I don't care if you have a boyfriend." He shrugged. "I'm not looking for anything serious, I just want to have a little fun. Why don't I pop open the champagne and you can take off that apron and relax."

"I care very much!" She gathered a baking tray and measur-ing cup and mixing bowl. "I'm quite busy. I think you should leave."

"If you remember, that's the one thing I can't do," he said with a little laugh. He looked at Louisa and there was a flicker of pain behind his eyes. "In fact, I've changed my mind. I'm going to fin-ish that bottle of brandy. Getting drunk in the afternoon seems like an excellent plan."

Louisa waited until Digby left and then turned back to the

counter. She hadn't done anything wrong; Digby made the whole thing up. Anyone could see she was only interested in him as a fellow chef; she never gave him a different impression.

Tears pricked her eyes and she wanted to curl up like the kittens she saw in the pet store window at Christmas. But she couldn't let Digby's words affect her. That wouldn't solve anything.

She greased the baking tray and turned on the oven. The kitchen smelled of cinnamon and vanilla and fresh cream like a farm in the French countryside. When someone returned, she would beg them to take her to London. Then she would hand Noah the cinnamon rolls and he would say they were the best he ever tasted.

Chapter Eighteen

KATE SAT IN THE LIVING room of her suite at Claridge's and tapped at her laptop. It was midafternoon and the wintry sun filtered through the drapes. Poinsettias flanked the marble fireplace and a crystal vase held yellow tulips.

She hoped she could remember everything about her suite when she returned to New York: the striped drapes that were made out of a fabric as stunning as any ball gown, the eggshell yellow satin walls, the art deco furniture. And the little touches she couldn't imagine having in her own apartment: scented soaps next to the bathtub and expensive lotions and a cashmere robe hanging in the closet.

There was a silver tray of finger sandwiches and scones on the coffee table. She wasn't the least bit hungry, but she hadn't been able to resist ordering afternoon tea. She was leaving tomorrow night and when would she have the chance again to eat roast chicken with Pommery mustard and cucumber with mint cream cheese and fresh scones?

She remembered all the times she brought Trevor raisin scones with strawberry jam when they were at St Andrews and grimaced. The memories would fade as soon as she stepped off the flight in

New York. She would have so much to do: choose menus for next week's show and go over wardrobe suggestions with Bianca and sift through an endless stack of papers.

Did Trevor return to Claridge's after he left the gallery or was he wandering around Trafalgar Square? No matter how she tried to stop thinking about him, she kept imagining him in a black tuxedo.

How could she allow herself to fall in love? It didn't matter; Trevor made it perfectly clear it wasn't going to work. And it had been a wonderful week: attending the ballet and shopping on Bond Street and dining at the Dorchester. Now it was time to concentrate on *Christmas Dinner at Claridge's*.

There was a knock on the door and she answered it. Noah stood in the doorway, clutching a Harrods bag.

"Come in, thank you for picking up the aprons." She ushered him inside. "You look positively frozen. Next Christmas we'll have to do the show in the Maldives or St. Barts."

"There might not be a show next year." He stood next to the fireplace. "Louisa has disappeared. I can't find her anywhere and she's not answering her cell phone."

"Didn't she tell you? She assisted Digby Bunting this morning," Kate said. "She's probably sitting in a hot bath in her suite. It's the perfect place for her. She must be nervous and a bath will help her relax."

"I asked the maids to check her room and she's not there." He shook his head. "I contacted all the staff in the hotel. The last person who saw her was the doorman when she climbed into Digby's Range Rover this morning."

"It's three o'clock," Kate said, checking her watch. "She said she'd be back by 2:00 p.m."

"I'm afraid she is still with Digby, and I have no idea where they've gone." He rubbed his forehead.

"Louisa seems very responsible, she wouldn't let us down," Kate assured him. "They're probably stuck in traffic and she'll rush through the lobby any minute. Taping doesn't start until seven. There's plenty of time for hair and makeup."

"I just have a funny feeling." He hesitated.

"What kind of funny feeling?" she asked, picking up a smoked salmon sandwich.

"That she isn't coming back," he admitted.

"That's ridiculous. The whole reason Louisa is in London is to film *Christmas Dinner at Claridge's*," she scoffed. "She's very focused on her career; she's not the kind of girl who would run off with a man. Why would you think she isn't coming back?"

"Something happened," he said uncomfortably. "And it's my fault."

"I know you feel responsible for hiring Louisa. But I am the producer and the show's success depends on me," she reminded him. "Whatever happened, I'm sure it can be fixed."

Noah looked up and his eyes were dark. "I fell in love with her and I think she felt the same."

"Oh, I see." Kate put the sandwich back on the plate.

"I know it's unprofessional and I fought it as long as I could," he began. "But Louisa is special," he said with a sigh. "It's terrible timing. I'm studying for law school and she's saving money to open a restaurant, so we tried to remain friends."

"I know what you mean," Kate said thoughtfully. "But what does that have to do with Digby?"

"From the beginning I thought Digby had his eye on Louisa,

but she was positive he was only interested in her skills as a chef," he explained. "It caused some friction between us."

"Digby is rumored to be a bit of a lothario, but Louisa is very talented," Kate replied. "Why would you have doubts?"

"All sorts of things." He shrugged. "He invited her to the Winter Wonderland and took her shopping at the Christmas markets and offered her a place in his master class. Then he asked her to assist him today and I told Louisa she shouldn't go."

"But today was a great opportunity, *Town & Country* was going to be there," Kate said. "And maybe Digby was just being kind, everyone needs help at the start of their career."

"I apologized to Louisa this morning and said she shouldn't miss out." He took a deep breath. "But then I noticed the diamond earrings he gave her."

"Diamond earrings!" she gasped.

"From Harry Winston." He nodded. "Louisa said he gave them to her for the photo shoot but I didn't believe her." He fiddled with his collar. "I insisted she not go. She accused me of not trusting her and putting my feelings before her career. We got into a raging fight and she stormed out of the hotel."

"That is a bit of a mess," Kate agreed. "But she wouldn't jeopardize everything because you got into a fight."

"Digby can be very persuasive," he persisted. "What if he convinced her to skip the show and stay in some luxurious country hotel? Or they could be on their way to Scotland or on a flight to Paris."

"I'm sure it's nothing drastic." Kate tried to stay calm. "Call anyone who might know where Digby is: his hairstylist and tailor and publisher. Find out the name of his dentist, maybe he's laid up with a toothache. And call his doctor, he could have had an emergency appendectomy." She paused. "And try his mother. But don't tell her Digby is missing. No mother wants to think her son disappeared on Christmas Eve."

"I'm very sorry." Noah walked to the door. "I didn't mean to cause you so much trouble."

"I don't want your apologies, you need to fix this," Kate said sharply. "Call *Town & Country* and ask them the location of the shoot. If we don't find Louisa, we'll need to get an understudy for the understudy and we only have four hours until the show."

Kate waited until Noah left and stood at the window. A gold Rolls-Royce idled on the pavement and the hotel canopy was dusted with snow like frosting on a cake.

Noah was right: falling in love was a terrible burden. It kept her awake at night and made her favorite scone with orange marmalade taste like cardboard. But she could as easily ignore it as she could fly the plane from Heathrow to JFK by herself.

It was Trevor's idea in the beginning not to talk about the past. It had been easier to just enjoy drinks at Claridge's bar and dinner at the Dorchester. She had to make him see what they had was worth fighting for. Love was as rare as the most perfect diamond. If you were lucky enough to discover it, you cherished it forever.

She gathered her purse and entered the hallway. The elevator door opened and she pushed the button for Trevor's floor.

"Kate!" Trevor said when she knocked on the door. "What are you doing here?"

"I need to talk to you." She suddenly remembered the scene at the gallery. Could she really confront Trevor when he had just rejected her?

"I'm busy," he said evasively. "Can it possibly wait until another time?"

"It will only take a minute." She entered the suite. The coffee table was set with a silver teapot and porcelain cups. There was a plate of shortbread and bowl of mixed berries.

"Help yourself." He waved at the tray. "The maid keeps bringing food and I'm not hungry."

"I feel the same," Kate replied. "It's a shame not to have an appetite the day before Christmas."

"Kate, I feel awful but nothing has changed." He stuffed his hands in his pockets.

"You're right." She faced him. "Nothing has changed, we're in love with each other. We have been ever since you corrected my algebra homework and I helped you study *Beowulf*. Do you know how rare it is to find the person you want to spend your life with? Love can be more painful than the worst stomachache but it's useless to fight it."

"I disagree," he said stiffly. "I've been quite happy."

"You couldn't have been in love with your wife. You've been separated for a week and don't even miss her," she fumed. "The only pictures you have are of your dogs, and you're going to spend Christmas Day alone."

"It wasn't the closest marriage, but it had some good moments," he recalled. "And many people feel strongly about their pets. I don't mind being alone at Christmas, I've always enjoyed my own company."

"It's fine being alone if someone cares about you," she urged. "Remember the semester when we didn't see each other for days because you were taking an impossibly difficult analytics course and I was writing a paper on Chaucer? We knew all we had to do was walk down the hall to see a friendly face." She stopped. "It's different when the only thing you come home to is Netflix and take-out Thai noodles."

"I'd rather be mildly content than live with a permanent pain in my gut," Trevor said. "You hurt me and I can't get past it."

"You never let me explain what really happened," she said. "If you had only waited, everything might have been different."

"What do you mean?" he wondered.

"At the Graduation Ball, Ian offered to get me a glass of champagne. I ran out of the tent, but he followed me. It was such a lovely evening with the sky full of stars and warm summer breeze, I thought it wouldn't hurt to sit on the steps and chat." She perched on the sofa. "Then suddenly Ian pulled out a ring and asked me to marry him. Apparently, he had been carrying it around all semester.

"I tried to return the ring, but he told me to keep it and give him an answer in the morning. I could hardly leave a diamond ring on the lawn. I put it in my purse next to your promise ring." She paused.

"I couldn't sleep. I finally dozed off fully dressed and then I overslept and woke up at noon. I didn't even have time to change out of my gown. I ran straight to Ian's room and gave him back the ring." She took a deep breath. "I told him I couldn't marry him because I was in love with you. He said he saw you at the brunch and I was afraid you overheard that I still had his ring. I rushed downstairs and you were standing in the foyer. You saw me in my ball gown and assumed I spent the night with Ian."

"What else was I supposed to think?" Trevor demanded. "It was almost noon and you were just leaving Ian's room. You had your evening bag and your hair was rumpled and you were wearing last night's makeup."

"When I woke in the morning I didn't even think about changing my gown. All I wanted was to say no to Ian and go find you. I ran after you but I slipped on the playing field and you disappeared. By the time I reached your parents' hotel, you had already checked out." She felt like a long-distance runner who can see the finish line. "You and I just had a wonderful week exploring London, and realized we both wanted to have a future. Then Ian Cunningham stepped out of a cab and kissed me and it all disappeared like snowflakes on the pavement. Are you really going to let him do that to us again?"

Kate's heart raced and she walked to the bar. She poured a glass of water and took a long sip.

"You can't imagine what it felt like to see you leaving Ian's room." Trevor twisted his hands. "It was as clear as the simplest math equation. You accepted Ian's proposal and didn't have feelings for me at all."

"You didn't trust me," she murmured. "If you loved me you would have given me a chance to explain."

"I was twenty-two. All I could see was Ian in his white dinner jacket and gold cuff links sweeping you off your feet." He clenched his fist. "How could I compete with a trust fund and a villa in the south of France?"

"There was no competition," she said quietly. "I haven't felt the same about anyone ever."

Trevor paced around the room and she was reminded of how handsome he was. His shoulders were broad under his wool sweater and when he smiled, something inside her melted.

"You don't know how many times, before I met Susannah, I longed to conjure you up, like stars at the end of a telescope. But it's like anything: one learns to live without it. Then I saw you at

Claridge's and thought we could just have a few dinners. I never meant to fall in love with you again." He paused. "But when Ian appeared at the Dorchester and kissed you, it brought up everything that happened. I can't risk feeling like that again, it's too painful."

"It doesn't have to be like that," she whispered.

"I don't want to hurt either of us again," he said. "Do you mind if I take a little time to think about it?"

"Of course, I don't want to get hurt either. You said you were falling in love with me and I felt the same." She stood up. "I have things to do, I'll see you later."

Trevor touched her cheek. He drew her close and kissed her. She kissed him back and his mouth was warm and tasted of berries.

"I do love you, Kate," he said when they parted. "That will never change."

Kate entered her suite and walked to the sideboard. She poured a cup of coffee and added cream and sugar. She would have to leave the maids a very large tip. Every time she returned to the room there was always hot coffee and fresh cream and a bowl filled with sugar cubes.

It was almost three thirty and she hadn't heard from Noah. She still refused to panic. Digby was one of the most well-known chefs in England. He wouldn't just disappear before the biggest television event of the year.

She ran her hands over her mouth and thought about Trevor. She was glad she went to see him. But now it was up to him; she couldn't give it any more thought.

There was a knock at the door and she answered it. Noah stood in the hallway, clutching a clipboard.

"I tried Digby's hairdresser but he was doing the hair for Victoria Beckham, and his makeup artist is on holiday in Singapore." He paused. "His mother was very friendly but she hadn't heard from him since her birthday. But I got hold of his publisher and he gave me the address of the country house."

"Did he say when Digby would be back?" she asked, relief flooding through her.

"He wasn't reassuring." Noah fiddled with his pen. "Apparently Digby has done this before. Alan, his publisher, had to cover for him."

"He's run off before an internationally televised program and no one said anything?" she asked incredulously.

"Digby is like a rock star." Noah shrugged. "Alan sends out an apology that Digby got laryngitis or came down with a twenty-four-hour flu, and he's forgiven."

"Then we'll have to get Louisa ourselves." She glanced at her watch. "I'll call the front desk and ask for a car. We'll be cutting it close, but we can make it."

"Alan said the house party includes some members of the royal family," he said. "Without security clearance, we may not be able to get through."

Kate sipped her coffee and remembered all the crises she had dealt with: when the Lincoln Tunnel was shut down and Bianca was stranded in New Jersey, Kate had hired a helicopter to deliver Bianca to Manhattan. The time a protest blocked Fifth Avenue and she had to pay a bike messenger to borrow his bike and transport three cartons of eggs and a bottle of vanilla extract in his basket.

"I'll pile my hair under a hat and pretend I'm the Duchess of Cambridge if I have to." Kate gathered her purse. "What's the address?"

"The house is called Yardley Manor." Noah consulted his notes. "It's in Sussex near Chichester."

Kate froze and her purse dropped on the floor. "What did you say?"

"The hostess is named Susannah Skyler. She throws a house party every Christmas and invites well-known chefs to cook the meals," he continued. "Digby was supposed to bake the puddings and leave them in the fridge."

Louisa and Digby were at Trevor's country house in Sussex! He could get her through security. But what if he didn't want to see her and refused to go? She wouldn't take no for an answer. The whole show depended on it.

"I know how we're going to get there." She picked up her purse and opened the door. "Follow me."

She raced down the hallway and pushed the button on the elevator. The door opened and Trevor stepped out.

"Kate!" he exclaimed. "Where are you going, I was coming to see you?"

"I don't have time to talk about us now," she said. "You have to take me to Yardley Manor."

"What did you say?" Trevor gasped. "You want me to drive you to Susannah's house?"

"It's the most important thing in the world, I'll explain on the way," she said and turned to Noah. "You should stay here in case Louisa returns."

Kate and Trevor stepped into the elevator and the doors closed behind them. Whatever Trevor came to tell her would have to wait; finding Louisa was the only thing that mattered. A shiver of excitement ran down her spine and she didn't know if it was from the strong coffee or finding Louisa or the fact that Trevor was standing so close to her.

"I hope you know some back roads, we have to get there quickly." She turned to him.

"I'll do my best." He nodded and a smile crossed his face. "I don't want to disappoint you."

Chapter Nineteen

LOUISA WALKED DOWN THE HALLWAY of Yardley Manor and peered into a room with a billiard table and walnut bar and framed portraits. A fire flickered in the fireplace and a silver tray held bottles of sherry.

She had explored the whole downstairs hoping to find someone: a guest who had fallen asleep and not gone with everyone else, a maid who was doing endless loads of laundry and didn't hear her and Digby arrive. But the house was empty.

She wondered if she had ever been so miserable. There was the time she sprained her wrist before the tenth-grade ski trip and had to stay behind. She was the only one in the grade who missed it and spent the day in the English teacher's classroom. The teacher let her watch *A Night at the Roxbury* and brought her brownies but it didn't make up for missing hot chocolate with her friends at the ski lodge.

And there was the time after she graduated from the Culinary Institute and had an interview at the Four Seasons as an assistant pastry chef. A deer jumped in front of the train and by the time the deer was rescued and the train was running, she missed the interview and someone else got the job.

But neither of those situations made her feel sick to her stomach: she was letting down Kate and Noah. Christmas was about doing things for others and she had only been thinking about herself. From now on she would spend every weekend at the Boys & Girls Club in Harlem teaching kids how to bake cinnamon rolls. Or she could sign up to deliver homemade desserts to a nursing home in Queens.

After she told Digby she didn't want to sleep with him, he had wandered upstairs. He wasn't used to a woman rejecting him and she probably wouldn't see him for hours. How could she have misjudged him? He was like a male model who was only real in the pages of a fashion magazine. Once you took away the smart blazers and expensive loafers, there was nothing there.

She had searched the mudroom for a pair of boots and jacket and was going to run down the driveway and flag a passing driver. But then it started to snow and she decided it was a bad idea. If she got struck by a car she'd create more problems for everyone.

She remembered when she met Noah and he said she had to come to London because it was her fault that Bianca's lips blew up like a blowfish. She'd gladly listen to any of his lectures if it meant he would talk to her. He had forced her to go to London even though she wanted to stay in her suite, and he had been so furious that she went to Buckingham Palace by herself and was almost late for the reception at the Fumoir.

She had every right to have been angry with him. He didn't trust her when she just said she was falling in love with him. But isn't love about listening to each other? If she had taken his advice, she'd be standing in her suite at Claridge's. Instead she might get Noah and Kate fired, and they would never speak to her again.

Gravel crunched on the driveway and she peered out the window. A black Range Rover pulled up and Louisa wondered if she was imagining things. What was Kate doing here and who was the man beside her?

She ran to the foyer and flung open the door. Kate jumped out of the passenger seat and strode toward her.

"Louisa!" Kate exclaimed, walking inside. "Digby's publisher told us where you are. I'm glad we found you."

"Oh, Kate!" Louisa wanted to hug her. "I'm sorry about everything, I feel awful. Digby's car wouldn't start and there's no cell phone reception and the house phone seems to be broken. I kept hoping someone would give us a ride back to London, but the whole house party went to Chichester and hasn't returned."

"I called Susannah on the way." A man entered behind Kate. "They're having afternoon tea at Amberley Castle. They'll be back this evening."

"Louisa, this is Trevor." Kate introduced them. "Trevor was married to Susannah. Yardley Manor is his house. Digby's publisher said there might be tight security because some of the house guests are members of the royal family."

"I guess the security guards drove with the house party," Trevor offered. "It's like when Susannah and I stayed at Balmoral Castle. You couldn't go to the newsagent without two men in a black car following you."

"Trevor is Susannah's husband, what a small world!" Louisa exclaimed. "I haven't even met her but the house is spectacular. I was so excited about preparing the desserts and it all came out wonderfully. But then we were stranded and I felt so terrible for letting everyone down."

"It's not your fault. You asked if you should go and I thought it was a good idea. Where is Digby?" Kate asked. "We need to hurry if we're going to get back to Claridge's."

"I don't think he's coming." Louisa bit her lip. "He made a pass at me and he got very angry when I refused. He started drinking and I doubt he's in any condition to do the show. He wasn't planning on going back at all."

"I'll go find him," Trevor said. "He can't get away with that kind of behavior."

"It's going to have to wait." Kate touched his arm. "If we don't leave now, we'll never make it to Claridge's." She turned to Louisa. "Sit in the back with me and I'll do your makeup on the way."

"You can do my makeup while Trevor is driving?" Louisa followed her outside.

"I'm a television producer," Kate chuckled. "I can iron a blouse on the hood of a car if I have to."

The car peeled down the driveway and Louisa peered out the window. Snow fell softly and it resembled a snow globe. Fir trees lined the road and there was the faint outline of grand country houses behind iron gates.

"When we pulled up at Yardley Manor, I felt like Cinderella arriving at the ball," she said with a sigh. "I was going to assist Digby Bunting and have my photo in *Town & Country*. How could I have been so stupid and think Digby believed in me as a chef? All Digby is interested in is a woman's legs."

"You believed in yourself, there's nothing wrong with that." Kate took out her lipstick. "I asked Noah to wait at Claridge's in case you returned. He told me everything that happened. He said he was falling in love with you, but you got in a terrible fight."

"He told you that?" Louisa gasped.

"He blamed himself for you running off with Digby." Kate

nodded. "You were angry at him for not trusting you. You thought he put his feelings before your career."

"I was furious at him, but I would never miss the show on purpose," Louisa insisted. "Anyway, I'm finished with love. I'm not going to let anything get in the way of opening my restaurant. Falling in love only causes heartache, and I almost ruined things for everyone."

"You and Noah should talk it out," Kate advised. "Love can be painful, but it can also be the best thing in the world. Life is empty without it."

Louisa remembered when Noah kissed her by accident on the Giant Observation Wheel. She pictured entering Selfridges and Noah saying she could pick out whatever she wanted. They shared an omelet at the Foyer and Noah said he was in love with her.

"I suppose you're right," Louisa said. "But sometimes I think it would be easier to get a cat."

The car pulled up in front of Claridge's and Louisa stepped out. She had never been so happy to see the hotel's striped canopy and revolving gold doors.

"Come up to my suite. I already called the stylist to finish your hair," Kate said. "I'll tell Noah you're on your way."

They took the elevator upstairs and Kate opened the door. A card was propped against a vase and Louisa recognized Noah's handwriting.

"Noah left you a note." She handed it to Kate and had a funny feeling, like when she stepped on an escalator that was moving in the wrong direction.

Kate tore it open and scanned the page. "You better read it," she said, giving it to Louisa.

"Dear Kate," Louisa read out loud. "I am offering my resignation, effective immediately. You are the producer but you can only be as effective as the people who work for you. I let my personal life interfere with my job and put the whole production in danger.

"It is better for everyone if I'm not here when Louisa returns. I booked myself a flight to New York this evening. I'm going to go stay at my parents' place in Wisconsin for a while. I'll be back in New York at the end of January when law school starts and I'll stop by the office to collect my things. Sincerely, Noah."

Louisa sank onto the love seat and her heart hammered. She smoothed the paper and folded it carefully.

"I guess I don't have to wonder if Noah will talk to me." Louisa's eyes glistened. "It's better this way; I can concentrate on my career. When we get back to New York, I'm going to ask Ellie if I can do double shifts at the bakery. Chloe and I will bake on the weekends and I'll volunteer at the animal shelter." She fiddled with the paper. "I can't have a cat because my roommate is allergic, but that doesn't mean I can't help animals. So many stray cats get picked up in Manhattan, I could help some of them find a home."

"Don't be silly." Kate snapped off one of her earrings. "Noah is just being dramatic, he'll come around when you're both in New York."

"New York is a long way from Wisconsin," Louisa responded. "Maybe he'll rekindle a romance with a high school girlfriend and forget about me. She'll move to New York with him and become a cocktail waitress to help put him through law school. I'll run into them in the East Village and exchange an awkward greeting."

Kate took off her other earring and placed it on the coffee table. She grabbed her phone and dashed off a text.

"I'm sending Dexter, the assistant camera operator, to Heathrow." She looked up. "I gave him instructions to stop Noah from getting on the plane."

"You can't force Noah to stay in London!" Louisa exclaimed.

"I'm not forcing him," Kate corrected. "Dexter will invent an emergency that only Noah can solve. If I know Noah like I think I do, he won't let the show down completely."

"Do you think it will work?" Louisa tried to keep the hopeful note from her voice. The important thing was that she do a good job on *Christmas Dinner at Claridge's,* not that Noah was stopped from going to Wisconsin.

"Leave it to me," Kate said confidently and picked up a hairbrush. "The stylist is late and you have to be on set in fifteen minutes. A little hairspray and lipstick and you'll be camera ready."

Louisa slipped off her wireless microphone and took a deep breath. Taping the show was over and the production assistants were milling around, removing gaffers' tape and turning off bright lights. The director huddled with Kate in the corner and the kitchen staff loaded the dishwasher and scrubbed down the marble counter.

When Louisa first took her place beside Pierre and Andreas and Alan, Digby's publisher, she had been terrified she would freeze. But then she pictured Ellie and Chloe huddled in front of their television and knew she couldn't let them down. If Louisa wasn't in New York baking cinnamon rolls for the Christmas rush, she at least had to do a good job so Bianca would promote the bakery on her show.

It had been easier than she imagined! The moment the assistant placed the ingredients for the croquembouche in front of her, she didn't think about Noah at all. All that went through her head was that the puffs should be perfectly round and the crust must be light and fluffy.

It was only when the cameras stopped rolling that she glanced around for Noah. But Kate had been wrong: he hadn't returned. He was probably on his way back to New York, enjoying a special Christmas Eve in-flight meal of turkey and stuffing and Christmas pudding.

The kitchen door swung open and a man appeared. He wore a brown leather jacket and there were snowflakes in his hair.

"Noah!" she gasped. "What are you doing here?"

"Apparently there was a camera malfunction and I'm the only person in London who could fix it." He approached her. "I was standing on the sidewalk at Heathrow waiting for a taxi, and Dexter pulled up in front of me."

Louisa looked up and wondered if she'd heard him correctly.

"You were waiting for a taxi?" she asked.

"It's impossible to get a taxi at the airport on Christmas Eve." He nodded. "I had just let mine go and there wasn't another free taxi anywhere."

"Why did you need a taxi? You were on your way to America."

"That's what I thought I was going to do, but when I reached the departure terminal I realized I couldn't leave Kate in the lurch." He dusted snow from his hair. "I ran back outside and tried to flag down a cab. Then Dexter showed up and said the whole production was in jeopardy unless I returned."

"I see." Louisa folded her apron. Noah was only worried about the show, he hadn't come back to see her at all. "Kate will be very happy. She said she wouldn't accept your resignation."

"You read my resignation letter?" Noah asked.

"Kate gave it to me. She can't do the show without you." Her voice wobbled. "You were right, Digby only wanted to seduce me. He's not even a real chef. His publisher writes his cookbooks and Digby shows up for the publicity shoots."

"I came back because I hadn't finished doing my job. But I also came to tell you that it's my fault, I should have trusted you." Noah shook his head. "You said you were going to return the earrings and I should have believed you. When you love someone you have to have faith in them."

"Digby did try something," Louisa said uncomfortably. "I told him I wasn't interested and he slunk off like a dog without a tail. His car broke down and the whole house party went to Chichester and I was stuck at Yardley Manor for hours. Kate and Trevor rescued me, and Kate showed me your note." She paused. "She sent Dexter to stop you. She said we were just having a lovers' quarrel and we would both calm down. Love could be uncomfortable and difficult but life without it is meaningless."

"Say that again," he cut in.

"Say what again?" she asked. "Don't tell me you haven't been listening. I'm tired and my feet hurt and I need a bath. I don't want to repeat the whole story."

"Just the last part of the sentence," he urged.

Louisa tried to remember what she said and frowned.

"I'll say it for you," he offered. "You said that love could be difficult but life without love is meaningless."

"I did say that," Louisa agreed. "Of course, there are other things that are important too. My career means everything to me. I've worked so hard to open my restaurant and I'm not going to stop now. And I'll always want to make time for Ellie and Chloe, they're like family. I really enjoyed writing the Christmas recipe cards for Chloe. Chloe and I might collaborate on a children's cookbook. After all, Christmas is all about children and it could be very successful. But—"

Noah leaned forward and kissed her. She kissed him back and the lights glimmered on the pots and pans like fireworks on the Fourth of July. His mouth was warm and he pulled her close.

Noah's hand moved down the small of her back and she felt a shiver of excitement. She pressed herself against his chest and her whole body was filled with the most incredible yearning.

He kissed her harder and then he stopped and rubbed his thumb over her mouth. He tucked her hair behind her ear and kissed her on the neck. She took a deep breath and suddenly had never wanted anyone more.

"Oh, Louisa," he whispered. "I want you so much."

"I want you too," she breathed, reaching up and kissing him again. He smelled of pine leaves and cologne and she felt light and happy.

"You kissed me while I was still talking," she said when they finally parted.

"I don't need to hear anything else." He grinned. "You told me the only thing that mattered."

The kitchen door opened and Louisa jumped. She had almost forgotten where they were and she was suddenly embarrassed.

"We should go," she whispered. "They have to finish clearing the set."

"Louisa, wait." He stopped her. "We hadn't finished."

Louisa turned and wondered what she had forgotten. Noah wrapped his arms around her and kissed her.

"Now we can go," he said and smiled. "I'm sorry I didn't trust you, I'll never doubt you again. You are bright and beautiful and you know more about baking than anyone I have ever met." He paused and kissed her again. "I realize how lucky I am. I couldn't have found a better replacement."

Chapter Twenty

LOUISA SAT AT A TABLE at the Foyer and sipped a glass of sparkling water. It was Christmas Day and the restaurant was the most elegant place she had ever seen. White tablecloths were set with gold inlaid china and Baccarat champagne flutes. The Christmas tree was strung with white and blue lights and gold candelabras held flickering candles. Silver balloons floated to the ceiling and there were fruit trees with oranges and lemons.

Christmas Dinner at Claridge's had been a huge success. Pierre's oyster with fennel and wild mushrooms was the perfect appetizer and Andreas's pigeon with onions and rhubarb was superb. The roasted duck was fragrant and tender and the sides of cauliflower cheese and Yorkshire pudding made her long to stay in England.

Digby's publisher, Alan, made a Peach Melba with vanilla foam that was so light, it floated down her throat. And he was terribly apologetic about Digby's behavior. Louisa brushed it aside and said it was Christmas. There were more important things to talk about than Digby Bunting.

The flight to New York was leaving that evening but they were all having Christmas lunch first. It had been so nice to see Kate and Trevor together last night. When Kate hugged Louisa after the show and said it had gone better than she hoped, Louisa could sense that Kate was happy and in love.

She had barely talked to Noah after they left the kitchen last night. One of the cameramen went on a pub crawl and took the camera with him. Noah had to find him and no matter how hard Louisa tried to stay awake, her eyes kept closing. She finally texted Noah and said she would see him in the morning.

But she was confident they would make it work. She would have to make changes in her schedule, but it would be worth it. She couldn't order up love when it was convenient, as if it was a cheesecake from Harrods. Noah was like no one she had ever met and she wasn't going to lose him.

A man appeared in the doorway and she recognized Noah's short brown hair. He wore a tweed blazer over a beige shirt.

"I'm sorry I'm late." He approached the table. "The maître d' wouldn't let me in without a sport coat."

"You didn't buy one!" she protested. "They must cost a fortune."

"I looked in the gift shop but I couldn't afford a single button," he admitted. "Apparently the concierge keeps a selection of blazers for this situation. It's a little big around the shoulders but it will do for lunch."

"It suits you," she mused. "You look quite British."

"Next time I'll pack a blazer." He sat down. "You look beautiful. Is that a new sweater?"

"It was a Christmas gift from Kate." She stroked the soft angora. "She shouldn't have bought me anything; she gave me the best week of my life. But it is lovely and it's perfect for Christmas lunch."

"It's gorgeous." He nodded. "And Kate was very pleased with the show. You did an excellent job."

"I bought you a present." She handed him a parcel wrapped in tissue paper.

Noah opened it and took out two knitted cup warmers.

"You put them around your cup to keep the coffee warm." She suddenly wished she had splurged on a tie or bottle of cologne. "To be honest they were all I could afford at the gift shop, and everything else was closed." She flushed. "But I thought they would come in handy when you were studying."

"They're perfect." He kissed her. "I can't think of anything I'd like better."

Louisa turned and a couple approached the table. Kate looked stunning in a cashmere dress and silk scarf. Trevor stood beside her in a navy blazer and beige slacks.

"We're sorry for keeping you and Noah waiting." Kate pulled out a chair. "I've been on the phone with New York. Bianca is frantic about next week's show. She wants to do a New Year's Eve menu, and she can't find bitter milk chocolate for the mosaic chocolate dessert."

"I know a chocolatier on the Lower East Side," Noah offered. "I'll track some down."

"This is for you." Kate handed Noah an envelope. "It's your Christmas bonus. Perhaps you and Louisa can stay at a bed-and-breakfast in Vermont over the holidays. And I put in a request for you to have an assistant." She smiled. "You have to study for law school and make time for your personal life. You shouldn't be trying to find quince for a chestnut puree on a Friday night."

"Thank you." Noah slipped it in his pocket. "That's very thoughtful."

"What gorgeous earrings." Louisa noticed Kate's sapphire earrings. "Are they new?"

"Trevor gave them to me for Christmas." She touched her ears. "We promised we wouldn't give each other anything too expensive, but he bought them anyway."

"They were the only thing I liked in the gift store and all the jewelry stores were closed," Trevor said. "Besides, they bring out the color of Kate's eyes."

"They're beautiful and I adore them." She smiled.

"We're going to celebrate my birthday next month in New York," Trevor said to Louisa and Noah. "Perhaps you can join us."

"New York!" Louisa turned to Kate. "That is exciting."

"Trevor was asked to give a lecture at Columbia," Kate began. "And I'm coming to London in the spring. Digby's publisher wants me to produce a television special for one of his celebrity chefs. Her name is Felicity and she's related to the royal family. We're going to film at Kensington Gardens."

The waiter appeared and they ordered venison Wellington and Parmesan gnocchi and heritage beetroot. There was a wedge and blue cheese salad and bowls of tomato and basil soup.

Louisa sipped white wine and they talked about her plans for the restaurant and Noah's classes. Kate told them stories about television and Trevor recounted meeting Prince Harry. Noah's arm brushed her sleeve when he reached for a bread roll, and she felt light and happy.

The waiter cleared their plates and passed around leather dessert menus.

"We don't want anything from the dessert menu." Louisa handed hers back.

"Of course we want dessert." Noah glanced at the menu.

"That's the best part of the meal. The warm apple crumble with vanilla ice cream sounds delicious or I might try the ginger and treacle cake."

"We're not getting anything from the menu," Louisa repeated. "I have a surprise."

The waiter disappeared and returned with a pyramid of golden pastry puffs coated with caramel and threaded with royal icing. It was wrapped in spun sugar like some fabulous diamond bracelet and decorated with sugared almonds.

The waiter set it on the table and for a moment, Louisa was afraid it would collapse. But it settled on the plate and she relaxed. It looked so lovely in the flickering candlelight, like a jewel-encrusted music box in the window at Tiffany's.

"It's my croquembouche," she explained. "We didn't get to eat it last night. I thought we could have it for dessert."

The waiter pulled it apart with silver dessert tongs and passed around porcelain plates. Noah took the first bite and Louisa held her breath. What if the pastry was too crunchy or the caramel was sticky or the slivered almonds got stuck in his throat?

Noah put his fork on his plate and wiped his mouth. He looked at Louisa and it was the longest moment of her life.

"It's the best thing I ever tasted," he said finally and kissed her.

All around her champagne glasses tinkled and silverware clinked and Christmas music played over the speakers. Little girls in red velvet dresses drank Shirley Temples and boys in trousers and suspenders clutched toy cars.

Louisa reflected on all the wonderful things about Christmas at Claridge's: the giant Christmas tree made out of metallic umbrellas and Brandy Alexanders served at Claridge's bar and wrapped ornaments in her suite. The Dorrington ham sandwiches served on green-and-white-striped china at afternoon tea and the English muffins with Cornish cream that were so fresh, they melted in her mouth. And the lobby! It was like the most luxurious British drawing room with a marble fireplace and sideboard set with decanters of brandy and sherry.

She turned to Noah and her heart filled with such happiness, she thought it might burst like the silver balloons that floated to the ceiling.

"I was hoping you would say that." She beamed and kissed him back.

Acknowledgments

Writing another Christmas book is very special to me, and I want to thank my wonderful agent, Melissa Flashman, and my amazing editor, Lauren Jablonski, for the opportunity. Thank you to the whole team at St. Martin's Press: my publicist, Brittani Hilles; Karen Masnica, Laura Clark, and Brant Janeway in Marketing; and my fantastic publisher, Jennifer Enderlin. Thank you to Jennifer Weis for bringing me into the St. Martin's family.

Thank you to my friends Sara Sullivan, Jessica Parr, Cathie Lawler, and Cindy Pintar. And the biggest thanks to my children: Alex, Andrew, Heather, Madeleine, and Thomas.